# *A*
# *Jewish Mother from Berlin*

AND

# *Susanna*

## *Modern German Voices Series*

Ingeborg Bachmann
*The Thirtieth Year*
*Three Paths to the Lake*
*Malina*

Manès Sperber
*Like a Tear in the Ocean*
a trilogy

Peter Härtling
*A Woman*

Eric Rentschler, ed.
*West German Filmmakers on Film:*
*Visions and Voices*

Wolfgang Koeppen
*Pigeons on the Grass*

Alexander Kluge
*Case Histories*

GERTRUD KOLMAR

# A
# *Jewish Mother*
# *from Berlin*

A NOVEL

# *Susanna*

A NOVELLA

*Translated from the German by*
*Brigitte M. Goldstein*

New York / London

Published in the United States of America 1997 by
Holmes & Meier Publishers, Inc.
160 Broadway New York, NY 10038

Published originally in German as *Eine jüdische Mutter* and
*Susanna* copyright © 1978 by Kösel-Verlag GmbH & Co., Munich

Book design by Colin Joh
Typesetting by Coghill Book Typesetting Co., Chester, VA

This book has been printed on acid-free paper.

**Library of Congress Cataloging-in-Publication Data**

Kolmar, Gertrud, 1894–1943?
  [Mutter. English]
  A Jewish mother from Berlin : a novel ; Susanna : a novella /
Gertrud Kolmar ; translated from the German by Brigitte M.
Goldstein.
     p.   cm.
  ISBN 0-8419-1345-5 (alk. paper)
  1. Kolmar, Gertrud, 1894–1943?—Translations into English.
2. Jewish women—Fiction. I. Goldstein, Brigitte. II. Kolmar,
Gertrud, 1894–1943? Susanna. English. III. Title. IV. Title:
Susanna.
PT2605.H54A4   1997
833'.912—dc21                                    96-54584
                                                 CIP

Manufactured in the United States of America

# A
# Jewish Mother
# from Berlin

# Part I

# . *1* .

ugust nineteenth, in the evening. Autumn was already in the air. The meager trees lining the streets already yellowed and shivered. A storm passed over like a big, long-legged bird with blackish blue, powerful wings driving the rain in sheets between rows of shabby, oldish houses. The cobblestones glistened.

The streetcar buzzed uphill, drizzling and spraying, past the dark red, soot-covered brick building of the train station. From the railing on the bridge, the view descended to the bottom of a deep shaft, where, not all too far in the distance, a fleeing mass of tracks became entangled, resembling a snake pit. The huddled houses receded.

At this point, to the right, pressing against the embankment, the fortification of the hospital with its reddish masonry and iron gates, its spire, its ivy-encrusted wall and a clock with gilded ciphers over the main portal came into view. To the left, the last of the gardens surrounding the suburban villas receded—old Franconian gardens with bushes growing wild and trees that enclose flat-roofed structures with decorative columns—incongruously southern, almost Italian. Others were in the style of Scottish castles, with graduated gables and embattlements. In the midst of an unkempt lawn, on an erect stem, glowed a saffron yellow rose saturated with heavy raindrops.

The streetcar left the hospital area and entered a world of summer shacks, of small gardens, a suburban world marked with signs like "Sunday Joy Colony," "Green Fields." The individual settlements were separated by expansive areas of wasteland, sparsely covered with wild overgrowth of thick, low-growing pines that under blue skies might have given the illusion of pines in an Italian landscape. Here enveloped in the cloudy, wind-swept dusk, they marked only the northwest corner of Charlottenburg. Above the open wire-mesh door were the words "Rosskaempfer Inn." A well-trodden path, lined by decaying birches, led through thin grass to the tavern, a dirty white, crumbling, rundown structure, situated in the far rear of the lot.

At the streetcar stop a single rider got off—a woman, tall, in a slender black-blue coat. She pulled out her umbrella and inspected it. The wind was still blowing, but it did not rain. She walked back a few steps toward the street she had come from and entered the unpaved footpath between the garden area and the Rosskaempfer Inn. To the right were rows of narrow square plots planted with vegetables and strawberries, unkempt bushes of purple and red dahlias grew around the shed. To the left, near the alley adjacent to the inn, was an overgrown garden, at its center a crumbling wooden hut inscribed with washed-out letters that read: Villa Grazietta. Everybody knew that the Grazietta belonged to a woman from Riga and that an old, rather grouchy man lived there like a hermit. As if to scorn the decaying, crooked structure, a solid yellowish wall rose next to it, supporting the posts of the wrought-iron gate; one wing was slammed shut, the other was wide open.

The dark woman hesitated a moment and looked around, then she quickly entered the yard.

The yard had unpaved, sandy ground, now muddied with puddles. Two maple trees cast their shade over it, darkening no doubt the windows of the unadorned gray multiple-floor tenement that faced the entrance. The building formed an elbow and its shorter arm delineated the space against the Grazietta garden. On the shorter side in the front, the wall jutted out at an angle, spied on by the green-leafed eyes of a magic garden. This was the spacious property of Binnwald Castle from which, nobody knows why, this rectangular lot had been carved. Maybe it was a former carriage- or caretaker's house the new owner had converted into rental apartments. The woman dressed in dark lived here in the squat building to the rear. She hesitated. She stood, key ready in hand, lifting her eyes, as if amazed, and gazed at the rain gutter under the roof and at the fresh, saturated leaves crowning the trees. For years and years she had been returning home like this, and she was still moved every time by what had touched her the first time she had discovered the alley and the silent house behind the wall, which made up for all the shortcomings of the accommodations. There was something monastic, peaceful, introspective, something of the secludedness of a convent, something that had long vanished although the building had received its last facade only shortly before the turn of the century. Structures like this always have western exposures, and the pallid window panes softly reflect the red glow of the sunset. Now it was dusk. The woman went inside.

The woman ascended two flights and rang a doorbell. A little, friendly old woman poked her head out, her white hair neatly parted, her bony cheeks, like apples, painted with red dots.

"Ah, Frau Wolg!"

"Good evening, Frau Beucker. Is my Ursa in?"

The old woman reached for the thin silver brooch pinned to her collar.

"Ursel, no she is in the garden with Anna and Elschen. They were probably waiting for the rain to pass, or they would be here already. I'll send her over to you as soon as she gets here."

"Yes, please. And here, Frau Beucker, thirty cents for the milk from the other day."

"There was no rush." She stuffed the coins in the pocket of her blue and white striped apron. "Good evening."

The cheerful, shriveled little old woman disappeared. The dark woman turned and unlocked her apartment just across the hallway.

A pitch-dark entrance hall. But the room was high and spacious and well furnished. Without seeming cramped or tight, it bore the massive mahogany bed that stood in the middle like a huge varnished crate storing the bread of slumber. It was covered with a fringed, yellowish, patterned bedspread of such fullness it rose like a high vault and almost reached to the edge of the footboard and the cannon-ball posts. More perhaps than the plush green sofa or the decorative carvings of the mirrored cabinet, and even more than the tile stove, it was this bed that gave the room an old-fashioned, somewhat conventional appearance. Missing were only a pearl-embroidered greeting over the door and a plaster bust of Schiller on the console. Instead there were two reddish photographs on the matte flowery wallpaper. The framed picture of a man stood on the nightstand next to the candle and a small, nickel coffee service gleamed on the white, knitted table cover.

It was all so clean, so neatly arranged, in perfect order. Yet these petit-bourgeois, polished surroundings looked askance at the woman who placed coat and hat on a hook and proceeded to take off her wet shoes. For she was a simple woman, unadorned, the way she stood in front of the mirrored wardrobe, loosening her heavy, dull hair knot as for the night, and then rolling it up again and fastening it in the nape of the neck. She lingered, looking forlorn at the severe features of her large face, stealthily pursuing the thin horizontal lines running from her nostrils to her brow and others edging toward the corner of her mouth.

Suddenly, surprised and hurt by this self-observation, as if it were something improper, she took a sharp turn and tore open the nearest window to chase the stale, locked-in air to the four winds. She followed it with her eyes. The secret garden of Binnwald Castle reached out with its densely growing elms, flat like silhouettes against the frail grayness of the vaulting sky. In the distance hovered a quiet streak of soft pale reddish yellow, placed there by an inadvertent, ephemeral stroke of the hand. The leafy branches rustled in the wind, single drops of water splattered down: pitter-patter, little drum music. From a small tube faint sounds of a music box flowed endlessly. Gold-beaked blackbirds flitted about but had ceased singing their black velvet songs in the evening. They had long fallen silent.

The woman in the dusk had already turned away from the window; she removed the fringed bedspread and folded it up. She gathered the pillows and covers, placed them on the plush sofa, and prepared a nest, a small resting place. Then she crossed the hall to the small kitchen area, and since it was not worth her while to start a fire in the cold stove, she mixed some milk and farina over the flame of a spirit stove, buttered a few pieces of bread and listened to the noises in the yard as voices and the sound of footsteps flared up.

A thin, shy ringing of the doorbell. She opened. Two young little arms grew in the dark about a round face that was damp and cool and sweet like strawberries. She bent down and kissed it, mumbling indistinct words; her serious, almost harsh expression dissolved, and she smiled for just a second. The little one toddled alongside her mother as she went back inside, climbed onto the chair at the kitchen table, allowed a bib to be tied around her, dipped the spoon hungrily into the porridge, and told her story.

"Mother, we pulled turnips from the ground. Elschen had one so big she couldn't even get it out. And I had one, a double one, with two legs, like a man. Frau Lange said I could keep it. But we put them all together in a basket and later I forgot. Mother?"

"Yes?"

"Did you pho-to-graph dogs?"

"No, not today."

"Yesterday?"

"No, not yesterday either."

"And the day before yesterday?"

"Yes."

"What kind of dogs?"

"Only one—a German shepherd."

"Is he pretty? What is his name?"

"Fida."

"Fighter? He is probably named that because he fights."

"No. Fi-da—a girl's name like yours—Ursula."

The child looked thoughtful. She played with her drink between her tongue and lips as she often did when she did not swallow in one gulp, but sucked it in sip by sip.

"Tell me mother, aren't mice tiny little dogs? There was a mouse in Frau Lange's garden shed. A disgusting beast," she suddenly added emphatically, presumably the way Frau Lange had said it. "Elschen said it was not disgusting."

"And what do you say?"

"I say the same thing. They are not disgusting. Dead cats are disgusting. We found one the other day. Erich thought that somebody drowned it. It was all dripping wet . . . Ugh!"

The mother pushed back her chair. She was not squeamish and did not shy away from listening to the story after dinner, she did not choke with disgust; but the plates were now empty, she heated water in the kettle, washed the dishes and for a while continued straightening up in the kitchen and the parlor. The child danced around her like a little flame that was soon to be extinguished. Then she took her few modest toys, the animals, a few blocks, and the ship made of newspaper, and spread them out on the threadbare rug in front of the wardrobe, but she put everything away again soon for it was time for her to go to sleep. There was no begging, or mouthing off or dawdling here as elsewhere, where children want to stay up at all cost. When the mother wanted to rest, the child could not play on into the night. On occasion she would disobey, then the mother would undress herself, without a word, without scolding, until the dreaded moment when she said, "I am going to darken the room." And every time the soft, frightened mouth would say in the end, full of guilt:

"Mother . . . ?"

"Yes."

"Won't you undress me?"

Now from her nest on the sofa, like a tiny flower girl, a white rose surrounded by green leaves, she eyed the one who, by the round soft light of the oil lamp, was still darning her stockings. She blinked her eyes as she hung up her dress, reached for a washcloth and soap. She was already half asleep; but just as somebody who is already full will spear a last crumb with a fork so as not to waste a single morsel, she did not want to miss even a tiny bit of the time as long as there was still light, and with great effort she forced her drooping eyelids to remain open. She saw her mother walking naked through the room, unfolding her nightgown and tossing it over her head; then she sat at the edge of the bed and braided her hair. Suddenly the child asked with a slow, sleepy voice:

"Mother. Tell me, are you actually beautiful?"

"Why?"

"Because Elschen . . ."

She became more animated. "Elschen once said that you are not pretty, and Erich said you are ugly. But Otto, who is older, he is learning to swim, you know, he said to them that they are both stupid monkeys and that my mother was beautiful."

"So."

The mother rose and stretched her limbs. She seemed very tall in the long, pale gown. "That depends, Ursa, how *you* think of me."

"To me you are beautiful," she said, a little tired but with conviction.

"Then all right, that's what I am. Let's pray."

She folded both hands.

"Dear God, I pray you will let me stay good and devoted to you. Give me a little star at night and sunshine by day. Amen."

The mother softly stroked her hair one more time and smoothed the pillows. She took the lamp outside to extinguish it and groped her way back in the dark.

"Mother, are you there?"

"Yes, Ursa."

"Are you already in bed?"

"Yes."

"Good night, my dear mother."

"Sleep well, dear child."

But she remained without slumber, her hands folded behind her neck, felt the darkness of the corner and the wall flowing into her eyes. Not until deep, clear regular breathing came from across the room did she close her eyes.

# . 2 .

Martha Jadassohn had come with her parents from a small West Poznanian town, named either Bobst or Meseritz, to Berlin where her father's only sister, a widow, was living alone. Martha was the youngest and only surviving child of the elderly couple, and since finishing her schooling, she had been keeping the modest household. Her aging mother still helped with the cooking; they had no other help. They lived quietly. Besides the aunt, they had few visitors and did not call on anybody. The couple, who had spent their life in withdrawn, modest circumstances, always felt a little intimidated by the sprawling wilderness of the city. Neither of them was distrustful and they never thought of protecting their child from social contacts with young people. But where should the daughter get to know other people? She lacked the opportunities others had to meet them at social gatherings or at the workplace. She always presented an impenetrable, aloof face, and not only when somebody tried to start a conversation with her in front of the store or in the hallway. Whether she was satisfied with her lot, with her work, nobody asked and nobody knew. Without many words she swept the rooms, worked at the sewing machine, passed her free time with a book, or went for two or three hours on solitary, far-flung walks. When the weather was nice in the summertime, she would sit with her parents on a bench in the park. Occasionally she would walk over to the train station and watch for a while the arriving and departing trains with a strange look in her eyes. This is how she lived in the last years of the decade of the twenties and she knew pitifully little of what people call experience.

As in other apartment buildings, a tenants' council had been formed in the building where the family lived. A meeting had been called to discuss above all else problems with the coal supply and the nightly gate closing time. Martha's father, who was already ailing then from the illness that was eventually to strangle him, was laid up in bed, but did not like the idea of having to forego his right to vote on the matter. And since the mother was at heart not adroit enough and too dawdling and fearful to speak up in front of a dozen people, or even finding herself in a position of having to contradict them, it was decided that the daughter should represent the family.

The meeting took place in the home of the wholesaler Wolg, an educated and apparently well-to-do man. The wholesaler's son, Friedrich Wolg, an engineer, had seen Martha Jadassohn before in passing but had hardly taken notice of her. On that day he really saw her for the first time as he listened to her speak, in her quiet, terse manner, yet determined and firm. The contrast with several of the other women who spoke excitedly all at the same time, moving from topic to topic and almost losing the evidence supporting their opinions in little anecdotes, made her appear in a favorable light. He even engaged her in a verbal duel, since he played the role of shield bearer for his father, and used this as an excuse to approach her the next day in front of the building. This was the first move and the rest unraveled like a ball of yarn whose beginning had been loosened by an invisible hand.

Old man Wolg took a hostile stand. His jovial, easygoing nature recoiled from the austere, reserved girl; he called her a wet blanket and cold. It also did not suit him that she was a Jewess, especially an impecunious Jewess. He warned his son that such a woman would eventually sap his freshness and vitality. He added that her severity—which the lover took for virginal shyness, immaculateness—would not die with the wedding and would prevent the wife from being a companion and friend to her husband. He might as well marry an antique statue.

"We are living in the twentieth century, not in Jacob's tent. She looks like someone out of the Old Testament. Her name should be Leah instead of Martha. You might think she is champagne on ice. I don't think so. Ice, yes: a big lump. Jerusalem at the North Pole. She is stronger than you, I can feel it by just looking at her. And if you should ever have a disagreement, she won't give an inch. Either you will bolt or she will break you to pieces. Without mercy." The warnings had little effect.

Martha actually loved Friedrich in spite of herself. At first it seemed to her depraved even to consider a Christian. The parents asked no questions. They knew enough since the engineer had paid them several visits under the faintest of pretexts and had spent hours sitting around the table with mother and daughter. And then one morning the father called the girl over with a weak whisper; the mother listened with concern from the dark corner. He did not object. A co-religionist would have been preferable, certainly. But since he was on his sick bed, he had time to weigh things and there was much he saw now in a different light from before. Otherwise there was nothing wrong with the young man. And the Wolgs were rich and times were hard, and he would like to see his child well taken care of before his passing. One week later he died.

Hans Wolg considered this death a particular misfortune for his son, who, as he scolded in front of his wife, sneaked over there "every moment, to console the weeping bereaved." He changed his strategy now to gain by surreption and trickery what had been denied him in open battle. He knew that Friedrich was a sanguine type like himself, whose feelings were intense but of short duration. So he pulled a few strings and packed the fool off to England—for a few years, he hoped. There he would get to see and taste plenty of other ladies and the spark for this one would, for lack of nourishment, slowly but surely finally die. The calculation might have been right, but all too soon, after six months, Friedrich returned and seemed madder about her than ever. Although his promise to be faithful, made at the moment of their painful parting, did not hold him to playing monk, to his father he made disparaging remarks about British beauties, about their blandness—what mush, milk porridge with raspberry syrup.

"If I want blue eyes and blond hair, all I have to do is look in the mirror."

He finally managed to ask his mother for a more favorable wind, and his father, who had just shown the iron determination of a weathervane, turned against his will, screeching, toward the undesirable side. Martha Jadassohn became Martha Wolg; she appeared calm and collected; Friedrich was madly in love and happy.

Disappointment followed soon, even though the young husband did not admit his error so he could give his father's warnings the lie. But he remarked very early to Martha with derision: "Actually I don't have a wife, only a lover." He spoke the truth. She lived with him only in a union of the night. Smiling he called her Vesuvius or Etna or Krakatoa, because her embrace resembled the eruptions of an apparently quiet, but secretly smoldering crater. In time, the erratic fluctuations between cold and heat tired, even plagued, him. And the woman he knew in the daytime depressed and bored him. He could forgive her for not understanding much of his work although she would listen and nod, what annoyed him was that she shared practically none of his interests. She did not like to go paddle boating with him, or sit on his motorcycle, and he was usually the only one listening to the radio that stood in the corner. When he went to the movies or a coffeehouse or visited friends, she always quickly found an excuse to stay home alone.

"Well, that's all quite convenient," he tried to persuade himself. "I couldn't wish for a more accommodating wife." Yet he did not want to feel that way. There was something peculiar, something strange, something . . . he searched for a name.

Maybe it was because she was of different blood, a Jewess. But she did not carry with her the practices and customs of her forebears. She did not observe Friday nights and never thought of going to the temple. But she did not abandon her faith. She did not wear it like a dress that could be washed or torn and be lightly tossed off. Rather with her it had become like a skin, vulnerable but incapable of being sloughed off, indissoluble. Friedrich had a sign of this; and it was this which led to their first brief spat.

They had gone into town shopping together. The pregnant woman stopped in front of a lingerie shop and looked for a moment at the tiny children's shirts and jackets. He nodded toward the window display: "This one, this would be a nice little dress if we have a girl, a baptismal dress . . ."

Awkwardly, she turned toward him in boundless amazement: "Baptismal dress? But our children will not be baptized."

He mumbled, "I thought . . ."

She replied calmly, "You promised me something, you know that."

He shrugged his shoulders: "Whether such a promise is binding is questionable . . . I read somewhere . . ."

Her voice was cold. "It doesn't matter what you read about it. If you don't want to keep your promise and incite the minister . . ." She interrupted herself. "It is useless to make threats if one does not know yet what one will do. But consider," she said softly, "that our child is still inside of me, in my womb and that you, once it is born, cannot take it with you to the factory, and if you take it from me, I will find it no matter where."

She walked beside him without saying another word. He continued to argue into the air a little while longer before beating his retreat, for she did not fend him off. She was victorious.

His parents were outraged, especially his father became quite outspoken. "A Jew . . . She should be glad if her brat receives a Christian upbringing."

Friedrich seemed very distressed. "I beg of you just one thing, don't fight with her, let her be. You don't know her. She is capable of killing the child; she is a Medea!"

"A vixen," the father grumbled. The mother looked at her son with deep pity and sighed.

Martha gave birth to the child and fell over it like a hungry she-wolf, as the in-laws remarked. It was her child, only hers. As if the lightness of the father had been battling with the darkness of the mother as it was coming into being, and as if her darkness had in the end demolished his light and devoured it, Ursula's eyes and hair were nocturnal, her skin yellowish, almost brown, and of an even deeper hue than the ivory tone of her mother's face. Her features likewise betrayed nothing of Friedrich Wolg. Of course, he found pleasure in the little creature, but his paternal pride was soon dampened since it was as if it banished him with tiny fists from Martha's life. His wife now often appeared to him like a savage he kept in a cage by force and whose only thought was to break free. Whenever he came near her, she held the child up against her breast, then she looked at him without saying a word, but with the strange, ominous glowering of an animal mother who trembles for her young. She never quarreled with him, she never complained. Most of the time she just pushed him unceremoniously away like a thing that was not needed just then. And if he tried to oppose her, insist on being accorded his due, then he would ram against a magic wall she erected around herself. The wall gave way, the blow landed in thin air, only his arm hurt, and she stood there untouched at the very spot where she had barricaded herself.

One day Martha happened to meet him in the company of a pretty young woman, an employee at the factory where he was working. He wanted to justify himself. "It is nothing, believe me." It really wasn't anything yet. Martha said in a bored, lazy tone: "Leave it be. I didn't complain, did I?" He continued his stammering; she wiped the crumbs off the table. Indifferently: "It's all right."

He could not bear this kind of behavior any longer. He did what his father had prophesied and fled. He escaped to America. He remained there almost a year, then he returned, gravely ill, and died. His parents were furious with the daughter-in-law who had driven him away; had he stayed in his homeland he would have, so they believed, lived a long life. And secretly they blamed her for his untimely death.

Martha's situation in the world was uncertain. She inherited nothing from her husband and very little from her mother, who had died. The elder Wolgs did not love her. But nobody would accuse them of letting their grandchild starve. And the eyes of strangers, who knew of Friedrich's marriage only as a happy one, needn't see, even now, that matters stood differently. Hans Wolg arranged an apprenticeship for the unskilled widow with Frau Hoffmann. And almost against expectations, Martha showed herself so willing and talented that after completion of her apprenticeship, the gentle old lady took her on as her partner. She had a special talent for photographing animals; she actually introduced animal photography to Lydia Hoffmann. A young Newfoundland, who just happened to accompany his master, started it all. Soon it became fashionable among the wealthy from the western part of the city to have their lap dogs, Angora cats, monkeys, and parrots photographed. Occasionally she would take the short walk from the studio to the zoo to take pictures of the sacred cows for a magazine. Her brittle bond with the Wolg family became ever more frayed and one day, without an audible sound, it just snapped completely. And Ursa hardly remembered her grandparents; what the mother offered her were worn, faded, unappealing little pictures, and she rarely asked about them.

Martha, who was then still unaware of how fate was to bend her, exchanged the expensive apartment in a new building for a cheap, smaller one. One room, a kitchen, and a pantry were enough for her even when her courage and purse swelled. An apartment of her own seemed a lofty possession, even one without many amenities, without steam heat, gas stove, electricity, and located "halfway out of the world," as Frau Hoffmann called it. Her immediate neighbors were Otto Lange, a clerk at the magistracy; Anna, his wife; Elschen, the daughter—a little girl with a pronounced limp—and Frau Beucker, the mother-in-law. And one day, Martha was locking her door and was about to bring her child, as usual, to the day care house, when Frau Beucker peered out from her cave and presented a wish. Since Ursa and Elschen were already good friends could she not stay with them? She, Frau Beucker, had time enough to take care of both children, and an extra spoonful of soup for lunch would not matter all that much, especially since the weather was so dismal today, just right for catching cold. From then on, Ursa was left every day in Frau Beucker's care, who also picked up in the kitchen and parlor, and received from Frau Wolg a weekly compensation for her labor of love.

# . *3* .

She stood on the platform, on the stone island, waiting for the train. The pavement had been bleached by a burning, cloudless sky. Endless lines of high-speed automobiles whipped up golden dust. The towers of the Kaiser Wilhelm Memorial Church shone a silvery lead mold that soon melted in the heat. And all the women and children passing by had gotten out their most beautiful, their lightest and softest dresses that fluttered and glittered, after days of constant rain. A young woman steered a grass-green baby carriage through the crowd; high above its shade danced a balloon, pink with silver windmills. On the lower verandas of the cafés, decked out with pots of pelargonias, the guests drank their mocha, their chocolate frappes. Into the lions' gate at the zoo flowed an inexhaustible human stream, and those without money or time to spare stood for a second at the fence to catch a glimpse of the elephant wandering about in front of his Indian temple. Oh yes, she thought, I had wanted to visit the animals with Ursa. I promised her. I should have arranged it with Frau Beucker. She would have put the child on the train and I could have met her at the station. Well, tomorrow, maybe, if the weather doesn't change. Her train arrived, she got on.

When she rang the doorbell to the Lange apartment, the city clerk himself opened the door, a frail, smallish, milky man with thin pale blond hair. He was surprised to see her. Weren't Elschen and Ursa playing in the yard in front of the gate with the other children? They had just greeted him as he was coming home. Martha thanked him, entered her apartment, unpacked her string bag, took off her hat, arranged this and that, then decided since the blue sky was so inviting, she would go down and look for Ursel. After all she couldn't be very far. Between the wall of Binnwald Castle and the area of the garden sheds, she descended into the Spree River valley. Her gaze skimmed the vegetable gardens. Far away, toward the East, swam a faded, pigeon-colored streak in the sky. And on a late afternoon, an early evening such as this, the flowers gleamed as if bathed in pure, transparent air. Black purplish bundles of dahlias, orange-

dotted student flowers, honey yellow, creamy white gladiolas, goblets
of nectar for bees and bumblebees who, here and there, still hummed
around the stem of the goldenrod, and the brimming, erect heads of
the golden rudbeckia. Even the nettles along the fences were of a
friendlier, clean green. And everywhere people labored outside their
sheds, propping up weighty tomato plants, taking away the rotting,
ripe fruits, turning over the bean beds, and gathering the few pieces
of fruit that had fallen from the young trees. On occasion, a white
butterfly, stirred from its dream, would wander off, a loving,
trembling soul.

Martha had been peering through chain-link fences for her child
but was unable to discover the little gray skirt anywhere, nor did
she hear the warm sound of Ursa's already darkening little voice.
Martha was separated from the flat river bank only by a bundle of
tracks that ran alongside the lazy-flowing Spree, pulling her barges.
She stood still and scanned the landscape Frau Hoffmann had dubbed
"German Northwest Africa" and "New Cameroon." For this was a
developing world, a world of the unfinished, of contrasts: a flurry
of irregular construction in a desert or steppe. Far above, the sheds,
fearful and small, looked down from their high mountain that sloped
like a huge, barren, steep sandy incline; somebody in need of sand
had dug up the slope in several places. And in another place, the
garbage dump ate its way in like a nasty abscess, the refuse: broken
pieces of porcelain, cooking pots with holes, cardboard, moldy rags.
In the treeless desert across the river a huge red factory rose abruptly
in the sky; farther away, however, a bucolic scene, an old man resting
in the abundant growth of grass by the river and grazing his goats.

Martha crossed the tracks near the switching station and the track
barrier. She discovered a little girl with blond braids who limped
all alone along a narrow strip of grass, carrying a toy fishing rod
made of a stick and cord and a rusty marmalade bucket. She stopped
and hollered across the water in the direction where the goatherd
was encamped, but got no response. By God, Martha Wolg thought,
how often have I told them, and Frau Lange too has forbidden them
to go near the water. It's useless. Nobody will come to their aid if
one of them should slip. This area is so deserted. If Ursa should

drown ... She closed her eyes. Then she called out. The little one looked up, dragged herself over, held out her hand, and curtsied.

"Listen, Elschen—first—you know, and should finally remember, that you are not allowed to play on the other side of the tracks. If one of you should fall into the water nobody will pull you out. That goatherd surely won't jump in after you. And second, where on earth is Ursa?"

"Ursa?" the child looked around, puzzled, as if she were only now missing her little friend. Then she remembered: "But she went with Max and Erich."

"Where to?"

"Over there." She stretched out her arm toward where, a short distance away, they could hear a racket from screaming boys, very shrill in the evening stillness. Martha quickly followed the sound; Elschen slowly traipsed behind, curious yet unsure whether she should come along.

"Which one of you is Erich and which one is Max?"

A little chap stepped up.

"You are Erich?"

"Yes."

"And where is Max?"

"He is gone—gone home."

"Tell me, weren't you playing with Ursula Wolg? Where did you leave her?"

"With Ursula Wolg?"

"Yes, Ursa, you heard me. Where is she?"

"She ... she is probably at home—the man called her away."

The man? In the clockwork of her heart a turning wheel cracked, stopped, for only a second. "What kind of man?"

"I don't know! I didn't know him." He answered in a boorish, insolent tone, annoyed at being disturbed. His friend held the brown football stiffly in his raised hands, ready to toss it as soon as this bothersome woman would be gone. She did not budge.

"Now come over here and tell me in exact order one thing after another. This is very important."

Children like to feel they are important and that they are the center of attention, and so Erich himself enjoyed giving his report, now that his friends had gathered around and were listening attentively.

He was climbing around on the sand hill earlier with Max and Ursa when from above, he pointed to where, suddenly a man appeared and kept calling: "Ursel, Ursel." And then: "Come here, come right away, your mother wants you." Ursa hesitated, she thought: This man is a stranger. But Max warned her: "You had better go, you hear him, your mother is looking for you." So she finally traipsed over there and left with the man.

He stood still, the whole gang of playmates stood still and stared at the woman, waiting for what she had to say that was so important. When she spoke again, none of them noticed, because they were children, how her big face had turned a shade paler, her hand had closed in a cramp, and her nails pierced the palm of her hand, how her mouth had opened without a sound and how she breathed in and then out again, gasping almost like a fish in the sand with ocean-distant, uncomprehending eyes. And the woman said:

"What did the man look like?"

"I don't know. I didn't look at him. He wore a cap, I think. Maybe Max . . ."

"Where does Max live?"

"Max Hinnes? He lives in the Fellenbach Villa . . . his father is the gardener."

"And where is the villa?"

A boy, probably the oldest of the bunch, generously offered his services: "I'll go with you. I'll show you."

She nodded. "Good."

The others quickly talked it over whether they should come along, but decided after a short exchange of whispers that they would stay and go on with their game.

It was the garden with the graying Roman-style house, with the lawn of wildflowers and gleaming, deep saffron-yellow roses on strong tall stems. The little iron gate seemed locked, but the boy knew the trick to open it from the outside. They entered through a rear entrance, two steps down to the gardener's apartment.

# Part One

She knocked. "Come in."

A kitchen, low-ceilinged and cramped full, darkened by lattice windows. The gardener, a big, sinewy old man in shirtsleeves, his bristly chest bared, returned her greeting and jumped up. He seemed the liveliest around. The woman and two grown daughters remained seated at the table, so coarse, so plump and bulky, chewing bread and staring at the intruder, hostile, almost growling like dogs who had been disturbed while devouring their food. A green cucumber in a piece of paper and a few empty beer bottles were on the table. Max, who had come home late, crawled out of the corner and was subjected to a brief cross-examination by his father. Nothing new was found out.

"Well, let's hope she will still be found," muttered the old man, apparently thinking that he should say something to reassure the suffering woman. The coarse face of the woman clearly read: What fuss she is making about her brat. Why doesn't she leave already? She left.

Martha left and the gardener accompanied her, since he had to lock up in the front anyway—this was how, to his wife, he cloaked this unnecessary courtesy. She was silent. Suddenly she asked, as if there were nothing more pressing for her in the world, even surprising herself, as if a stranger spoke: "The rose ... do you know its name?"

"The yellow one? Melody with a 'y' at the end."

"Melody," she repeated softly. And she felt: My Ursa was a dark yellow rose. "Was?" she thought trembling. "Was ... ? My God, she is, she is still, still alive. I know it ... I want to know it!"

She staggered across the embankment. And this reserved, severe woman called forth the people, she called them to their gates and to the fences of their small vegetable plots; they leaned their shovel, their harrow against the wall, put down the bucket, obliging or unwilling, curious or bored. No, they had seen nothing, they had just now come back. No, they had been busy planting strawberries and were minding their business. Yes, a man passed by with a little girl—blond in a blue dress, wasn't it? Martha's heart sank. She was like a blind beggar. She groped her way, stretched out the hand:

here nothing and there nothing, what was offered turned out to be a worthless button that was completely useless to her. And then she had to bear the cruel, terrible words of pity: "Yes, that's the way it is—one hears so much that is terrible these days; there are too many criminals in this world. Such an innocent child . . ."

And then again—may God bless them: "Come on now, you mustn't get all worked up about it." Everything will turn out for the best. Our Hertha was picked up once. He had a little one in a baby carriage and she was supposed to watch it for a while so it wouldn't fall out while he went to a store. The languishing woman eagerly and gratefully devoured such talk.

Frau Beucker ran up to meet her. She had heard enough from Elschen. "I have asked around everywhere," she reported, "but unfortunately . . ." The old, wrinkled mother compassionately stroked the younger woman's arm.

"All right, and now Frau Wolg you must first come home and have something to eat. You must be exhausted. And tomorrow morning—if by then the child hasn't been brought back, for by now everybody around here knows about it—then you will go to the police. Today they are probably already closed and they won't do anything at night even if you report it. My son-in-law has gone out too—to attend his course."

The police! Why didn't Martha think of that herself? She had thought of it. But the nearest precinct was quite a distance away toward the town, and then she would have to wait around, would have to answer questions, minutes would rush by, and her child would shriek and she would have heard the scream had she been here! For she must be here, nearby, she still wanted to believe that. And then there was something, a thought, thin as a hair: If I carry my child to the police it means I am giving her up for lost. It means I no longer have any hope. So far the whole thing was something sad, an event, an exciting story, now it would become a criminal case. And all that could come of it was misfortune, a crime, murder. She did not draw any conclusions. She was herself not aware of what she was thinking.

Frau Beucker held her hand: "Did you check at the Rosskaempfer Inn?"

She barely mumbled a sorrowful no. She tore away like someone
who at the last minute had just remembered something she had
forgotten to do, and rushed under the frail birch trees to the small,
run-down establishment.

Here and there one of the guests looked up from his glass amazed.
A youngster, who was playing catch with the cardboard beer coasters,
stopped what he was doing and turned around. The innkeeper's wife
was reading behind the bar by a greenish, cheesy ceiling light; she
put down the newspaper. "Oh, God!" she sighed. "How can a person
possibly do something like that to children."

Martha felt a stab in her heart. Then the husband was called—
he was as spindly as she was hefty and coarse and spread out—they
tried to remember for a good, long while who had been at the inn
this evening and fixed on an unknown young man in a stiff cap
whose motorcycle had been waiting outside while he drank his beer.
The innkeeper was sure it had a side-car, but it was empty. Frau
Rosskaempfer had noticed the motorcycle but not the side-car, and
they started to argue about it.

But her hands tensed up and folded against each other as in fervent
prayer. She looked at the couple without understanding, as if they
were speaking in a strange tongue and she could but barely guess
the meaning from their gestures. She hardly listened anymore. It
would never have occurred to her that someone should take her child
far away, abduct her in his vehicle. At first, she would enjoy the
ride in the cart, she would take a liking to the man who was speeding
away with her. But then he didn't bring her back home as he had
promised. He was bolting through the cold night and she was shed-
ding bitter tears, calling out, and the noise from the motor was
drowning her cries.

She was petrified. Only her heart beat in her throat. She felt like
vomiting, spitting it out of her mouth. On the other side of the bar,
on the grimy wall, between the faded, dusty pictures, was a shiny
new one. A little girl, with healthy cheeks, black curls, in a bright
red velvet dress, held up a mug of malt beer with an impish smile.

She didn't look at all like Ursa, but the mother became completely engrossed in the happy, fresh face, and suddenly, as she wanted to say good-bye, a sound issued from her throat, just a short one: a groan, a sob. She winced, pulled herself together, and merely nodding left the inn.

She stood alone in the deserted, wide, dusky street. A man came by, probably a worker, carrying a tool bag on his back. She ran up to him, stopped him and babbled something incoherent about a motorcycle, a side-car, and her child. He shook his head slightly. No, he had met nobody. He spoke to her softly, almost apprehensively, as one speaks with a raging, insane woman so as not to provoke her. She let him go. But several stragglers, following in the light from the street lantern and late on their way home, were frightened by the trembling woman who darted out of the dark: a stammering madwoman.

# . 4 .

She awoke. She was resting half dressed, in her dressing gown, on her bed, shivering as if she were outdoors. The cool night air prowled around her and stroked her with its fingers. She had opened the windows wide, one in her room and one in the kitchen, and both doors. Her bare feet were cold. Her face was hot. She shuddered, turned over and stretched. She yawned. In an apartment below, a clock struck twelve times—she counted the peals. She sighed. She leaned heavy on her elbow, unrefreshed, so tired. She had been sleeping after all. Not very long but she did sleep, an hour maybe. Suddenly she sat up: Why am I cold, why am I awake and not undressed? She saw the nest of pillows on the sofa gleaming pallid in the darkness. Quick like a snake she slid over, feeling it with trembling, flying hands. Nothing, nothing. She threw herself on it and dug her head into it. She embraced its yielding softness, pressed it with her arms. You. You. Oh God, and I fell asleep. I was able to sleep. I was able to . . . She smoothed out the pillows, careful and tender, as if this still had a purpose. Then she stood up and listened.

It was nothing, no. But what if she did not hear the scream in her dream? That couldn't be, she would have heard it, with all the windows open she would have had to hear everything. And she doesn't shriek anymore, she thought listlessly. After all, she is dead.

"She is dead," she repeated aloud, bluntly. "Ursa is dead." She shook her head wildly, the black strains of her hair twitching like the snakes of Medusa. No. No.

"I am going out of my mind," she muttered, "I am mad. Nothing brings me joy anymore. Nothing gives me pain anymore. I am dead myself."

She sat down on the sofa, right in the child's little bed, and buried her feverish, hot face with her hands. She remained this way for a long time. She was no longer thinking.

She moved. Her foot touched something square, hard. She bent down, picked it up and felt, without yet seeing it, that it was a colored part from the set of mosaic building blocks Frau Hoffmann had given her little girl. She had been playing with it yesterday and had lost a piece. The mother thought: "Tomorrow I will tell her . . ."

Suddenly she knew: I had a child that will never return . . . my child . . . She sobbed, choking. She buried her flushed head in her lap, and suddenly, helpless and beside herself, she began to cry.

She wiped her eyes, her inundated cheeks. Oh God, oh Lord, she realized, imploringly, I believe in you! For years I have not been to temple, I did not always think of you, even when I prayed with my child in the evening . . . What did I do? Only yesterday I closed the door in the face of a beggar. He looked as if he would spend every dime on alcohol. I have often been stubborn and harsh. I have not always been good. Oh punish me, just let Ursa . . . my child . . . !

She fell on her knees. Her brow hit the hard wood. She remained this way, enveiled by her tangled hair; she whispered with hands intertwined like a penitent.

Somehow she felt stronger, calmer after the prayer. She pulled the dressing gown tighter around her, crawling deeper into it; sweat turned cold on her skin, and her undergarments were sticky. She walked to the open window. And like a fugitive calming himself with a cup of cool water, she looked out.

Star-bright. The Big Dipper had come to a halt before her gaze; sharply glittering, the star formation of its handle jutted into the sky. There were other worlds, unknown to her, that flourished and gleamed. The elms rustled. They looked so weightless, bodiless, nothing but a flat area, like ink runs and spots on bluish gray paper. Over there, far in the back, however, they were massing, together, into the jagged ridge of a camel's hump. The ridge on the back of a black-green dragon. Or a fish griffin bathing its scaly tail far away in the waves, refreshing the faces of the thirsty with a sea-cool breeze. She leaned forward on the windowsill and found the moon, who was waxing almost formless like a pallid compressed lemon. She contemplated it for a while. "From high above, through the opening of the cupola, the moon cast a pallid, silvery blue light . . ."

She knew not how these words came to her, where they came from. As a fifteen- or sixteen-year old, she had read on her own the story about the picture of Sais in her school reader and had often searched in her solitude for the secret behind the veil. She never found it.

Now she stood at the window and gazed into what had no life, no individuality, only a nocturnal landscape; the silence numbed her pain, while the little worm already lodged in her heart, the little worm of hope, whispering and nagging. What if, like little Hertha, this man too took Ursa only on a harmless errand. Or what if he is the kind of thief who quickly undresses children in a secret place, taking dresses, stockings and shoes to sell to a fence? Then the poor thing would be found covered only by her underwear and would be brought home in the morning with a nice cold. But she had a strong nature and would quickly recover. Into bed with her and something hot to drink . . . She wouldn't report the thief, no; she would thank him. Oh Lord, she sighed, please make it be so. Oh God—suddenly she made a mad dash for the kitchen.

A scream had just come from there. There was a scream; she had heard it clearly. From far away, a thin, very faint scream, a little scream, a whimpering. Her eyes pierced the crowns of the maple trees in the yard. Trembling, she listened, her eyes bulging, every fiber of her body taut, ready, at the first repeat that would give her a hint of the direction, to fly down the stairs and out of the building. Seconds: she still heard nothing. There—now quite close: twice, three times, four times, many times. "Tooit, tooit!" She breathed a deep sigh of relief. The owl. She had reassured Ursa and now she let herself be scared.

"Mother, what is this crying, what is it that cries like that?"

"Nobody is crying. It's a little bird, an owl, that calls and is happy."

"If it is happy, then shouldn't it be singing?"

"It can't sing."

"Mother."

"Yes."

"Why doesn't the owl go to sleep?"

"It sleeps in the daytime."

"In a tree?"

"Yes, or in the tower of Binnwald Castle or under the roof of Grazietta. You must be good and close your eyes now, do you hear?"

"I am scared—will you stay with me?"

"Yes, Ursa, I am here with you."

"Always?"

"Yes, always, my child."

"Always," she whispered. She held this dialogue here as if with her hands. She saw it before her, saw Ursa's low, gentle little voice: her eyelashes became moist. Slowly, like a sleepwalker, she closed the windows, first this one, then the one in the parlor. She pulled an old coat over her dressing gown and left, in soft, velvety shoes, the apartment, the building. With hasty steps she crossed the slumbering yard, the heavy gate had been left ajar, and she wandered into the sloping street toward the river valley.

A slight shiver came over her. Summer was still blooming, but this starry night already had something of the translucence and crispness of October. The contours seemed firmer down here, not as dissolved and blurred as from the window above. The garden sheds rose black and sharply delineated, like silhouettes, from the dull blue ground. Creeping plants, fine like filigree, had been trimmed. And through a gap between dark leaves flowed the hoary light of the moon. Underneath the moon fruit, wispy tufts of clouds crawled along, transparent, giant caterpillars. And no wind.

Martha vacillated. She raised her eyes toward the milky fog in the vaulting firmament above her, while it descended around her, gentle and heavy like peace. Everything was asleep. Ursa too was asleep. She was no longer able to moan and groan in this pure stillness.

A call rang out: "Ursa! Ursa!"

The sound cut far through the air, piercing like the lament of a huge bird. Nothing answered it.

Once again, higher, shriller: "Ursa! Ursa!"

Silence.

She started. A train with illuminated window panes speeded into the night like a hissing, gold-dotted otter. She turned back. But she walked past her yard until she reached the street. The eyes of tired street lanterns blinked forlorn from afar. Above the entrance to the Rosskaempfer Inn smoldered still a yellow, oily light. The young birches rippled gently, the silent birches. And again she lamented: "Ursa! Ursa!" Now a dog was barking far away. Nothing else stirred. She crept home.

The stairs creaked. She stopped several times to listen while she ascended into the shadowy darkness. It seemed to her that any moment a hand would have to rattle the gate below, and if she turned back and opened, she would find a stranger outside. Are you Frau Wolg? Here I am returning your child. That was rather unlikely. Now, at night, nobody would come. Tomorrow, yes, tomorrow in the morning.

She searched for the keyhole, feeling her way, carefully she unlocked the door to the apartment. Again she opened both windows. Took off the coat and buried herself in her bed. But she was unable to sleep. An eerie, strange brightness filled the room, the objects were infused with life from an evil, darting spook. The handkerchief on the floor became a gray rat. She only recognized it as a handkerchief when she picked it up with a doubtful hand. Now she sat in the armchair, very much overtired and yet barred from sleep. She lowered her eyelids . . . Ursa. And I am sitting here. I am sitting here quietly. She rose with a start. It seemed a crime to be sitting. Where are you? What are they doing to you? She quickly turned her head in fright, her tear-filled eyes darting about. What could one possibly do to a child? What do monstrous people do to children?

There it was. The wolf, dagger-toothed, spider-gray, he had been locked up, hidden deep inside a narrow, underground cage. Now he broke loose, crawled up to her, scornful, with red, laughing eyes.

He whispered: "Sundry news items . . . a child murdered in Riesa . . . gruesome discovery . . . sex crime against eight-year-old . . . boy's murderer on trial in the town of Pforzheim . . ."

And as through some diabolical magic, a white sheet of paper, dirty and torn, flew into her face. In the darkness, she read the black letters imprinted on it. "In an isolated area he pretended to play blind man's buff with them. He placed paper bags over the children's heads, led them to the river, and pushed them into the water. The suitcase opened to a gruesome sight. On top of a pile of old clothes and sheets lay a ten-year-old boy, suffocated, his hands still pushing against the lid in a desperate struggle with death. Apparently one of the children, before being murdered, had written the address on the package in which the dismembered bodies were mailed to the unhappy parents . . ."

She groaned. Too much. She could take no more. Suddenly she flung up her arms and crying out she sank to the floor.

# . 5 .

She trembled. Her teeth chattered as she washed herself in ice cold water. She yawned. She had apparently trailed off at dawn into a chaotic, oppressive, enervating sleep, but like someone in a feverish trance, she felt compelled to leave the bed. As she tied her hair in a knot, the drawn, livid face of a penitent, lids of bluish shadows and swollen with tears, stared at her from the mirror. She felt miserable. She heated some milk—oh, she had so much of it. Ursa's evening milk had remained untouched. Slowly, almost with pleasure, she swallowed the hot liquid. But she ate nothing with it. Sipping the milk, she kept her eyes fixed on the kitchen window, listening for any sound down in the yard. And every strange sound or voice that was only a buzzing in her ears pulled her halfway to her feet: They are here! They are bringing my Ursa, my child.

Nobody came.

She wrapped herself in a silk scarf and a warmer coat even though the sky promised a beautiful, sunny morning; but she was cold. On tiptoe, she stole into the stairwell; she was unable to talk, did not want to meet anybody from the Lange family. But the door opposite hers was already ajar; the neighbors might be spying on her, they might be lying in wait for her already. At that moment, Frau Beucker emerged, the proper well-groomed little old lady appeared unkempt and sleepy in her old-fashioned Chinese braid. After a subdued "Good morning," she stood there, hands crossed in front, and knew not what to say. The fatigued, pained demeanor prohibited any inquiries. She coughed lightly. "Hm . . . if I can perhaps . . . if there is anything I can do for you, Frau Wolg."

Martha, who was already on the first step of the stairs, turned around. "Yes. Please be so good," she said in a hoarse, unnaturally controlled voice, "would you go to Rosskaempfer's and call Frau Hoffmann—Steinplatz exchange 8873. Eighty-eight seventy-three. Tell her I won't be in today . . . that I am not feeling well."

Her voice, too taut, broke, tore apart. Frau Beucker's hand reached down, pushing Elschen, whose fearful pale little face had been peeking out from behind her skirt, back inside. Martha noticed the child. Quickly, as if stirred by the sight, she suddenly walked over and without a word placed her trembling hand on the little dull-blond head. Only for a moment. Before a word could be said, she turned and precipitously rushed down the stairs.

Yesterday she had been afraid that a visit to the police would be a waste of precious time, now she paced back and forth at the streetcar stop with restless impatience. After a few minutes, she was sure that the car would not come anymore. In vain did she scan the horizon and was just about to set out on foot even though she knew that the yellow car would speed past her as soon as she was on her way. At long last the streetcar appeared on the deserted, straight platform, it seemed to creep along like a snail. Martha got on. The seats were all taken. She walked to the front door, scrutinized the passengers as if she hoped to discover among them the man who had taken Ursa away. This way she arrived at her destination faster than she had expected. The police station was directly opposite the streetcar stop.

Closed. She pushed down on the door handle two or three times; she persisted with determined defiance. It seemed malicious to her that they still did not want to open the door. Next door, in an unremarkable high-rise apartment building was a watchmaker's shop. A look at the hands of the clock, which jumped forward suddenly or advanced gradually, threw her into a fit of despair.

Countless, precious moments had gone by, trickled away. She could not bring herself to leave, to look elsewhere. After all, there was nothing to see: a green-blue waiting taxi, a baker's apprentice on a bicycle with baskets. Two soldiers, who had apparently come from the nearby military barracks, and a few women with market baskets. At the grocery store across the street, a thin, red-headed fellow was rearranging the display in the window. She tried to pay sympathetic attention to the pyramid he was building from little boxes.

Again she looked at the clock. And then it suddenly seemed to her that she had missed everything. She should have gone to the precinct yesterday, should have alerted the police criminal investigation unit by telephone rather than wait twelve hours. But since she still had hoped that it would not . . . A key creaked in the lock. She hesitated a moment, then she entered.

A narrow corridor, then a bleak cavernous room with several cabinets and tables. She stood at the barrier and heard herself mouth something she had memorized, something alien that might as well have nothing to do with her: "My child is gone; somebody has abducted her." One officer looked up briefly from his work; then he continued to read, at least he pretended to be reading. Another wandered over to a worm-eaten cabinet while she was talking; he opened a drawer and took out a piece of paper covered with writing.

"Here it is. Martha Wolg, widow. Ursula Wolg, born February 11th—five years old," he mumbled, satisfied, as if locating this piece of paper already explained half the mystery.

"And what does she look like?"

Oh God, thought Martha, what should she look like, the child. She is a sweet little thing.

But she started to describe her: "She was wearing a gray dress with colored embroidery on the chest . . ."

As she was depicting her, the child stood before her in a light gray linen dress with green and pink embroidery, with brownish arms budding round and soft from the short sleeves. She lost her balance, was overcome, her speech fluctuated, she swallowed hard: ". . . and brown stockings and shoes." Suddenly she felt something moist on her cheek as if she were ashamed. She crumpled the handkerchief in her hand. The officer busily took down the details.

The other one, who was presumably reading, spoke unexpectedly as if into thin air: "In June we had a little girl here for a day and a half. A lady had found her somewhere. The girl was quite healthy and cheerful. The mother lived far away, down in the Schlosstrasse. She had been looking for her everywhere, except here."

One of them said: "Why don't you come back, if you like?"

Then she was outside again. She had been given short shrift like someone in need who had been hoping for a few coins or a cup of soup and had been gently pushed out of the door with empty talk.

She did not take the tram back. Her feet, unwilling and heavy, made their way home along the gradually ascending road.

She read a brass sign: "Fellenbach" and stopped along the way, pondering. What was she to do next. First I'll go to search the garden areas, not only ours, all the others too and the deserted lot, then, I'll go walk down the avenues and stop people along the way. I don't care what anyone thinks. She raised her forehead. In the garden she saw the rich bush of saffron roses. She leaned her head against the fence.

"Melody," she whispered, "Ursa . . ."

This dark yellow, fragrant song was her child. She pulled herself together, crossed the embankment and entered the Rosskaempfer Inn with determined, quickening steps.

The coarse innkeeper's wife met her right away with a distressed look on her face.

"And you still haven't found her? Too bad." Then she remembered. "Old Frau Beucker was here earlier and made a telephone call."

Martha nodded. "Frau Rosskaempfer, a favor please," she uttered assiduously, "if you could please talk with your patrons, tell them about it. Perhaps somebody saw the child and that man somewhere."

"Talk about it? Of course. My husband does too. We haven't been talking about anything else. Isn't that so, Wilhelm? It's just too terrible." She sighed. Suddenly she was a totally different woman who spoke.

"Although we have no children—it's also more convenient—but if I had a child and such a jerk came along and they caught the creep, I'd tear his guts from his body like the pig that he is."

Martha tugged at her scarf. She pulled her felt hat lower. She breathed a barely audible "Thank you" and stuffed her handkerchief in her mouth.

And again she walked. She walked and walked. She looked at people in a strange way, distrustful, crazed, glowering, with questions in her dark eyes and on her sealed lips. She looked at men as if she were reading secret evil deeds from their blank brows; at women as if they were all suspect to her as accomplices. But she did not place herself in their way. Instead she strode over to the lumberyard to question the people who were carrying window frames from a storage shed, the worker who was sitting on a pile of wooden planks leisurely eating his breakfast. They shrugged their shoulders, shook their heads surprised. No, they hadn't been here yesterday. Martha, pushing herself to continue, no longer heard as somebody, pointing a finger to his forehead, said: "Who knows if it's true. She looks not quite right in the head."

A car with darkened windows whipped by. She stared after it as if it contained the abductor. Then there was a man sitting on the coach box, a woman straggling alongside the horses swinging a bell. She must have been sounding the bell up and down the avenues, calling: "Lad-ders! Lad-ders!" There were still several on the wagon underneath wooden posts, hoes, and baskets. And the horses trotted away from the town toward more rural communities. If some tale-bearer had whispered in her ear that wandering gypsy vendors had put her child in a wicker basket and had tied on a lid, she would have believed it.

She approached a more remote garden settlement where the clerk from the magistracy had acquired a small piece of real estate. The wife used to spend much of her time there in the summer with Elschen and Ursa, but Martha did not know the place. The garden plots lay deserted and quiet in the waning morning hours. Wherever a living soul showed itself, she called out, just to receive an answer that was like an empty, shriveled pod without a kernel to bear fruit.

At one point she stood near a fence waiting to see what was causing the commotion from an open shed; it was a pitch-black dog, glowering at her and starting to snarl when she did not leave immediately. Above the adjacent fence a dark sunflower face appeared, surrounded by a golden beam. It looked at her. She contemplated it and suddenly reached for it, grasping it with both hands: "Ursa . . . !" she groaned. She felt somebody touching her sleeve; a voice had been rushing after her, the voice of the sprightly young woman with whom she had just spoken.

"My husband thinks you should go and look over there. Back there. Second alley to the left. We call it 'Colony Refuse Disposal.' Everything gets dumped there; the plots are totally run down, nobody takes care of them. You won't get any information, since there is hardly anybody there. It's only ... but the fences can be easily breached by climbing over or crawling under them. Sometimes all kinds of shady characters hang out there. Not so long ago, a whole gang settled in for several nights. If you'd rather not go alone— sometimes you might find such a character sleeping in one of those seedy shacks. Herr Weinküpers, who owns the field at the corner, is out of work and putters around the garden all day, he surely would be glad to go with you."

She accompanied Martha a short part of the way, explaining one thing and another; Martha stopped.

"I thank you," she said softly. The woman, who had the impression that this strange woman did not understand her very well, nodded: "I'm only doing my duty as a human being," and turned back. Martha continued on her way alone.

The torn wire mesh and the gray, ramshackle huts came into view. The plots were overgrown with nettles and all sorts of weeds. Strewn in between were broken appliances, pothandles, doorknobs, bed-springs, as well as torn shreds of cloth, bottlecaps, pieces of paper, and empty tin cans. She found a passageway to the first building, a longish, open shed. Inside she found a few rotted wooden boxes, nothing more. Then she wavered. For the next miserable thing, separated from the shed only by a few trampled-down barbed wire pieces, was a windowless cube with a door almost like that of a construction booth, high enough to reach the shingled roof, that looked more like an outhouse. She strode forward: neither key nor doorknob, it had apparently been torn off. It hit Martha like lightning that she had to breach this hut at all cost; she forced her fingertips and her nails with grim determination into the gaping crevice and was almost disappointed when the door gave way with minimal effort.

She flung the door wide open. It was dark inside, a darkness of cobwebs and filth. Her foot knocked over a bucket, leftovers of fruit, shreds of newspaper. There was a sleeping bag, seagrass stuffing welled from the slit in a red pillow. And there ... She stared, a second only, and did not believe it. She did not believe it. Then she fell screaming to the ground.

She screamed. She threw herself over it. She fell down in the corner where it was lying, thrown into the refuse, crumpled up, a scrap of paper, a shoe rag. Dead.

Oh God! Her beloved child. She pulled it up; it groaned. Oh God! Oh God! She trembled, gathered it in her arms and stumbled outside. She stood in the light. Its little head drooped like a wilted flower. In one piece. It was still breathing. Suddenly she pulled back the hand that had supported it by the bottom. It was wet. It was full of blood. And suddenly she knew that her hand had felt the child's naked thigh, not its undergarments, its panties. She drew back the little skirt. Mercy! She fell on her knees. She was blind with tears, deaf from moaning. Somebody said: "No, how can this be possible." Somebody said: "Such a cute child." Somebody said: "Men are worse than animals." Somebody said: "Come now, you must get up. You cannot remain stretched out like this. The child belongs in the hospital, maybe it can be saved."

She obeyed, took her miserable burden without shaking the sand from the dress. A train of people formed, she walked in the middle, still weeping, her head inclined toward the child that became heavier and heavier. Somebody wanted to take it, to carry it for her. She would not have it. Somebody called out to a passing car, but it whizzed by. Behind the gate to the hospital they were stopped by the gatekeeper. Martha did not speak, the others spoke for her.

The gatekeeper quickly waved to somebody in the yard. "Sister Ida!"

She came rushing over, listened and nodded.

"I'll go with you right away. This way. Let's see if Dr. Heidingsfelder is still here."

The people stayed back at the gate and told the gatekeeper what they knew.

Now she stood and waited in a hall with potted plants, indoor trees; there were wicker chairs near her, but she did not sit down. The little nurse was flitting around—whispering everywhere, searching. A man in a white coat appeared, slender and bespectacled. He placed his hands gently on the child and she let him take it without a word. He looked at her unobtrusively, only furtively.

"Do not despair," he mumbled. "We shall do all we can."

The nurse touched her arm lightly. "Please come to Admissions now."

She found herself in a large room where clerks at their desks were busy writing, fiddling with heavy files. Sister Ida leaned over the barrier.

"Here—a child," she whispered. "Sexual assault. So you won't ask the mother."

Then she pushed Martha forward. The clerk filled out the forms. "What is the name of the child?"—"And what is the date of birth?"— "What is your address?"—"Do you have a telephone?"

Martha answered softly, apathetically, almost unwillingly. She was handed a form with instructions to stop for payment at the cashier's office during her next visit. The nurse explained everything to her as if she were speaking to a dim-witted child.

"All right, and now why don't you go home. If you want to, you can come back again in the afternoon. Ward 5B. So. For now everything that needs to be done is being taken care of. For now we can only hope . . . Good-bye."

Everything was being done; one could only hope.

Outside the gate were two of the women who had accompanied her. With them was a policeman who stopped her as she walked by.

# . 6 .

By the dim light of the lamp, she sat on her bed in her nightgown. She let her hair down, flung it back and ran the comb through the black strands, combing it again and again, and did not know what she was doing. She had subdued her fluttering heart, had held herself in check, and had gone to the hospital only toward evening, hoping that the later she came, the more there would be to learn about her child. Now she was not taken to see the child, but was briefly, professionally given encouragement. The child was alive, being taken care of, bandaged, but still unconscious. Tomorrow morning, around ten, she could come back to see the child, even outside visiting hours. Once at home she managed to write a few lines to Frau Hoffmann, and when she came back from the mailbox, she was confronted with the task of softening her neighbor's self-recriminations.

"One just can't leave them alone . . . if I had only suspected it. Ten times one watches them when it isn't necessary and the eleventh time one gets lax . . . no . . . no that our good Lord should permit something like this . . . that he wouldn't send a lightning bolt from heaven and strike the Satan dead. For this can only be a Satan, yes, certainly."

She put down the cake platter she had been gripping tightly with stiff, bony fingers while she was uttering her lament.

"Here, I just baked some cookies . . . one must have some pleasure . . . Ursel always loves them . . ."

She had meant well when she spoke, but was immediately sorry. No groan came from Martha, but tears trickled down her eerie, frozen face which she kept under control only with the utmost effort. And with a manic, almost savage gesture, she grabbed one and took a bite.

"Frau Beucker," she muttered heavily, her voice breaking, "I thank you."

And choking, "It is not your fault. It is . . ."

Abruptly she flung herself around in the chair and pressed her face against its back and clutched it with both hands. And the elderly mother stroked her shoulders, mumbling words commonly used to comfort and calm a child.

"She will get better . . . doctors nowadays can fix a lot." Finally she added, "If she is well otherwise . . . she is only five, the other thing will be forgotten."

"The other thing will be forgotten." She repeated the words aloud and finally placed the ivory comb on the night table and began braiding her hair. But she did not believe it. Slowly she shook her head. No. She had never forgotten, no, not she. She was eight or nine then. She saw it clearly before her. She had passed with a school friend through the gateway—it was Lucie Weigeler, she still remembered that. A man was standing there. He did not touch the children, only exposed himself shamelessly, and they quickly ran away.

"What a pig!" Lucie said later in disgust. "He looks like such a fine gentleman and is such a pig." She said nothing. She had been shaking in every limb.

Then the nights. She could not sleep. For it came to her then, gleaming, the abhorrent gruesome thing. It put her under a spell. Sweat broke from her every pore. She was burning hot. She wanted to scream, but could not and did not dare move. Completely motionless, she lay alone in the dark and stared with wide open eyes at this . . . this terrible thing. In the daytime she avoided her parents, no words came over her lips; she never even spoke about it with her companion in misfortune. One year—these horrifying secrecies lasted . . . more than a year.

She breathed deeply. She felt the heat on her brow; she felt her cheeks burning merely from remembering. She leaned her head back, pressed the palms of her hands hard against her temples. Moaning. She fell back onto the bed and pulled the covers around her shoulders. She had not opened the window or put out the lamp. She could not yet stay prostrate like this, in the dark.

She tarried and brooded. I don't want to think. She fought in vain. And yet nothing had actually happened—only an image. Nothing compared to what Ursa had gone through; that was indescribable, unimaginable. Again she noticed something sticky, the blood on her fingers. And suddenly she was seized by an insane, anxious thought: Maybe this unspeakable deed happened only this morning. Maybe she could have saved her, if she had only searched longer in the evening, if she had kept on roaming through the night. And another sudden thought: Maybe this was only the latest, the end in a chain of tortures.

She screamed. No, she did not scream. She emitted a peculiar sound, like a muffled howl. She shrank back from herself. I can't go on. I am losing my mind. It is too much. Too much.

She tossed about. She pressed both hands against her bursting heart. She folded her fervent hands and began to pray, whispering in haste, confused, desperate things. Little verses she had known as a child, biblical passages, Hebrew phrases from school, which had barely remained and whose specific meaning she had long forgotten.

Then again and again: Oh God—please help me—help me! Then suddenly she said out loud: "God does not exist, nothing exists. There is absolutely nothing."

And as she spoke, a huge black veil descended gently over her eyes. She was blind. I am talking nonsense. Please forgive me.

She sat erect on the bed, her hair matted to her skull. She thought: I cannot permit this to happen. I cannot forsake myself like this. I must help her. I must be there for her. I am her mother.

She stretched out on the sofa, calmer. Her child. Only two days before, in the evening, she had been jumping about like a frog, without a chemise, stark naked; she had been afraid that she might catch cold. Then she had, as usual, washed the round little face, the soft body, the little breasts that still seemed like weak unclear stars, the tummy, and the strong little thighs, and her ... Her vulva, a glowing, budding flower, an unopened flower . . . so lovely, so sweet. She wept.

She was unable to tear herself away. She had been cast into this inhuman world, unable to escape. I must sleep, she commanded herself. I want to sleep. She remembered a jar of pills she kept in the medicine cabinet next to the bed. She had hardly ever needed it after it had been prescribed. She rose and found it right away. She took some, after having put out the light and opened a window.

She rested with eyes closed. She slept.

# . 7 .

She had fallen into such a dead, dreamless sleep, she awoke disoriented, stunned. It was from that stuff. She had always been healthy, was unaccustomed to doctors or medications. She poured some cologne into a bowl, washed and was refreshed. Then she glanced at the clock. Thank God. A quarter after nine. It was good that she had rested this long. She got ready and stole from the building before a neighbor could accost her in the stairwell today.

She walked at a leisurely pace, for she did not want to arrive too early. The thought of having to wait again in the hallway seemed unbearable.

"Hello! Frau Wolg!"

Frau Rosskaempfer stood under the grove of birches, hanging stockings out to dry.

"I heard the news already, Frau Wolg. You found the child. Well, if she is still alive now, then she will live, I'm sure of it. You must believe that. The doctors, they'll fix it. Good thing the hospital is so close. Come on in. I have something to show you."

They went inside. The only guest was a construction worker, arguing with the innkeeper about politics. The woman leaned across the glass counter of the bar. With an almost triumphant look, she put down a page from a newspaper and underlined the boldface words with her stubby finger: "Crime against a Child . . . yesterday afternoon . . . five-year-old Ursula Wolg . . . in a rundown shed . . . found there by the distraught mother . . . immediately admitted to the hospital . . . so far has not regained consciousness. The girl's playmates . . . hardly any leads . . ."

Martha pored over the paper. Sentence fragments flickered, danced before her eyes. She looked up into the almost proud, searching face of the innkeeper's wife, the guileless face of someone who surprised a friend with the news that he had received a special award of which the recipient was still unaware. She seemed to regard it as a special distinction and honor that an inconsequential name like Wolg should appear overnight in all the papers, for everyone to read, in big headlines at that, and everything described in exact detail.

Only her well-meaning sympathy made her point out to the poor
tormented mother the pillory once again. Not that she expected a
big show of gratitude; the contorted face, fighting back the tears,
did not make her shrink back. She just gave a nod of compassion,
repeated that the doctors would pull it off for sure, and turned to
greet two staggering old men, who looked like fraternity brothers,
just then entering through the doorway.

The hospital clock pointed to ten after ten. Martha quickened
her step. The gatekeeper blocked her way in front of the gate house,
but when he recognized her he touched a finger to his cap and,
without any questions, let her in. Her footsteps resounded on the
wide, stark white pavement, then abruptly seemed to become something silent, empty, something that was chasing away the distant
day whose hem fell on the expansive lawn between the two gigantic
chestnut trees at the far end. The massive buildings that lined the
green looked like reddish flesh-colored bodies enshrouded in wild
vines and leaves blurring into brown-red, Bordeaux red, pale green,
and yellow, which gave them the look of wondrous objects of precious
bronze. And near the wall, a pumpkin was stretched out in the thin
sand, still carrying its yellow wilting flowers instead of balls of
fruit; but its grotesquely huge leaves were incredibly overgrown,
almost tropical.

In front of the entrance she passed a group of recuperating patients
who were basking in the sun. They seemed world forlorn, like
strangers, in their blue and white striped smocks. They eyed Martha
suspiciously as if she were some peculiar, bizarre creature.

Section 5B. Through the inner glass door she heard voices arguing
in sharp though muted tones. It was an unequal battle. A frail, meek
old woman struggled with the head nurse, who was a robust, grayish-
blond person; her enraged blue eyes sent daggers through the gold-
rimmed glasses.

"These are the regulations, and you know it. There is nothing I
can do about it."

She blocked Martha's path.

"Where are you going?"

"I am Frau Wolg. My child was admitted yesterday, a little girl."

"Oh, yes. First door to the right at the end of the hall. You may stay for a few minutes."

Martha thanked the nurse. The poor old woman's hateful eyes followed her. "Of course, the lady can pass, but for people like us there are regulations," she complained bitterly. The nurse took one step toward her, she whispered something with a sharp hiss. The woman, filled with fright, stared at her, changed her demeanor, becoming uncertain.

"No . . ."

"Yes," said the head nurse in a milder tone. "And now, why don't you go home, and thank God that there is no need for you to visit your boy outside of visiting hours."

The miserable little woman muttered something to herself and stole away.

The hall which Martha entered was called the "Children's Room." The little ones were resting there in rows of oversized beds. Many were wretched, very quiet and pale, some tried to speak, here and there was a wilted bunch of flowers, and some had little games in front of them on their blankets. Ursa had nothing yet, no toy, no flowers. She lived close to the wall in the corner. Her neighbor, a bold little fellow with flaxen hair, pulled Martha's dress as she sat on the wrought iron chair between the beds.

"Hey, lady, what's the matter with the little girl? Is she very sick? She must have a broken leg."

Martha nodded. But she hardly looked at the boy and did not hear whatever else he was asking. She bent over her child.

Ursa lay quiet. At a casual glance one might have thought she was asleep. But her breathing was labored and her dark little face on the bluish white pillow gleamed with a wan, waxen glare. Martha's hand twitched. Her hand wanted to lift the cover so she could see the wound and the bandage; but she did not have the courage. She immersed herself deeply in her child; she probably was without sensation. She spoke very softly to her.

"Ursa . . . Ursa . . . can you hear me? I am here."

She took the limp little hand into hers and stroked it with trembling fingers.

"Ursa . . . !" She waited.

Suddenly she threw herself over the child and passionately, desperately kissed her soft mouth, her eyelids, her cheeks, and her pure brow, kissed it eagerly, thirstily, like someone who has been languishing for something to drink.

"I will give you whatever you want, your mother will give you anything . . . I want you to have a boat . . . a really big one . . . that we can float on the Spree . . . you can play near the water, you may . . . the water isn't all that bad, people are worse . . ." she sobbed, "and when you are well enough, we'll go to the zoo and look at the animals: the monkeys and the lions and the tigers, the parrots."

Slowly she straightened herself and placed her hands against her temples as if she could squeeze out a thought that had sprung into her mind, a thought so disturbing, it made her reel. Yes. On the day when it happened, when the unspeakable occurred—she found it hard to believe that it had been only the day before yesterday—while waiting for the tram at the stop she had thought of calling the Rosskaempfer Inn and sending for her child to take her to see the animals in this blue, golden weather. Somebody would immediately have taken the message to Frau Beucker and she would have gone out to look for the child, and Ursa would probably not have . . .

She placed her elbows on her knees, the fist against her forehead. It was too terrible to ponder: You could have prevented it. You should have known that you could have prevented it. Could have thwarted it. It is all your fault. You too . . .

The child stirred, moaned.

"Ursa," she murmured fervently. "Ursa, forgive me. Forgive me. I am only a poor woman. Only your poor mother—I am so rich, Ursa. After all I have you. Only you . . . nothing else . . . nothing!"

"The woman is crying," noted the boy in the next bed.

She lifted her face like a heavy burden from the ruffled pillow. "My dear Ursa, right? . . . my . . . my . . ."

The door flung open. A white bonnet blinked with gold-rimmed glasses.

"Your time is up."

Martha rose obediently. When she took her hat from the rack, her gaze fell on the dolorous little sun, dimming, becoming cooler and mute, a sinking star without luster.

. *8* .

The little owl wailed. She did not know then that it was nicknamed "hen of the dead" or "bird of death" otherwise she would have taken the call to mean: "Come along, come along to the cemetery!"

She heard the heart-rending lament, the child's whimpering fear.

"Be calm," she begged, "be calm."

She pulled the corner of her covers over her ears, crawled deep into its warmth, and found no rest. Long after the graying of dawn her lids finally fell shut.

The Sunday bells rang her out of her slumber. She knitted her brow. She clenched her teeth; she pitted a sudden, incomprehensible hatred against these peals. The sound was somehow soulless, cheerful, so completely self-satisfied. Empty and loud. The chow signal, she thought, for the hungry souls. They are all cattle in a cowshed. If the minister didn't fill the hay rack, they wouldn't find a single sheaf of straw.

She remembered a Jewish wedding she had attended about eight or nine years ago in a big hall. The little bride's name was Anni Seidemann. Martha hardly knew her, but the parents had been friends. The preacher of the Reform congregation, in a gown and bareheaded, spoke of Goethe and Schiller, and Schopenhauer and Kant.

"What a splendid speech!" somebody praised the sermon afterward. "So open-minded, not at all like a Jewish clergyman." Frau Cronheim nodded: "It's only a shame there were no church bells. Then nobody would have noticed any difference." That was her aunt, Henne Cronheim, née Jadassohn, her father's only sister. She must be close to eighty. She had moved to Liegnitz years ago to be with her grandchildren; Martha hardly knew anything about her life. From her aunt her thoughts wandered to father and mother and to the elder Wolgs.

The mailman rang and threw a letter into the slot. Baffled she held in her hands a letter from her in-laws. The letter was good, almost warm. They had learned of the horrible deed through the newspapers. It was a terrible shock. Too dreadful. They were deeply shaken. They knew all too well what a mother's heart must suffer these days. They wanted to help and comfort. They wanted to know where the hospital was and when would be a good time to visit the poor little creature.

Martha tore the scrap of paper into tiny pieces. If they were all that concerned they would have found their way here already. She judged them unfairly. The old couple probably thought they would not find Martha at home if they paid an unannounced visit. Martha thought: They shouldn't come anyway. I don't want them. I won't answer; they must not have any part of Ursa. For it seemed to her that sharing the suffering she endured for her with others was giving away her child.

This time, at the hospital, she was left standing at the door without an explanation. It wasn't a good time, a young nurse said, since visiting hours were from three to four o'clock today anyway. She could see the little one then. Her condition had hardly changed, a little better maybe. She had been moved from the children's ward to Room 70. Why? The nurse shrugged her shoulders. Who knows? They probably needed the bed.

Martha went home. She recognized from afar the lady walking back and forth in the yard near the wrought-iron gate. The other woman now also recognized Martha and with quick strides, she came up to meet her. Without a word, she pressed her hand. "I had to come," she finally said softly. "I just couldn't leave you alone in your sorrow. Although it occurred to me that you might be at the hospital." She had already been upstairs and had rung the door bell. Martha unlocked the door to the apartment, apologized for the disorder. She tidied up the place herself on Sundays and today she had not yet made the bed. Frau Hoffmann moved to the couch.

"Please go ahead with picking up. Don't let me get in your way." She put her hat down next to her; short, hoary hair puffed up around a pleasant, refined, almost youthfully fresh face.

"Now," she declared suddenly. "It is nice enough. I am your guest, you must sit with me."

She wanted neither the cup of milk nor the buttered bread. Martha pulled the armchair closer.

"Has Frau Reich come back meanwhile?" she asked in a tone that did not seem in keeping with the harmlessness of the question.

"Yes, she came. She said something about a mix-up of the photographs, a misunderstanding. I couldn't really make heads or tails of it. But she did pay. We probably won't see her again, and that's the end of it."

Martha nodded. After a while she said softly: "And what about the people with the unpronounceable name?"

"The Rumanians—yes. They came back with their daughters. People like them, with little facial expression, always make for good pictures. Calmness is part of their nature. The little Frau Mutzenbecher, by contrast, now that takes skill. She is only pretty and only herself when she chats and laughs, and to catch that exact moment . . ."

She interrupted herself and, falling silent, studied Martha with lively gray eyes.

Then she said slowly, "My poor woman. You are very hard."

Martha twitched.

But Frau Hoffmann repeated very softly: "You are very hard."

And after a pause: "On yourself. You are forcing yourself to speak to me of things that don't concern you at all. Right? For you, all that exists is your child. You shouldn't force yourself . . ."

Martha stammered: "What should I . . . ?"

The older woman took the dark, drooping head into her hands and lifted it up.

"You should cry. This rigidity . . . I cannot bear it . . . When this wretched man . . ."

"What wretched . . . ?"

"This pitiable man who did this to the little child . . ."

"You feel sorry for him?" Her voice trembled.

"I feel sorry for the mother who gave birth to him."

Martha shook her head, almost imperceptibly, hostile. Her old friend leaned forward, grasped Martha's hands. "But my dear . . . You must understand what I mean . . . I only want . . ."

She fell silent. Martha had pulled away, more with the wildness of her gaze than with any abrupt gesture.

"No," she gasped. "No, no! I don't need this. I don't need this kind of pity! The kind that is neatly divided up—one for my child and the other, the bigger piece, for the murderer. Thank you. Thank you from the bottom of my heart!"

And sharply: "Please go now. I want to be alone. I didn't ask for your sympathy. I am not a beggar! I want . . ." Her voice broke. She beat her forehead against her arm and against the table, sobbing uncontrollably.

Frau Hoffmann sat still and sad. "My poor . . ."

After a while her hand began to search for a handkerchief and wiped away the tears.

"Please forgive me. You see. It goes better when I force myself. I am so miserable, so strained, I no longer know what I am saying. I am not well. You can hardly imagine this . . ."

"Believe me, I can guess it." In a lighter tone she added: "I would like to stay with you until this afternoon, if you don't mind. We could go out and eat somewhere. Down there is a small place, not very trust-inspiring, but . . . You would rather not?"

Martha lowered her head, watching her fingers draw a figure eight on the satin cover.

"No," she said softly. "Frau Hoffmann . . ."

"Yes?"

"You mustn't—you mustn't be offended. I—It is not easy for me. I don't want to be impolite or seem ungrateful. But I can't speak about it with anybody, with any human being. I have to bear this alone—all this—by myself. Some mothers in unhappy circumstances . . . like to be comforted . . . or even distracted, I know. Not I. I am, I am different . . ."

The old lady got up. She tried hard not to take it personally, yet her words betrayed the mild disappointment of someone whose gift offering had been rebuffed.

"One never knows one's neighbors. One tends to judge others in terms of one's self. I meant well. Don't take this wrong."

The golden hand of the clock pointed to three. A crowd gathered and blocked the main entrance. Relatives and friends of the patients. More people kept coming. On the sidewalk, a booth had suddenly been set up, offering sweets and fruit. Flower vendors paced up and down. "Beautiful roses? Carnations?" They also offered more modest little bouquets for sale—snapdragons, purple and ivory colored, then tender cosmos of faded lilac with a light veil of greens. Martha carried a few yellow roses wrapped in silk paper. "Melody," she thought. But these were much lighter, more a canary-yellow.

"Oh," she thought and waited sadly, "here I am bringing flowers, who knows if Ursa can see them . . ."

Gentle drops began to fall from the gray sky.

Hardly was the first wing of the gate open, the mass of people rushed in, swelling and roaring like an ocean wave. Martha was swept up. She found herself in the yard where the flood divided into trickling little streams. She entered the building with several other visitors. She stopped a nurse and searched for her room number. Softly she opened the door.

The large, friendly room apparently had once been reserved for second-class patients. As everywhere, unadorned white walls and white iron bars. Only a brown rectangular table was wedged between the row of beds. In the bed near the window was Ursa. An old face crawled out from inside the bed near the door. A black sign above the headboard was inscribed with prominent chalk lettering: Ramtow, Emilie—housewife. And underneath: Sixty-two years old. The gray streaks of hair moved; Martha said hello as she passed. She filled an empty pickle jar with water from a can and put in the flowers. Ursa's eyes were open, lifeless, as if she saw nothing, nothing of the green, of the matte gold that was sliding toward her. She saw nothing of the eye above her that spoke as lovingly as her mouth. No batting of the eyelashes, no sign of recognition of her mother. Only when she seized the thin little arm, like someone famished seizes a piece of bread, did the little hand close tightly around the eager fingers.

She lamented, she no longer pleaded. She sat so still, so dejected, and big tears rolled down her cheeks. The old woman coughed lightly. Martha turned toward her. The sick woman probably had been already waiting for a while; she began immediately, chatty and friendly.

"The little mouse will be all right. She is already a bit better today or she wouldn't be in here."

"Why?" Martha asked puzzled. Disquieted she rose and approached the strange bed; again the sick woman coughed slightly.

"I don't really know," she continued, "if I should tell you . . ."

It was just talk, nothing more, but Martha leaned forward almost begging: "Please, please tell me; I am the mother! I am completely in the dark. The nurses talk so evasively and the doctor isn't here either. I won't tell anybody. I promise. You must understand . . ."

But the old woman who was dying to continue her blabbering was already talking on.

"Yes, last night she was screaming so horribly over there, in the other room. Not exactly loud but like . . . you know . . . that one could get the creeps. A few of the little girls woke up and cried. Because she also started to talk about the man. You understand. So the nurses moved her. One has to think of the other children . . . when they hear something like that." And she added almost impishly: "I am an old woman who doesn't need special consideration."

Martha said: "Yes," sounding spent.

She should have turned her back on the woman, called out: "Enough!" She couldn't. She was left without strength in her misery.

"She hasn't made a sound since," noted the blabbermouth, "only in the morning when she was being fed, she was twitching in a strange way—it was like a convulsion—probably pain . . . then something like calm came over her . . ."

The door flung open. A party of visitors swept in, shouting and laughing. Herr Ramtow, his daughter and son-in-law, brothers- and sisters-in-law. Noisy exchange of greetings, with flowers and fruit, cheery apologies for being late.

"Well, when one has made plans!"

"Yes, when one makes plans with Lene!" Lene defended herself. She would have been on time if it hadn't been for Hans . . . Now Hans defended himself.

Someone made a "psst" sound. The lively crew eyed the bed in the back with veiled curiosity. Frau Ramtow introduced the lady whom she hardly knew herself.

"My husband, my daughter and my son-in-law, Herr and Frau Jürgensmeister—Frau Wolg, isn't it?"

Martha nodded, mumbled something and turned away. The conversation continued with a whisper and the recurrent words "the little one" "the child."

Martha did not hear them. Her fingers were dug deep into each other, her head was shaking slightly in disbelief, she sat and stared at this, this thing lying there in such a dull state, blind and destroyed, that had been a pearl around her neck, in her heart.

A touch, the voice close to her neck startled her. The old Herr Ramtow approached the bed with a bunch of grapes in his hand.

"She might still eat these after all," he said in a friendly manner. He dangled the blue, gleaming berries in front of the little face. The demeanor changed.

"There, you see, she is already getting quite lively." He leaned forward. Just then the child was seized by contortions, the face was a grimace, the eyes were horror. She began to scream. She bawled. Hopelessly. Not high and penetrating, but uncanny. Inhuman. Then as if muffled, choking. Someone pressed her throat: she gasped. In mortal fear. In torment . . .

The mother, agitated and without a word, threw her arms over the bed, as if to protect the child, and drove the man away. He retreated in shock.

"She'll come around," he mumbled, insulted.

She made no reply. She placed her hands on the child's hair and brow, caressing it gently, ceaselessly. The child groaned and twitched. She kept stroking. It was a frenzied, ugly dream in which she did this, was forced to do this, she was unable to extricate herself from the veil that enveloped her. She saw the trees outside the window. And in her unreal, suspended world, she heard two voices coming from a distant, solid house.

One said: "How inconsiderate to put such a bawler in with an elderly sick woman who needs rest herself."

The other voice called as from a door: "The visiting hour is over!"

# . 9 .

She remembered. It was about a year and half ago when the child died. The little face hadn't been all that bad, very pale; the all too large, floppy ears seemed ugly. And the sky-blue, unseeing, demented eyes. Frau Lange didn't have to whisper to her that the child was disturbed. That much was immediately apparent. And then it died so easily.

The mother consoled herself sighing: "God knows . . . perhaps it is for the best this way."

"Yes, it is better this way," said the women in the neighborhood.

She also remembered a discussion with her husband soon after they had been married about a news report. A woman, educated and from a good family, a widow, had only one son—around twenty years old—who had homosexual tendencies, which he actively pursued. Filled with fear, the mother tried in vain to get him to mend his ways. One evening she got hold of him and tried to talk sense into him. He resisted. In the end he rebuffed her rudely, and she recognized from his words that somebody, or maybe he himself, had concocted a code of ethics that approved and even glorified his vice. He left and she waited all night for his return home. Then when he was asleep, she entered his room and shot him in the head.

Friedrich Wolg mentioned this deed; he thought it inhuman. Martha read. Then she said calmly, "No. I understand her."

Friedrich became agitated. "You understand this? A mother executing—that's what it is—executing her own child for no other reason than that he happens to have an unfortunate predisposition? She might as well kill him because he was ill. Mothers of criminals and scoundrels of all sorts are sometimes very honorable women; if they all reached for a gun . . . Strangers can condemn, a mother should always forgive."

He spoke this last sentence not as if it came from within him but as if he had heard or read it somewhere. Unsure he added, "One must have pity for those who are sick—people with abnormal desires . . . especially a woman."

Martha flared up: "And no pity for their healthy victims?"

"Of course," he replied, "I am not talking about hardened criminals, murderers . . ."

She rested her chin on her hand, and pensively: "For the love of one's child, one can do anything. One can let one's self be killed by him. One can kill him."

They both fell silent. Friedrich, searching for a reply, rummaged through his briefcase. Then the doorbell rang vigorously. She went to answer the door and when she came back, her husband's thoughts had already turned to something else.

Everything came back to her. She still remembered that as a very young girl she met a woman she did not know, at her aunt Henne Cronheim's house. When the visitor was gone her aunt declared: "She is very unhappy. She has a daughter . . ." The rest was nodded and whispered in Martha's parents' ears. Her father stroked his beard. "It would be better if such children weren't born in the first place." Her mother blinked her eyes in embarrassed discomfort. And the nineteen-year-old pondered all the way home what this terrible, secret thing that she was not allowed to hear might be. She never was to find out. Maybe it was . . .

Her gaze fell on the clock. Twelve minutes to ten. She jumped up, threw on her jacket, tore her hat from the closet. Twelve minutes to ten. And she wanted to stop at the store, the small stationery and toy store of the Benthien sisters.

"Mother, there is a ball in the window—you know a really big one, this big!"—and Ursa spread out her little hands—"with stars. You should see it. Yellow and red and green and blue. Frau Lange says nobody can afford to buy it."

She decided to get it today, the priceless ball. Already about to leave the room, she turned back once more. She went to the night table, took a little bottle from the drawer and put it in her purse.

Not a soul met her in the hallway of high ceilings and bare walls and the wafting smell of medication, nobody in a white coat or in a blue and white striped dress. She did not wait for them to ask but walked toward door number 70 and swiftly opened it.

Frau Ramtow's demeanor was greatly changed and had a vexed expression. Her clan had apparently stirred her up yesterday.

"You had better not even go there," she grumbled after a curt greeting, "or she'll start up again. She just stopped a moment ago. Half the night she had cramps. It was impossible to get any rest."

That Martha should offer no apology greatly angered the old woman.

"Others are sick too and in need of care. I would like to know what I am getting for playing babysitter."

Her voice broke off, frightened. The strange mother placed herself in front of her bed, suddenly, taking strong strides, standing very tall. Horrified she stared into her face: She wants to choke me. Martha did not bend down.

"Frau Ramtow," she said unexpectedly controlled, as if her voice were kept suppressed by a fist. "You call it cramps, I would like to know . . . Frau Ramtow, what you know? Please explain it to me . . . I am sure the doctor talks to the head nurse during the examination of the child."

The old woman pressed her chin deep into the pillows. "I don't know anything," she murmured, somewhat reassured. "The doctor, I believe, just said that something has been 'smashed' or 'crushed.' I didn't pay much attention." She cleared her throat. "We have enough troubles of our own," she added maliciously, but in a cautiously low voice.

"You don't know anything more?" Like a superior, a judge.

"No," the old woman turned over and closed her eyes as if she was going to sleep.

Martha walked over to her child. Up to now Ursa had seemingly been resting peacefully; but when she saw her mother, or should have seen her, a disquietude came over her features. Again this twitching fear, her little body, too, fearful, she made motions, weak, useless, like somebody in shackles who is attempting to flee from a place of horror. From her throat escaped rattling sounds, since she was already too weak to scream. A human face had done something so horrifying to her that now everybody made her shudder. She fled. The child fled from the mother.

Martha's face was stone. Her heart wept. She pulled back and stretched out her arm holding up a huge rubber ball in a net of wide thin mesh.

How it glittered. The glow of the brilliant silver stars and bright colors intensified in the child's gaze. A diffident trace of joy flew over the face, a heavenly sweet smile. A crazed smile . . . The child struggled to raise her little hands, to grasp the beautiful wonder. The mother lowered it onto her chest on a long cord. The child puckered her lips, gasping, groping, toward the ball in the net, just as a baby has to put everything into its mouth. "You are thirsty," Martha said aloud. There probably is no drinking glass here, she said, hoping. There was a glass. She left the colorful ball on the blanket cover, and went outside with the glass. In the hall was a faucet and a sink.

Somebody will see me, she still hoped. Someone will come and ask me what I am doing. I won't be able to pull it off. Nobody came. Well, yes, a male nurse's aide, carrying a pile of white sheets, walked by. Now she was alone. She opened her purse, the little flask, poured out some of it. If it does not dissolve in the water, I'll pour it out. It dissolved well. She returned with the mixture and administered it to her child.

Her last, final hope was that the child would refuse it. In spite of the unpleasant taste, the cool smooth drink seemed to please her. She did not resist. At least not right away. The first few sips slid down smoothly, without difficulty. Then she started to writhe, turning her little head. Then the mother held her constrained and forced the drink down her throat. The child groaned, resisted weakly. She held up the brilliant good-luck ball again for the child to see; the child smiled—lovely, crazed. The woman in the neighboring bed had her back turned like a stubborn brat.

Martha washed out the glass in the hallway, sipped a few drops herself. As if she had been summoned by the splashing of running water, the head nurse suddenly appeared in the hallway, asking in a sharp, surprised tone.

"Frau Wolg—you are here? Who let you sign in?"

With a bad conscience she whispered: "Nobody."

"You can't just do that. You mustn't misuse our kindness this way. You cannot go inside today."

"I've already been there."

"Oh, yes? That's very unfair. Please, you must leave now."

"Couldn't you at least tell me . . . ?"

"No, nothing. I don't have time. Sister Kate," she called a young woman who was quickly passing by. "Has Herr Ulrich been here? Did you take the form to the front desk?"

The doorbell rang. She answered. A young boy stood outside.

"What do you want?"

"I am Heinz Kopecki, my mother works in the kitchen . . . Sister Hildegard sent me. She wants you to come." Self-consciously he added: "I think your child is dead."

She felt faint, she tilted her heavy head against the wall, completely drained. Her eyes closed, she pictured the child the way she saw her later: The big ball still glowing at the foot of the bed; yesterday's flowers spread out on the blanket; and a yellow, dying rose on Ursa's chest.

# Part II

# . 1 .

Today was the anniversary of her death. One year ago today. She checked the return schedule one more time before leaving the station. A thin drizzle fell. A light wind blew. The shoulders and front of her grayish green raincoat looked stained from the moistness. She held the two flowerpots of asters awkwardly pressed against herself.

The entrance to the wooded cemetery was diagonally across the train station, separated from it only by a wide square of decorative flowerbeds. They appeared so new, geometrically drawn, artificially clean; also new and bare in its frozen polish, the asphalt embankment poured forth. A car jerked forward and backward, not knowing exactly which way to go. Martha waited. Something leaped down beside her—a chestnut, a spiny green ball fallen from the crown of the tree onto the hard asphalt. It split open and released a shiny brown fruit. Martha bent down and picked it up with difficulty because of the two flowerpots.

"Tesna," Ursa had called it when she was still small, "Tesna." She recalled Ursa and Elschen coming home, each with a heavy long chain of globules around the neck, proud of the ostentatious, barbaric jewelry like the African tribal chiefs.

Close behind the white wooden gate to the cemetery was a little house, also white. In front of it was a gathering of flowers—most were red—under a drab gray sky. Martha had already bought asters at the train station, but she liked the little plant. Like a little tree, green with yellow and scarlet red berries that looked like small blood oranges. The saleswoman, who did not tire of picking the hardiest specimen, did not know its name either. She let her borrow a carrying basket for her pots because she still had quite a way to go.

She passed by the new administration building, by a farmhouse of dusky mauve bricks. Mauve was in vogue. From the main path, wide and lined with trees, the side paths branched off like the arms of a river embracing wooded islands along their course; along their banks, under melancholy, ponderous pine trees, were the graves.

# A Jewish Mother from Berlin

"Under Brandenburg pines in the sand . . ."

Very few people. Here and there the moth-colored lost figure of a woman, cutting geraniums or moving fuchsias to the mound. The blue and pink hydrangea were faded. Above the gray stone urn was a shrub pregnant with the plenitude of rose hips, but nobody claimed it. For here were interred ash containers, and there caskets. A narrow path led through the grove of urns, upon the cross followed hewn blocks, tablets with Jewish names. She passed unmarked gravesites that were, not unlike the others, enclosed in rows of hedges. The dead slept in the woods. In the woods without hunters, with silent humans, and lively animals. Among the pine needles on the ground beneath the trees rustled a gathering of thrush; finch and titmouse hopped along the edge of the water bath; a dainty squirrel dashed up a tree trunk, then hesitated and looked around from above.

Here it was, the trunk of a pillar in a mahonia bush—her marker that she had to turn. She approached the family gravesite, the Greek temple rising cool and distinct in the clearing between two French poplar trees. Here a granite rock stood out with its gold inscription: Eberhard Weil. There, there was Ursa's resting place. Her grave was framed by an even, low growing, fresh thuja hedge. The mound was green with young ivy, overshadowed by the branch of a pine tree—a gray, rough-hewn rock stood guard.

Ursa, my child

Nothing else. Neither epigram, nor place, nor numbers. One day a roving gaze would also read the mother's. The plot offered space for both.

No flowers. Later, she would bring some bulbs, cream and pink tulips, and in the spring snowdrops, bluestars, and yellow crocuses will bloom again. From the rounded dwarf bush the last deep yellow bud burst forth. Melody. She had ordered the Melody rose and the gleaming Ibis tulip from a gardener some distance away as a present for her child. Ursa, black velvet bumblebee. Disturbed, it flew to the neighboring crypt, buzzing and dipping its tongue into the tightly folded orange flowers.

# Part Two

The drizzling had stopped. No more raindrops fell and through the milky sky broke a veiled, gentle sun with a pallid, blinking gleam. Martha squatted down. She took the white, violet, and reddish asters out of their pots and sank them with a small spade into their home soil. She placed the little fruit tree among the ivy, took a dried twig and pulled the weeds from the narrow path. Then she wiped the bench with a bundle of newspapers and sat down.

Only now did her eyes blink with moisture. As if, as long as she was weeding and planting, she too lacked time to search for tears. She did not weep on the way to the cemetery, had pulled herself together in front of all those people; she was able to do that when she had to. And yet . . . the sweet little girl who sat across from her on the train, holding a big, flat object wrapped in paper of which she absolutely did not want to let go and which obstructed the view of her face. She came from farther away, from the northeastern part of Berlin, the part of hard cobblestone streets, and she was on her way to visit relatives for a few days in the western suburb. They had a house and garden! There was a large, beautiful meadow, that's why she brought along the kite; it was new, yellow and lilac with a green shredded tail, and she lovingly pressed it against herself. Martha listened, she looked at her, and she remembered that Ursa never had a kite although the deserted fields of scabious and spurge were ideal for flying kites. But she seemed too little then. Some bully could easily come up and snip the cord. Had Ursa ever asked for one? Not even that she knew. It didn't matter. She had to ask and would surely get an answer.

She contemplated the tangle of ivy as if she wanted to find her child underneath, lying in her little casket, pallid with roses strung around her head and chest, quiet with gently lowered eyelids as if she had gone to sleep for a while. And the mother had knelt beside her and had kissed the dead girl, whispering, pleading like a woman gone mad: "Ursa . . . my darling . . . yes?" And she would certainly have woken and would have smiled between soft eyelashes, would have placed her arms around her mother's neck, if someone had not just then closed the lid of the casket. She sighed.

Abruptly she threw herself from the bench onto the knoll, burying her hot face, flooded with tears, in the cool, quivering foliage. It crossed her mind how soiled her clothes would be from the earth. She mumbled: "I don't care . . . I don't care."

She rose. It was a good thing that she had chosen ivy instead of flowers. Flowers on the grave are prettier, friendlier to look at, but ivy is soft and warm, a blanket so she would not be cold in the wintertime. For she would have to remain here in ice and storm. "My Ursa." Tears. She cast a wild glance at the sky, the pallid white gray. "Ursa, I . . . I am going to kill him."

Again she sat on the bench. Some living creature rustled behind her in the thuja hedge. It was crawling, dragging its feet, then it hobbled across the path, she stared at it—a powerful, fat, mud-brown toad. She was about to chase the thing away, when she held back with a smile. Ursa was so wonderfully innocent and new, not like adults who are burdened with useless, shriveled prejudices.

"Look what we have here. Something beautiful. A big brown frog. It's real tame, I always stroke it, and it jumps only a little." She patted it, with some caution, but without disgust or fear. "Jump! Jump!"

"Leave it be!" warned Frau Beucker. "That's a toad, not a frog. It's poisonous."

One more reason to pat it again. The little creature slipped through the fence.

"It probably has its nest over there."

"Ursa!" Elschen corrected her sternly. "Frogs don't have nests, they swim in the water."

It had been the sunniest holiday after a week of rain. She had taken a walk with Ursa along the avenues, and on the way back, they met the old woman with her grandchild. Ursa always liked to come along. Full of joy. After all, her mother only rarely took her for a walk. On weekdays there was no time and on Sundays she often did not feel up to it. She was either too tired, too lazy, or the weather was nasty . . . But even then, she only lived for her child. In the evening she sat at the edge of the sofa, told her fairy tales and other stories.

No, she needn't have any regrets, needn't reproach herself. No, she had not been an inattentive, neglectful mother. Serious, perhaps too reticent, a mother who did not heap affection on her offspring as if ringing little bells. She kissed her in the morning before she left; that was a blessing, a shield against harm; when she returned she kissed her with the fervor of a lover. But her mind was not on frivolous fooling around, on tricks and teasing, or little games and little songs, all the shimmering cuteness other mothers let swarm and sound around their children. Did the child feel something was lacking? Hardly. She knew that she would not just lazily give her presents of whatever money could buy, not just try to give the child pleasure in her own way, but also in Ursa's. She remembered the Saturday before—that day . . .

"Mother . . . Elschen is going to church tomorrow. Can we go to church sometime?"

"No."

"Why not?"

She was about to tell her child something she could hardly comprehend; she held back, something else had come to her mind.

"We are going to temple instead."

"Temple? Where is that? Is it nice?"

"Yes, very nice. We will go on Simchas Torah, in October."

As she spoke, suddenly the temple of her birthplace was before her, the parade of children with colorful little flags—an apple stuck to each point and inside the apple a light—and the sweets and showers of raisins that fell on their heads. She had to tell Ursa. And then, then came Sukkos and the day of rejoicing in the law went by unnoticed. She never kept that promise. Was never able to keep it. She had not been in a synagogue since . . .

Suddenly she was startled out of her thoughts by voices behind her. People had come to a neighboring gravesite behind her. Gardeners—she had not even heard their footsteps. Now she was as startled as if these men had caught her in the midst of wild, forbidden thoughts. The taller, darker one peered at her with sharp eyes. She rose, sent a last glance toward Ursa, and left. On the other side of the hedge slumbered a much beloved, very young woman, dead at age twenty.

She slipped past the mausoleum, past the huge boulder that had been erected by the parents of a son killed in the war, a fighter pilot who had crashed. It was almost black with green moss crawling along its temples. She stopped in front of a spindle tree to touch the strange shape of its carmine red fruit. At the gate, she returned the basket she had borrowed from the flower vendor.

As she got off the train and left the station, somebody was handing out flyers in front of the soot-covered building and placed a scrap in her hand too. She glanced at it briefly:

> Your *future?* Your *fate?* Your *happiness?*
> *The stars don't lie!*
> What would you like to know?
> The gifted lady to whom the *deepest secrets* are revealed
> —Sandra Oreta (opposite Stern's department store)

She crumpled it up ready to throw it away. Then she suddenly changed her mind and stuffed it, crumpled up as it was, inside her coat pocket.

# . 2 .

She had not eaten a warm meal since morning. When she had come home from the cemetery, she had curled up on the sofa and had fallen asleep right away. Now she stood at the stove, cooking soup and frying a few eggs in the pan. She took out a cold piece of schnitzel, a few slices of sausage meat from the kitchen cabinet and devoured it all, although to be hungry seemed to her like disloyalty to Ursa. Opposite her own simple place setting, she set out a small colorful plate, contemplated it with a strange look, and then put it away again.

"No," she felt, "this is necromancy. This can't be. I want her to sleep in her grave."

She thought of the glass, filled with grape wine like all the others, from which the prophet Elijah drank on Seder nights of her childhood. A window wing had been left open. And while Martha was having her quickly prepared meal, she heard the voice of a child in the yard below:

"Frau Lange! Frau Lange! Herr Lange, is Elschen home?"

"She can't come down. She was away all afternoon and has to do her homework first."

He shut the window.

Homework. She saw the little girl sitting, serious, her head bent forward, and the red busy tip of her tongue moving back and forth between the lips, as she drew large letters in her notebook. She did not know whether Elschen worked that way, using her little tongue, but she knew Ursa, her child, did when she concentrated hard on her playing. After good work, the schoolbag was packed: an arithmetic book, a pencil case, and a primer. The case was of brown, varnished wood, with golden ears of corn carved into the lid. Frau Hoffmann had confessed, softly and hesitatingly, almost with a sense of guilt.

"I had bought the pencil case already, and wanted to give it to Ursa for her sixth birthday, since she was to start school after Easter."

And Martha with faltering voice:

"If . . . if you don't mind—you can give it to me . . ."

The pencil case. Over there in the cabinet. It was earthen brown with golden ears of corn. Like her child. She walked over. Driven by a desire to redeem herself, she knelt down in front of the drawer and reached for a book. The Bible. A present of long ago from Aunt Henne Cronheim for the little niece. A black volume with a golden seven-branch candelabrum on the cover and beautiful pictures inside. There was Eve under the appletree with the crafty snake. The artist had justly given the worm feet; for that "thou shalt crawl on thy belly" was the punishment for the evil counsel. And Cain walking behind the bulls with the plough and Abel tending his sheep; and Abraham riding ahead of his clan on a camel under palms and stars. And King David dancing around the ark and King Solomon sitting in judgment. She stopped leafing through the book.

"No," she thought. "I don't know. I probably could not have done it even if it had been my child. I could not have given it up . . . to the other woman, I don't know . . . No."

She lingered and read over carefully Solomon's judgment. This was one of the Bible stories she had wanted to tell Ursa. When Ursa would have been older. She had thought about it at times: her child should receive her faith at home, not in school. She herself wanted to be her teacher.

"And at that time, two women came before the king. And one said . . ." Ursa listened to what they said, her head tilted to the side, an innocent, dear question already on the waiting lips, with warm pure eyes. Those dark, thoughtful eyes. Always her child . . . oh God . . .

She turned the page. This page suddenly seemed painted with horrible grimacing faces, with terrible things written on it. And there, where she happened to end up, she began to read obdurately. She read about Jonah in the belly of the big fish and the shady plant, the gourd that, to his great sorrow, had withered. Then she looked up, empty, as if drained of energy. Why did she do this? What did this do for her? It brought no answers to her brooding, left her unconsoled and helpless. It shed no light on her dark pain. She closed the book. The prophet, the plant, and Nineveh, what did those have to do with her? Why was she still pleading with God? If there was a god, how could such a horrible deed be perpetrated against a child?

He was not.

She was hardly aware that the faith of her ancestors had become so much a part of her that a mere desire to be rid of it was useless and that she was no longer capable of an effort to mutilate herself.

She took out a pile of wash in need of mending; took darning thread, needle, thimble, and scissors and moved closer to the light. Only for a while did she pull the threads through with great care; soon she let the work sink into her lap. Dusk had settled on the room. Outside both windows was an expansive, rosy copper sky painted over with fluorescent gray—an unreal, gentle, seemingly mythical sky. The crowns of the elm trees cut sharply into it with their bronze-carved leaves, leaves of green bronze. Toward the south, it was streaked with clusters of fallow clouds, a staircase of suspended evanescing steps, silvery bluish, gray-violet. In the west, its rosy copper above a lusterless brassy yellow into the matte gold of a blurring sun. A quiet shimmering ocean ebbed softly away from a happy, virgin shore. The evening's soft, wind-blown mantle flew out to sea, absorbed completely by the mantle as far as it glimmered. Martha, who saw this tiniest of mirrors going blind with matte-golden water, lifted herself up in her chair, rising slowly as if she were held down by a heavy weight. Because her gaze fell on the washstand, she picked up a piece of almond soap she had bought on her way home, and unwrapped it. She pulled off the tin foil and smoothed it into a glimmering coverlet.

She was startled. What was she doing? For whom did she straighten the edges: Who could use such a silvery coverlet but Ursa, her child? Frau Beucker used to cut all kinds of patterns with scissors.

She remembered. She had once brought home a different brand of soap; Ursa was not happy about it.

"This one doesn't have any silvery foil, what kind of soap is this?"

"A very fine kind. Flower soap."

"Flower soap? Is it used for washing flowers?"

"Yes," the mother answered with a smile, "little dirty flowers like you."

She suppressed a yawn.

"It is still too early," she thought. "At least I can go to sleep; I am tired despite the nap before the meal. The mending will keep till tomorrow."

Slowly she began to undress herself. She had lit the lamp and, while rummaging through the drawer, she inadvertently pulled out something. A nightgown of soft apricot brocade with brownish filigree and brownish lace. Friedrich Wolg had given it to her. She had hardly ever worn it before his death, much later three or four times because Ursa liked it so much. What should she do with it? For a gown like this a woman had to be married, have a husband, a lover— I am a widow and will remain so.

She was thirty-seven. She was not tied to a dead man through a secret oath to remain faithful. But she had never looked again nor had she found. It was just that no man had come. She lived alone.

She had never complained, neither consciously nor unconsciously. She had been mother to her child and maybe as a matter of course she had forgotten how to be a man's wife. And yet men entered the photo studio every day. It was possible that none of them discovered the door to her face, an impenetrable, walled-in face. She was polite and quiet, and always wore a dark, elegant dress.

Frau Hoffmann had been teasing her about a lawyer named Pommer. "Fritz Pommer, Doctor of Jurisprudence, Berlin W 30, Geisbergstrasse 11"; she was surprised that she still remembered this notice a year and a half after he had invaded the studio with a whole troop of little nephews and nieces who were to be in a photograph for grandma's birthday. She wore the brown velvet dress with a collar of gilded leather, and he remarked, not even in jest, that she looked like "an old Dutch master." She had taken the remark, which was flattery, without much thought, but Frau Hoffmann had insisted afterward that Herr Pommer had had a favorable eye for her. It didn't matter. It didn't matter then and still was the same to her today. What was she to do with a male friend? He could have helped her that is true, could have advised her, and represented her.

She would have sent him out. There must be taverns, frequented by the likes of this swine.

Her eyes darkened as if filling with blood. She was glowing, hot. She tore the shirt from her shoulders, stood naked in front of the undraped window. Let them look at her through their binoculars if it pleased them at distant Binnwald Castle. She was not ashamed. Yet, she suddenly blew out the lamp and flung open the window.

The air was mild, the air of a summer night. It was pouring. No wind. The dancing, rolling drops spoke in even tones, soft, benumbing. She planted her arms on the window sill, her chin in her hands, she bored her febrile brow into the darkness that was caressing her softly as with a cotton ball. Seconds; then she was gliding upward. She stumbled toward the closet and groped for her old loden coat; she threw it over her shoulders and stole out of the apartment and the building.

She wandered through spaces of dusky oceans, undulating, storming, and whispering with fluid shadows of huge plants that shot up from the ocean floor with the shadows of fishes and hulls of ships that floated above her head. Algae beards matted against drowned planks of wood. Her soles treaded muddy sand. She pulled open her coat; it slid off her shoulders and chest. How white were her naked breasts in the dark. How hot . . . and how cooling was the drizzling rain. It splattered, kissed her lips. What if a man came by?

"I want to belong to you, you must do it, must find him." No man came.

She turned back home. Her skin was cold now and moist; she shuddered, wrapped the loden cloth tightly around her body. It was warming. Something scurried near the wall of the yard. Maybe a rat. Hurriedly she unlocked the front door. She was not afraid of animals, but she thought that the rat could jump on her feet unnoticed and look up her coat. Even while she was climbing the stairs, it seemed to her that she could still hear the clambering and leaping of the tiny claws.

She slipped into the room very quietly, as if she feared disturbing someone who was asleep. She lit the yellow candle and removed it from the nightstand. She tied the coat around her hips, knotted the sleeves together; the coat draped her ankles in black, heavy pleats. She stood in front of the mirror. She looked at herself, the straight shoulders, the strong, even body, the breasts, shallow, rounded, and large like precious bowls, without flaw or fold, spreading softly and merging with the smoothness. Fatigued, she extended her arms, gripped and supported her neck. And she tilted her head back slightly; her eyes stared. She was powerful, tall, a picture of antiquity, serious and oppressive in her nakedness like the stone Niobe that had recently been uncovered in Rome.

But she did not know her.

She turned away with a sigh, loosened the coat and put it on the proper way. Then she took out some writing paper, ink, and a pen. Hurriedly, as if no time was to be lost, and without relighting the lamp, she sat at the table by the fearfully flickering candle; she thought for a moment and began to write:

*My dear Doctor:*

*I don't know if you will remember me, the photographer who last year took pictures of your little troop. You said at the time that you liked the pictures and you added that since one never knew where life was leading us and if I should ever need advice in a difficult situation, you would be glad to help me. This is why I am now asking you for a few minutes of your time at your earliest convenience. It might be better if I made an appointment with you by telephone instead of writing directly, but since it is not a matter of law that concerns me, it is not legal counsel I need, but rather a sympathetic human ear. You may have read about my misfortune in the newspapers. This is what I would like to talk with you about if you can grant me a visit.*

*Kindly let me know. I greet you with utmost gratitude and with the expression of greatest respect.*

*Sincerely yours,*
*Martha Wolg*

## Part Two

She re-read it and knitted her brow.

"Full of mistakes," she thought, "so formal and awkward, so politely overwrought. He'll think I don't want to pay anything . . . oh well."

She folded the sheet, stuffed it in the envelope and sealed it.

## 3

She wandered down a long, straight, boring street, between houses that all looked alike; middle-aged women devoid of charm, who had lost their outward freshness and who had not yet managed to attain the dignity of old age. Periodically she felt for the crumpled-up piece of paper in her coat pocket, pulled it out and examined it as if it were an identification card she had to show to the authorities. And each time she unfolded the little piece of paper, she looked around furtively, making sure no curious face was looking over her shoulder. Then she felt ashamed. It was all nonsense, superstition. She was well aware of that. If she went there nevertheless, it was only because one shouldn't heedlessly refuse a hand that had been extended, even if it seemed too weak and offered little support and guidance. For Ursa's sake she had to believe. Maybe God would forgive her and bless the strange astrologer with real secret powers. Thus she edged ever closer toward house number 46, still with a feeling inside of wanting to turn back, quietly fearful, the way she had felt as a child every time she was sent on a visit to the dentist.

"Across from Stern's department store." The signs were already coming into view, then the store windows, the first one was filled with aluminum pots and earthenware bowls, the next with woolen goods, ribbons, and collars, with coats and clothes exhibited on mannequins. Martha crossed the street and stopped in front of the fashion exhibit. Stiff white little paper plates, marked with prices in black lacquer, were attached to either the lapel or belt, looking almost like targets at a shooting gallery. With apparent attentiveness, she looked over the fabrics and prices, while still considering whether she should not wander back down the street without having fulfilled her purpose. Then, her gaze fell on the exhibit of three pairs of little girls' underpants, three of the tiniest undies of wool and silk, one airy blue, one pink, and one light green. Sweet, adorable little things. Ursa usually wore a gray pair because it didn't get soiled so easily. She embraced them with her eyes, she glowed. Then abruptly, like someone who had been startled out of her thoughts and hurries to make good on a forgotten errand, she dashed from her corner of the store window back to the other side of the street.

A small enameled plaque at the entrance to the building directed her to:

SANDRA ORETA

Garden House

*Second staircase to the right*

She suppressed a certain scornful satisfaction. Such eminences lived in the rear building, yes. As she passed in the yard the heaping full iron container gaping at her, she still was not quite ready to throw bare knowledge, cool reason in with the rest of the refuse. "I want to be won over," she thought with yearning, "I won't resist. I will become a better person, Ursa, for you."

She climbed over the well-trodden linoleum to the second floor. On the stairs she met a woman coming from the opposite direction in a slovenly black skirt and jacket with a worn, baggy leather bag, a woman who, judging from her commonplace demeanor, went well with the antiquated, ordinary tenement buildings. But maybe she did not live here, maybe she had only sought consolation or a warning from the astrologer? When she had disappeared down the stairs, Martha regretted not having stopped her to talk with her, but even if that possibility had occurred to her in time, who knows if she would have spoken to her. For she would have had to give her an answer.

To the right, a little brass tablet read: Orth-Oreta. Underneath a piece of cardboard, attached with thumbtacks, was inscribed: 10–12 5–7. She rang the doorbell. A teenage girl in a white apron opened, and showed her the way through the dark hallway to the waiting room. What a surprise. Old, worn furniture, worthless oil paintings; but it all was friendly and simple, almost tastefully arranged. A quite comfortable little living room. A lady and gentleman were already there. A married couple apparently, well dressed, quietly withdrawn, not at all as Martha had imagined the clientele of a seer. On the table were magazines and astrological brochures. Had it not been for these brochures, she might have thought herself in a physician's waiting room, waiting with a heavy heart to see the doctor. She picked up a magazine and leafed through it, without actually reading any of it. She eagerly looked forward to meeting the astrologer who might at any moment ask those ahead of her to come in. Instead there was some rattling outside at the door.

The lanky young girl looked in from the hallway and mumbled: "Please." The married couple followed obediently. Martha got up immediately. She had pulled herself together in front of the strangers, but was too anxious now to remain in one place. Charged with restless energy, she ambled between door and mirror, between chairs, and gazed through the window down into a miserable, barren stone courtyard, but without actually seeing it. She glanced distractedly at the pictures on the wall: a still life, a lute with colorful ribbons, a pewter tankard added to it; parforce hunters on horseback, clad in scarlet coats, just before the unleashing of the pack of dogs; a landscape, meadow with boy tending geese, in the background the village. Underneath was the picture of a man with a walrus mustache; he closely resembled the old official who had given the information the time before. She wanted to go back to Alexanderplatz police headquarters soon, even though they would send her away as usual, without hope, the way she came, with empty hands, as an ungrateful, bothersome beggar. The police had better things to do than to bother with searching for the murderer of little Ursa—the assault against such-and-such, the stolen pearls of the film goddess X. She twisted her lips as if she had a bitter taste in her mouth.

"Frau Hoffmann thinks I am very unfair. Nonsense. They would track down the brute, I just don't have enough money. From the beginning they have been dragging their feet."

"Please." She was startled by the young girl's sudden appearance in the room before she heard her coming. "Please." She turned away quickly. She almost stumbled like a schoolboy who had been caught dreaming and rudely awakened by the calling of his name.

"I rehearsed exactly what I would say," it occurred to her, "and now everything is all jumbled up in my mind and I don't know anymore . . ."

# Part Two

The girl opened the door, showed her in, and closed it shut behind her. She was caught.

This was her first peculiar impression of the parlor far removed from the light of day. Only later did she discover the window hidden behind the plush, darkening curtains. The opaque, pale pink glass of a hanging lamp poured a soft flowing gleam over the walls which were submerged under the silken, silver-hemmed priestly garments, underneath deep green velvet coverings with golden fringe and embroidered with golden stars and signs. The floor was decked out with carpets, but otherwise the furnishings were sparse. A low bookcase stood in the corner, its moss-soft curtain partly pulled away, and it was crowned with the bronze bust of a bearded man and a copper chalice supported by three snakes.

And the woman herself was velvet. She wore a violet robe, over it silver chains; she had a pale face and kinky reddish blond hair. It occurred to Martha briefly that this hair might be dyed to give the astrologer a bizarre, mysterious appearance, but since she was not sure she immediately abandoned the supposition.

"Good day," said Sandra Oreta in a somewhat artificially pleasant tone. "Please have a seat. Why have you come to see me?"

Martha, who had intended not even to give her name so she would not prejudice the wise woman, answered awkwardly, as it seemed to her, and without sitting down.

"I would prefer not to say anything . . . Fraulein Oreta. I have to explain this later."

The other woman nodded, hardly surprised, and not at all insulted.

"I am Madam Sandra," she corrected, as she probably wanted to be called, and repeated quietly. "Please sit down, please."

She turned off the ceiling light and turned on the long-stemmed slender lamp on her cluttered, black antique desk. She rummaged around, searched, then handed Martha a large yellowed sheaf of paper painted with twelve round black plates, each bearing a strange golden object.

"Here. Now, think of what it is you desire; try to make a connection between your desire and one of the pictures and then show me the picture. One or two, whatever you wish."

Martha contemplated the face of the clock, which was only missing the hands; she did not know that it was the zodiac. After a while she pointed at the two naked, golden children, two boys holding hands and exactly alike in appearance. Sandra Oreta nodded, but remained silent and watched her, attentively but reticently, with eyes that were no less soft and deep, but that shimmered in the glare of her dress. If Martha were to remember this hour several months later, it would surely seem to her that this advisor examined her with a sharp eye to discern whether she was infertile and hungered for a child.

"How old are you?" she then asked directly. "If it is permitted to ask."

"Thirty-seven."

"Hm." And shaking her head after a pause: "So far this doesn't tell me anything. Let's try again."

Martha searched again and pointed at the golden warrior with bow and arrow, at the scale.

"Good," Madam Sandra said finally. She fell into brooding, propped up one arm against her chin and looked at the melancholy woman as if she wanted to hypnotize her.

The silence bothered Martha.

"I thought maybe you would cast my horoscope . . . whether or not I will be successful with certain plans."

"To cast a horoscope" was the only thing she knew about astrology, although she had no idea how this was done. The redhead seemed to smile diffusely.

"No," she interrupted herself suddenly, almost bitterly. "Madam Sandra, you know already. Tell me what you know. I want to believe . . ."

The fortune teller thought for a while. "I don't know much. Somebody has done you an injustice, against you through your child—presumably a man—and you want to—you want revenge."

When Martha later thought back on the course of the conversation, it did not seem so wondrous anymore that the soothsayer had guessed everything; she was probably very experienced in such matters, and with some skill was able to put things together from Gemini,

Sagittarius, and Libra. Then, however, she was disturbed by the surprising accuracy of this solution.

"Yes," she breathed. And more firmly: "I also want to tell you my name ... it was in the newspaper ... you must have heard it ... I am the mother of the little girl ... Frau Wolg."

Madam Sandra lowered her forehead. "I know ... Now I will cast your horoscope, as you call it," she explained in a friendly manner, mumbled something about "nativity" and asked when Martha was born.

She was dissatisfied.

"We have the day and year, but not the hour. This is awkward. In that case I can do very little."

Martha thought for a while. "Around noon—yes, it was around noon."

Madam Sandra hardly seemed to listen. She leafed through several thick tomes, stopped, knitted her brow with displeasure and spoke to herself, half aloud, words Martha did not comprehend, probably was not supposed to comprehend.

"The moon rules in the fourth house ... the aspects ... Albertus interprets it favorably, but ..." She shrugged her shoulders scornfully. "Hm." She pushed a white cardboard full of disks and rings across the desk, also a cardboard with numbers, signs, and lines attached so they would spin around. The whole thing looked like a study aid for geometry; Martha had never understood much about geometry. The wise woman did not deign to explain in detail, but ran her finger across it.

"Here is the moon ... here is the sun ... this Saturn. Do you see the angle this creates? This should be removed, but it cannot be changed. The aspects are hostile ... I can promise you little luck for the future."

"Yes," Martha said matter-of-factly. Her voice was as sallow as her face, but lodged in her eyes was an eerie black fire that ate away at her. The astrologer looked at her, stared in front of her, knitting her brow, brooding. Then she started to fiddle with a delicate iron ink pot in the shape of a devil's grimace on dog claws; red felt pieces of blotting paper had been stuck into the slits that were the ears, on the horns rested a pen. It seemed new and was downright tasteless.

After a while. "All that matters for you is reaching a certain goal?"

"Yes."

"And you wouldn't mind if somebody else reached it for you? Consequently you must find somebody toward whom the stars are more favorably disposed and who will make your plans his own, isn't that so? You need not despair yet."

She hesitated, probably waiting for a sign of agreement, but Martha remained silent.

"All right, this is what you came to find out. By the way your tool can be either a woman or a man. Circumstances will tell. A man might be better still."

Martha rose. "Well, that's all," she said calmly. "I thank you."

She pulled her purse from her coat and held it up uncertainly.

"Five marks," Sandra Oreta nodded. "I am sorry I was not able to foretell much good for you."

As if a more favorable constellation would have commanded a higher fee.

Martha paid. Madam Sandra held her hand for a moment and carefully stroked her fingers.

"Your occupation is . . . ?"

"Photographer."

"Yes. But this is not the hand of an artist, more the hand of a thinker, a reflective person."

Martha left. At the door she almost collided with a young girl who was about to ring the bell. She looked so pale, so haggard and miserable, in a vulgar cheap dress.

## 4

It made her uneasy that she still had to think of the little dog which had traipsed after her in the morning—a rather young little animal, yellowish brown and black, of uncertain breed with crooked ears, bow-legged, curly tail, but pretty eyes. It sniffed the garbage heap and hopped over to her when she stopped, and wagged his tail at her. The dog quivered around her shoes, jumped up and left a few sandy paw prints on her dress. And as she turned, it ran after her, ears flapping and full of trust. It was no use that she turned away.

"I don't have anything for you. Go home."

It would not let go. From the trolley stop came a worker with a knapsack; he snapped his fingers to attract the dog's attention. It gladly trotted over to him and, begging, jumped up on him. And while the man bent down to talk to the dog, the bell of the trolley rang and Martha was carried off.

Now her workday was almost done, and she had not forgotten about the dog. She was not given to wistfulness. The little critter probably belonged to someone from one of the cottages nearby and had eventually leisurely strolled back home after a brief, forbidden foray. The owner probably missed it soon, called its name, went to look for it, and found it. But she couldn't rid herself of the thought that it had somehow strayed, maybe already the night before, had crawled into a shelter overnight, and then was walking into the morning, courageously, but hungry and helpless. Could the man have taken it in? She thought of Ursa, she too had been so cheerful, so lively in the evening, and then traipsed along just as guilelessly, just as unprotected with a stranger.

Ursa . . .

She took a deep, strong sip as if she had to wash something sharp, something burning and biting, down her throat. She covered the second, still steaming cup with the cake plate since it was slowly getting cold.

Frau Hoffmann was in the next room, answering a customer who had just come in, disturbing the cozy coffee break—the voice of a stranger, she did not know him. The exchange did not last long. Should she go in? She listened and suddenly heard the name "Wolg," then again. She was baffled. Somebody wanted her. She stirred the coffee in her cup, finished it, and entered the studio.

The stranger who was speaking with her partner stood with his face turned toward the door. As she entered he looked up and took a step in her direction.

"Madam," he said with inquisitive demeanor. And then with a bow: "Renkens."

"Oh," Martha lifted her hand in a friendly gesture. "This is a surprise."

"You know me, Madam? Your husband spoke to me about you, but about me . . ."

"He wrote often and later spoke frequently. Albert Renkens, isn't it?"

"You even know my first name."

She smiled. "I know more. Please."

She arranged the chairs. He assured her that he had to leave soon, but took a seat anyhow. She sat in one of the carved chairs while Frau Hoffmann quietly disappeared to drink her cold coffee.

Martha observed her guest while he spoke of the deceased friend, of their stay in America, and of their life together. I had pictured him differently, the newly graduated engineer whom Friedrich Wolg met one day in Plymouth, Massachusetts, and who had attached himself to him almost passionately like a homeless dog. She had pictured him as more boyish, a nice young man, but less distinctive, less well formed. Years leave their mark. He was probably somewhere in his mid-twenties then and was now over thirty. She had always painted this companion in her mind as a younger, less defined copy of her husband, and if blond hair and blue eyes, an elongated beardless face with a straight nose are similarities, then Albert Renkens and Friedrich Wolg were not all that different. But Friedrich did not have this firm chin, such a small mouth, reddish skin, and that distant look in his eyes—an ocean gaze, the gaze of a sailor. The eyes were the most peculiar feature about this man . . .

" . . . if it hadn't been raining, I would not have sought shelter in the entrance of this building. And as it happened, while waiting like that, I looked at the photographs on the wall. God, I thought Martha Wolg ... Martha Wolg ... isn't that ..."

So today he climbed the stairs to hear from the older lady that he had not been wrong, this Martha Wolg was the right one, the wife of his friend. But the friend was dead and the widow lived with the child—he knew that Friedrich had a daughter.

He hesitated, confused. Frau Hoffmann, who had returned, suddenly showed displeasure by furrowing her brow and making vigorous signs behind Martha's back.

As if she had felt the motioning and warnings, Martha turned toward her.

"No," she said in a frighteningly dispassionate tone that seemed to come from another being. "What does it matter? Herr Renkens was in America and couldn't possibly know. He'll just have to be told."

Frau Hoffmann quickly moved toward her and took her hand. Softly: "Telling him, yes—but not you. It makes you ill; for you this is hell, you always brood so much about it. I know how difficult forgetting ..."

Martha contemplated her lap.

"I cannot forget," she whispered, and suddenly, throwing back her head, with trembling voice: "I don't want to forget."

And with an abrupt motion of her arm, as if she wanted to push away the friend, the intruder between the guest and herself, she leaned forward: "Herr Renkens. Please excuse this chatter ... You will understand ... It is true, I had a child, a girl—murdered by a fiend."

Albert Renkens stared at her. He was too surprised, too overwhelmed to mumble the usual condolences, but also not touched deeply enough to say a soothing, sympathetic word to the poor woman. He lowered his head and took a deep, audible breath. That was all.

Martha nodded: "I thank you."

He looked up, surprised.

"People always want to comfort me; you don't comfort me. That . . . that is good."

"People would like to help you," Frau Hoffmann said with gentle rebuke. "If you would only accept their help, then maybe you would be less miserable, at least you would be calmer."

"I don't need this kind of help." Her eyes burned. "If somebody wants to help then he should find the murderer . . . and bring him before his judge."

She whispered passionately, pensively, as if she were all by herself: "If somebody came to me, holding an ax with bloodstained clothes and said: Look here, and I had to believe, would have to believe him that he really killed him: then . . . I would not refuse him anything, whatever he wanted as a reward. Nothing."

With flickering stars.

The old friend sadly shook her head disapprovingly. She looked at the man's face; it seemed a shade redder. The eyelashes twitched, as if this confession made him uneasy, embarrassed him. He got up, excused himself with polite words: "I am sorry . . . an appointment . . ."

Martha dismissed him politely, as if suddenly sobered, already remote. "It was very kind of you."

When he was gone, she found his calling card on a little table in the vestibule and put it in her pocket.

An hour later, Martha wandered down Kurfürstendamm. Its bustle before the rising dusk seemed hazier and at the same time subdued. The vehicles rolled along in softer shades of gray than the harsh light of the higher sun; their honking and rattling would soon resound more clearly in the black, star-cold night. Martha was barely aware of it. She took note neither of the ringing of the streetcars nor of the clatter of the motorcycles, nor the short-breathed, heavy buses, nor the quieter, elegant, elongated private limousines, and not at all of the stream of a divers human mass that carried her along and swept her forward.

She did not feel like a drop in the wave. She was a hunter on a secret prowl, careful not to lose her game, the guileless prey, from sight. This is how she became fixated on a slender coat of dark blue, fine fabric, legs in black shoes and stockings, and a dark, broad-rimmed felt hat on bluish black, corkscrew curls. She had spotted the hair and the gentle face when the young girl turned into Kurfür-stendamm coming from Grolmannstrasse. How old might be that round little face, this pink and white with the strong mouth, the little nose, the huge nights of her eyes, and indistinct Slavic trait? Fifteen? Seventeen? She reminded Martha of somebody. Of whom? She followed, deep in thought—and found a similarity with her sister Regina. Regina was eight years older and had died at the age of sixteen. The picture of her that hung in Martha's memory was covered with dust and cobwebs; the appearance of this very young stranger suddenly restored it clear and plain. And Martha was surprised to realize Ursa resembled the sister in many ways, so that the dainty, unknown young girl also reminded her of Ursa. True, her child's hair was simple, black-brown, without the bluish sheen, her skin was darker, her lips thinner; the Slavic trait was missing. How did she resemble her then? She did resemble her strongly in the roundness of the chin, the swelling of the cheeks, the indescribable line around the mouth, and the radiating expression of the eyes. There was a seriousness, a thoughtfulness, something strong, feminine already in the child's weakness, a quiet strength lay far behind the gaze, a dark abysmal depth. All this in Ursa and this girl. Ursa was sixteen, seventeen, and her mother ran after her; she did not turn her head.

The slender little neck. Passing between the low-lying strips of a window lattice, the girl approached a haberdashery store, stopped and turned quickly in front of the mirror and looked at herself in the store window. Martha stalked closer. Surreptitiously, she examined the pretty profile, and before she knew it, she was already picking out a hat for her daughter. The most expensive, most beautiful one, the big one in caramel brown velvet. Ursa would like this one. The coat, of course, did not match; she would have to buy a new one. The funny old Franconian coachman's collars were very popular again. Thus brooding, searching, and probing, she went back into the tumult of the street.

# A Jewish Mother from Berlin

Two young fops came by; that's what Martha called them. They let the slender girl pass under impertinent stares, they followed her boldly with their eyes, and one of them called after her in a low voice: "Cute!" Martha's hand itched. She could have slapped the fellow's face. After all, she was the mother. She actually had to restrain herself not to confront him because of a remark that, though crass, was hardly insulting. Her protégée now quickened her step; she only blinked at the hooligan with disdain. She had to move, had better hustle. And soon she crossed Tauentzienstrasse and turned into Budapesterstrasse.

No more human stream, no more tossing breakers; here only a peaceful rivulet was at play. A beggar sat next to a dark wall, his bandaged leg stump stretched out on the pavement, a quavering, whimpering little hurdy-gurdy in his hands. He touched his hand to his cap: ". . . my dear lady." The girl stopped, searched her pocket and quickly leaned over. He continued his noodling; as Martha passed, the left hand went to the cap. ". . . my dear lady." Martha too found a coin. She didn't know whether she gave because the girl had given. She now stood on the street's embankment, waiting for the yellow light to slow the cars and the green one to make them stop. Then they hurried across the roadway at the same time and headed toward the main entrance of the zoo.

A man stepped out from the red wooden lattice between the two stone elephants. He was of medium height with the beardless, energetic face of an American Jew. He was well dressed, not foppish, and seemed far more than twice the age of the flower-like, very young girl, whom he greeted almost respectfully. But his manner, as he leaned over the small, gloved right hand and kissed the white wrist above the pearl gray leather strip awoke in Martha a thin flame of jealousy and suspicion. Who was this man? What was he to the girl? Only a friend? The fiancé? The lover?

A lover? The two were already talking in a land that Martha had never entered. Like the small stones from a demolished mosaic, she had retained three shopworn Polish phrases from her childhood, enough to guess that it was a Slavic language, but too little to name the language or make sense of the words. But her ears were wide open with torturous curiosity and strange sounds after all always seem to stand out from familiar ones. This girl had such a dark-sounding voice. Melody.

They entered the zoo and Martha followed them, despite the ticket vendor's polite reminder that the gate would soon be closing. She followed jealously, unreasonably, just as a hot-headed hunter follows his game, a warrior an ardently hated enemy, as a sick, betrayed woman pursues the faithless friend and his new love. Now the girl turned around and extending her right arm pointed at Martha knew not what, maybe the whirling leaves. For the trees already stood there sadder, poorer, with a sparser, more apathetic song, and the leaves were strewn over the ground like so many dead birds. The cage of the beasts of prey was already empty. The big cats had gone indoors for the night. And over there the precious porcupines also wanted to go to sleep: two of them pushed through the door at the same time, and one pushed the other aside with erect bristles. Then they seemed to stare at each other confused, unable to understand that they could not both go through at the same time, and then trying again. A little boy, glued to the fence, squealed each time with delight at how dull-witted they seemed to be.

"Now one more time! Look at this! Now again! And another one, all three of them in a heap! Oh, they're funny."

Martha turned, half alarmed, as if the child's delight had distracted her from a duty, from something she was supposed to do. Where were they? There up front, they were wandering along, then halting, maybe because their chattering made them forget to go on, maybe too because they wanted to look at the distant structure of trees and brushes with its drizzle of leaves blurred in the bluish pale light like a suspended fountain of golden, bronze waters. And Martha ran after them almost for everybody to see, she held back for a moment underneath the stone blocks of the goats' barren mountain with its steps, reefs, and fissures. Near her, the brownish ram ate from a roofed hay-rack. A tahr. A strong, beautiful, masculine animal with noble, twisted antlers and despite its valor, still somehow gentle with its soft, flattering mane. With the gleaming, quiet eyes . . . It was good that such animals still existed, so clear and unique in contrast to ambivalent, unclear, and noisy humans.

"Tahr."

She pronounced the syllable half aloud with a start. For the pair was unexpectedly turning back and almost grazed her in passing. The two seemed so totally absorbed in each other, shielding each other, so that any look sharpened by suspicion bounced right off to no effect. She let them gain a little on her and then continued her pilgrimage, following them to the bird pond of the black swans, bridal ducks, pelicans. There the pink flamingo stood wondrously in blackish water on one glass-spun thread-like leg, with a filigree neck that seemed to have escaped from an artisan's foolish whim.

The girl seemed to have a similar thought, for she nodded and, smiling, raised her hand. And the man, who stood next to her, quickly stepped in front of her. Martha heard him speak softly. What he was saying she still could not understand. She could not see his face and its expression, for he stood with his back to her; but this quick stepping in front of the girl was something of a signal, like a code word, a secret meaning.

She thought: "He must be her boyfriend . . . her lover."

Ursa. Oh, God if she knew that Ursa too, with a man so much older . . . She would no longer have been enough for her. Her daughter would have grown apart from her like a young tree away from a gardener who at first had to bend down and once had spread branches over it. Ursa with green branches. Would she have provided her mother with shelter and shade in gratitude? She was such a serious, thoughtful little creature, she would have become a passionate woman. She is *my* child. And were this man to force her into his arms, into the bed of his whores . . . at seventeen . . . so young . . . And yet one day she would press her hair against her mother's cheeks and would weep.

She lowered her head. She held her forehead and groaned. Oh, no. No. She would have been a happy mother and would not have known it. A happy girl Ursa would have been and would surely have known it. She would have matured into love, would have loved; where was the outrage? A warm heart and her sensuousness, her glowing body: the strawberry mouth and the firm, round feminine breasts, and her pudenda that still hovered like a still unfolded, dreaming poppy flower. And when the man touched her, unlocked her, then it was right and was joy . . . Yes, it was good . . . was good . . . this surrender, this smiling . . . a virgin become woman—instead came this horror . . . tearing . . . slaying a still living child . . . God! She buried her face in her hands. Tearless. She only covered her eyes. Away. She did not want to see anything. But the screaming . . . the screams.

Her arms sank quickly. She lost herself completely after all. Where was she? At the zoo. She glanced about fearfully. There were people and there and there and soon somebody would have pity and would ask what had happened to her.

Back there her lovers walked past the empty concert shell. But she turned around, determined, suddenly disregarding, discarding what she had been searching for. She took long aimless steps, as if she had to get away as far as possible from the pair; then she stood still, thought for a moment, and then she knew whereto. To the big birds with sharp claws, humans call them robbers when they slay a living creature, and ignoble when they feast on carrion. She wanted to greet the condor. For she loved this wonderful bird, the one bird that soars to the highest loneliness, into ice-clear, silent air, the bird of the sun oceans—one wing pointing toward Ecuador, the other toward Tierra del Fuego, under whose claw Chile crumbles, on whose black feathers still melts the snow of the Cordilleras. He was a captive here, destitute and strange, he sat, in his narrow, reddish gaze the frosty melancholy of the exile, of one wilting away. She no longer found him. He probably sat crouched in the rocky cave, motionless in the dark; he slept. And as she sadly turned away, the zookeeper came to meet her, then waited until she was gone, past the monk- and white-head vultures, crowned with steep peaks. Then she heard the iron gate behind her rattling and closing.

## . 5 .

November branches of the elms beckoned at the window like a beggar's fleshless, desiccated, naked arms—black, rotting pieces of leaves still sticking to the wrists. Martha contemplated them, shivering. She stood in front of the stove, still wearing her jacket and hat; she had only slipped off her thin black gloves and held up her stiff fingers against the not very warm tiles. Frau Beucker had probably just gotten the heat started. She was chilled through and through, scourged by the wind, whipping and cutting the skin as with steel rods, defying all layers of clothing. It had been cool also in the temple, cool and rather empty. A few lonely old women on bare benches in a semicircle upstairs, a few old men downstairs. In addition, the preacher spoke German. Was that the reason she understood him only poorly and could hardly follow? The little Hebrew she knew had long been buried under the rubble—glass pearls in a bag full of holes she had owned as a child. But this talk too passed her by, unstoppable, numbing like the drizzling of seeds flowing through fingers. She caught herself, to her shame, searching the unadorned hall for a piece of filigree, a decoration on which to fix her gaze. She left the house of God with the feeling of an easily fulfilled duty.

Had that been her only purpose in entering? Since Ursa's death, she had been to the temple several times, always with the vague hope of finding consolation for her plight, an answer to her questions, and every time she left somewhat disappointed, sobered, with empty hands.

She swore, "It's nothing. It offers me nothing. I won't go again," and still she came back again, almost in spite of herself, as under a certain duress, like someone visiting a childhood friend who had become a stranger over the years. He struggles in vain to uncover those features he had once loved so dearly, to recognize the bond that had united them; he finds nothing, all is gone, and yet through lingering affection and inhibited by memories, he gains the courage, not the harshness, to close the other's door behind him, never to return. That's the way it was.

Martha stretched her limbs. With a sigh she placed her hat and jacket on the bed. Then she sat, her face glowing by the light of the fire as she leaned over the stove to rake the embers. The coals were not completely burned through, the little flames licked, leaped, transparent blue and red, hissed, laughed with snake's necks and heads. Adders in a narrow, walled-in pit, into which they had been cast by human hands, intertwined with each other, their bodies copulating, flickering, lusting for nook and crevice through which to slither out. Full of dancing frenzy, they bit the iron tip.

A noise, a rustling sound coming from the window made Martha look up. A butterfly trembled at the windowpane. It seemed all black as long as it was making fluttering motions. But it shivered quietly at the window frame, large with outstretched wings. Colorful: a peacock's eye, it looked at her with fox-brown sheen, gentle sulfurous rings, an amethyst-gleaming gaze. The soft rhythmic raising and lowering of the wings whispered of deep breathing, drinking air. A miracle. As by magic, her old-fashioned chamber had brought forth something that was beautiful and fleeting and pleasing. Did it mean good luck? How should she have good luck—what luck?

Following a sudden impulse, she went to the vestibule door and unlocked the mailbox. She was never in a hurry to check its contents; mostly there was nothing anyway. Or just advertisements or, like yesterday, a tax bill, useless, unpleasant stuff. Well, here was another useless scrap. Businesslike paper, a company letterhead; she twisted her mouth in scorn. She took it, crumpled it, took it inside where it was light, and stared at it:

Julius Siegel, Esq., Attorney at Law and Notary.

And below in the left hand corner: Dr. Fritz Pommer, Attorney at Law.

Now a response, after so many weeks! She turned the envelope over in her hand without opening it, as if she did not believe it yet. Then she tore it open with a strong hairpin.

It wasn't much. A polite, impersonal note, typed. First a brief excuse for the delay; his work as a lawyer had detained him in southern Germany for a long time; then a request to visit him in his office on Wednesday. "Yours sincerely"—hasty scribbling—"Fritz Pommer." It looked carelessly hurried.

Somewhat disappointed, Martha put the piece of paper in the drawer. She had expected less businesslike brevity, something friendlier, more responsive to her lament and hope. But what did she want? Why should he bother writing her about edifying things. He was going to receive her in Gertraudtenstrasse and speak with her.

The lawyer was tied up on the telephone when she entered. He nodded at her, receiver against his ear, bowed sitting and pointed with an obliging gesture at the heavy leather chair. "Si duo faciunt idem. No, I cannot negotiate later. I have to be in court in Schöneberg at twelve . . . five-hundred-fifty . . . Out of the question . . . can't be done . . . all right, I will see to it . . . Good."

He put down the receiver, got up, and tendered Martha his hand. "That's the way it is," he said smiling, "and especially today, the telephone has been ringing all day without interruption and I have to pick the line up myself. Bothersome, but what can you do. Well?"

"Doctor Pommer," Martha declared softly, "I already wrote to you about . . . the purpose of my visit. It is . . . you know about my misfortune."

The lawyer seemed a little embarrassed, just a bit. "Madam," he said hesitantly, "I must confess, since we don't have mutual friends . . . I am sorry . . . Will you explain what it is all about?"

Martha was taken aback even more. She had, surely without reason, presumed that he had read the brief notice under "Miscellany" in the daily newspaper and had not forgotten about it. She felt, though barely recognizing it, how something gentle and warm began to harden and cool inside her as under a thin breeze. She filled him in with a few spare words, and he even found a few sympathetic polite phrases.

After a fitting pause: "All right. What you want then is—even though you believe that the police have done their duty sufficiently— you want to try a detective?"

Martha nodded. She had secretly decided on something else; but she did not remember anymore what it was.

"Madam ... I would hardly advise you to do that. Nothing is likely to come of it. The results of such investigations are usually in no proportion to their costs. In cases of continuing, repeated offenses like adultery or pandering, which would have to be attested to and documented, but in this case ... You will waste a good sum of money, and what will you get in return? Nothing, a few empty leads—nothing open and shut—with which to establish a case."

"I see no other way," Martha said defensively, almost bitter.

The lawyer bethought himself. "If you absolutely insist, I can give you an address, a former criminal inspector. He is quite good. At any rate, he is better than most and therefore also not inexpensive ... but if one wants to have anything to do with such people in the first place ..."

He rummaged through the piles on his desk, scribbled something on a note pad, tore it off, and handed Martha the piece of paper. "By the way, I could contact the man myself, if you would prefer. But maybe you should think it over ..."

"Thanks," Martha cut in and repeated, "Doctor Pommer, thank you very much."

She wanted to get up, turn toward the door, but such sorrowful fatigue, such dejection pulled on her limbs like lead. She only lifted her arm from the rest, but let it fall again, and did not move.

The lawyer watched her calmly. Then a probing, inquisitive expression gradually spread across his face and he spoke in a barely changed voice, only his words were groping, unsure: "Madam, it seems ... I am not quite sure ... I mean, you actually did not get what you had been looking for. As far as I remember, what you wanted was not so much practical help from a jurist ... but simply personal advice. So I would like to ask you first ... may I ask you something?"

"Please." She straightened herself, but as if gripped by fear, as if she had to fend against possible hostility, an attack and assault.

Her opponent ran his well-groomed hand a few times over his temples. "I would like to ask you, would it help you as a mother—will your pain be eased, if the murderer is brought to justice?"

"Yes." Clear and firm.

"In what way?"

Martha did not reply. She sat, her hands folded, stiff, with big surprised eyes. With uncomprehending eyes. What was this supposed to mean? If a young woman longs for a token of love, a letter from her lover, somebody might ask: "What does this piece of paper do? Does it bring him closer to you? Is he holding you in his arms thereby and kissing your lips?" And she would have replied: "Yes, he is closer, very close!" This is how Martha felt too—

"Will your child be brought back to life?" he continued. "No. Isn't that so? Why then . . ."

But Martha had searched her mind meanwhile and had also found something. "As long as he remains unknown . . ." she mumbled, "there are still enough children walking around unprotected in Berlin, for such—for such a man."

"But this reason for punishing the crime—and I must admit it is a reason—did not occur to you until this moment."

"But it did."

"No. And if it did, then it was only a secondary thought, just a little thought within a big sentiment, and that sentiment is called revenge."

Martha blazed, went on the defensive. As if she held this revenge already in her hands and somebody wanted to deprive her of it by force. The way a rabid animal, driven into its hiding place, with hair standing on end, defends itself tooth and claw.

"And say this were so? Would it be so unnatural? Somebody has torn my child to pieces! I am not a Christian. When somebody slaps your right cheek offer him your left . . . something like that, I don't know it word for word. I am a Jew and a mother . . ."

The lawyer shrugged his shoulders. "We are of the same faith, Madam," he noted matter-of-factly, "but I am more tolerant . . ."

She twisted her mouth. Hard: "More tolerant? So is the rabbit, it does no harm to the hunter."

The man remained calm, looked at her pain with almost scornful superiority, so it seemed to her.

"I still have not heard an answer to my question. Or, rather, the one answer: you want revenge. Let's for the moment leave aside the justification—the moral justification, I mean—for your desire for revenge, and let's assume simply that . . ." he searched. "You believe when the misdeed has been atoned for, you will gain peace. Good. But can there ever be atonement?"

He is right, Martha thought, and immediately: Oh God! What good is this hair-splitting? Didn't he offer to help me; is this how he wants to help me? What to her was flesh and blood, warm blood and painfully convulsing flesh, he had neatly peeled off, exposing the bare bones. Now he dissected the skeleton and lectured about it. He cleared his throat and again rubbed the receding corners around his temples with his hand—a gesture that was apparently a habit.

"Hm. Let's presume: the police investigation and your own . . . efforts succeed in tracking down the perpetrator, the alleged perpetrator! He is arrested, indicted, and proven guilty on the basis of a confession, circumstantial evidence, or both, and he is sentenced to so many years' imprisonment in a penitentiary."

"Penitentiary?" Martha asked surprised. "A murderer?"

"It is not murder. It is . . ." he quickly swallowed the word. "It is quite possible that the punishment will seem too lenient to you. In such cases we are often dealing with sick individuals suffering from hereditary disorders and inferiority of mind."

Martha lowered her head and stared at the faded, trampled-on flower pattern of the rug.

"Yes," she said seriously in an inaudibly soft, dying voice. "I have read about it."

And hesitantly: "Frau Hoffmann has a thin little book, actually just a treatise, an article. 'Expert Opinions on Capital Punishment' by a professor in Kiel. His name is also Hoffmann, a relative, I believe. He talks about a criminal in Hamburg who had committed thirty-one assaults against children, the longest sentence was two years' imprisonment. Then came his thirty-second crime—he killed a child, a boy, by stabbing him repeatedly with a knife. He was sentenced to death and executed. The professor calls this judicial murder because his father was an alcoholic and a forebear of his mother was allegedly insane. I don't know . . . sympathy for the sick monster and none for thirty healthy children . . ."

"You must not demand a clear-cut agreement from me now, a

yes or no, Madam. I am not familiar with Professor Hoffmann's assessment. By no means do I doubt the truth of what you have said, but I would have to read the case myself, and especially within the specific context, to form an opinion. Professor Hoffmann is an opponent of capital punishment—I presume—is he not? As a jurist, I should actually know that; but so much is written, it is hard to remember everything."

"Yes, he opposes capital punishment," Martha confirmed, dejected, and continuing ponderously. "He also speaks of another murderer who was confronted in prison with the stepmother of the murder victim while he was detained pending his trial. The poor woman was so agitated she attacked him with her umbrella and injured his eye. The professor is indignant about this effrontery. He has probably never had a child of his murdered, and he has no idea how it makes one feel . . ."

The lawyer leaned forward.

"Madam, it appears that you are not in a position to examine such opinions objectively. That is quite understandable. You cannot do that."

"No. I cannot do that. Nobody can do that. You see, Doctor Pommer, not so long ago, there was a play on the radio by Reinhold Kagartz, you might remember. I did not actually listen to it myself. Frau Hoffmann told me about it. 'Murder of the Murderer'—a—how shall I say?—an attack against capital punishment. The hero is an unemployed young man who was found guilty of murder he allegedly committed during a robbery, although he was innocent. A few days later, the same Kagartz wrote in the newspaper an obituary for a dead friend who died young; he had been shot in hand-to-hand fighting during a political brawl. He concludes by lamenting the unatoned-for crime. 'The murderers got away without punishment; our mourning remains unredeemed'—or something like that. He thinks he knows who the perpetrators are and he can condemn them. Because it was his friend . . . With those few words he renders null and void his entire fictitious piece . . ."

"As far as opposition to capital punishment is concerned," retorted the doctor in a schoolmasterly and somewhat self-satisfied manner, "unlike opposition to other human institutions, where there may be multiple reasons, there actually is only one: its irrevocability, since there is no way to undo an injustice or to make amends. That is its only disadvantage, which in my opinion is sufficient to demand its abolition."

"What is the ratio of murders and judicial violations?"

"Individual violations are never recognized as such. An error of judgment always weighs heavily. Justice cannot err, for then it becomes injustice."

Her head sank deeper.

"I don't know . . . I find . . . For those who have to suffer like this, it is always painful just the same—without all that fancy stuff—I guess there are various ways of dying, but only one death. And the murderer does not ask whether he might be making an error or whether he is justified or something like that . . . Oh God, just to think that the one who—who tore my child to pieces . . ."

She was inflamed. "And even if I were myself the next victim of judicial error, I would hold out my neck and would not let out a scream . . ." She cowered down. "I believe I find you hard to understand . . ."

"Yes, Madam. Unfortunately I cannot dispute what you are saying. I had hoped to reach you with a few words of reason, to cure you, so to speak, of your desire for revenge; but I can see that I have overestimated my power of persuasion . . ." The telephone rang, shrill.

The lawyer picked up, held it against his ear. "Yes? This is Pommer. Colleague? I shall propose it to her . . . Good. Anything else? In the case of P., the verdict was negligence. . . . All right . . . Good-bye."

Toward Martha: "One second, please."

He rang the bell. The office manager, a thin, gray, faceless little man entered. "Herr Kilch, if Frau Floege should still come . . ."

"Frau Floege is already here. She is with the counselor."

"Good. Then I will . . ."

Martha rose. "You have expended your efforts long enough on

me, Doctor Pommer." She unsnapped her leather purse. "What do I . . . ?"

"Nothing, no. If I may ask you for one thing, Madam, think about what I have said. I would like to disabuse you of this primitive notion: Spilled blood cries out for revenge. Revenge demands the head. It is not that simple."

Martha nodded. "You are probably right. I am such an impetuous creature." She thought: Only my mouth lies like that outwardly, and inside there is something that is true and puts you in the wrong.

But she did not show it.

# . *6* .

There he lay, a fluffy, quivering silver-white gently flowing fur, the narrow, noble head resting on his paws with attentive eyes. Martha had to look into those eyes which, in the tender overrefinement of the body, childlike in its purity, lightness, and courage, still had preserved the luster of the fifth day of creation. She lightened up, was somehow reconciled to her existence.

"If I could find such a dog," she thought, "then I wouldn't know . . ."

Frau Hoffmann often tried to encourage her to adopt an animal as a friend. Hers was a yellow, lively and disobedient dwarf dachshund, the dutiful "Männe." And when her niece was looking for a good home for a Prince Charles, she offered it to Martha, who sadly shook her head. She did not like such lap dogs, she despised them; these were fragile toys rather than dogs. If she were to take to a dog and keep it, it would have to be a creature like Allegra or Herr von Alten's Kongo. The German mastiff Kongo was black as night, the Great Dane Allegra was trout-gray with dark streaks. But how would such a giant fellow fit in her little room, Frau Hoffmann demurred. Yes, Martha had already asked herself the same question, especially since mastiffs need exercise, and she knew she had little time for frequent long walks.

Frau Hoffmann did not give up so soon. After all, there were dogs of other sizes as well. Wolfhounds, Dobermans, and boxers. "Boxers are ugly." But she thought: I don't want a dog. If I were to set my heart on a dog . . . that would be robbery. Ursa shall not lose anything.

Just this Borzoi. He was the only one who could have seduced her, could have melted her loyalty. He was lying there like a smile. From time to time, when the saxophone sounded too many wrong notes, or the drums banged and droned, he did not howl, but cowered more deeply under the table, and a quiver ran through his white hair, which was fluffy and loose as if it were about to stream out into a silvery brook. He looked up at his master: What am I doing here? Why did you bring me to this place?

Martha observed the master. He was long and thin with somewhat elevated shoulders, dressed with slightly foppish prettiness. Under the flaxen mop was a small, indistinct face, sagging, debauched, hardly masculine. He leaned back in his chair, a derisive line around his mouth, his eyes grazed the dancing couples. Martha turned away, a repugnant sweet taste in her mouth; the morbid affectation disgusted her even before she consciously recognized it as such. Sure enough, he did not speak to the animal.

Martha moved her glass and sucked up a gold-green drop from the high-stemmed, lily-shaped goblet. Maybe that was the man. This unmasculine man. At any rate, she stared at him, pondered. It could be—as well as any other. He brought this beautiful dog, meaning that he was a regular guest just like the other one—the rapist of boys, the murderer of little Herbert Diem, who had been arrested here. The newspapers noted only in passing: in a dance hall, here and there, where he had been a regular for weeks—a short errand had sufficed to find out which dance hall it was, since there was only one on this street. She only had to think of that misbegotten man's crime to make the wild blood rush to her face. She clenched her fist under the table and could have smashed the table, assaulted the people, torn them to pieces—the drinkers, the dancers, the jazz musicians, the whole rabble. She held herself still as if with her own hands, closed her face. I must not think. I must be cold, icy clear and tough. Only that way can I force it, only that way. She stayed in her all too dark, all too simple dress and sipped the green drink.

"Mexican Aguila Band." Were these really Mexicans? It was true, they looked very foreign behind the big drum and the shiny, noisy brass, olive skins with oily black hair. The one in the front sat motionless like a bloated, fat pagan idol—now he disappeared from view behind the silky girl, a chrome yellow flower. She had planted herself diagonally across from him. She colored her lips with the help of a tiny mirror, now she pulled out a little bag, a little tin, and took out a cigarette. Martha didn't smoke.

Martha looked up. The air was filled with bluish clouds of smoke.

And everywhere winged lanterns hovered inside the smoke like red sparrow hawks. Above her head, suspended from a poppy-red lampshade, was a black cloth doll with a pointed cap, white face, and thin, lanky limbs. I am this doll. I am suspended on an invisible thread from a bloodstained light. It glows . . . She lowered her chin to her chest in shame and played nervously with a bow ribbon. The waiter probably watched with scorn the way she was staring into space. She could not betray her purpose. He rushed past with a tray of glass plates filled with colorful concoctions of whipped cream and sweet fruits. Over there, the blond one of two girls was served a delicious, gentle structure, a funnel-mold, brownish foam mountain with towers of wafers and snow.

Ursa would have liked this. She recalled a visit to the pastry shop with her child. She had buried her gleaming warm face completely in the steaming cup and took deep, long sips. Then she found the crumbly ladyfinger on her plate.

"Mother, we didn't order a cake like that. And not the water either."

"You don't need to order it, it comes free with the hot chocolate." Ursa then thoughtfully touched the dry dough before she began to nibble on it. Then she had to try the water and found that it tasted wonderful.

The blond girl cut up the soft mountain of delicacies and dug into it. How cheerful her laugh was! Young. With her fresh stubby nose, her bobbed hair, she almost seemed like a boy dressed up as a girl. Her somewhat smaller, dark companion also wore light blue— a flimsy little dress; they might have been sisters.

The white dog came wagging over and rubbed against the blond girl's knee; she took his narrow head in her lap and fed him some wafers. His master called him by some foreign-sounding, incomprehensible name; he gracefully crawled back to the place between the table and the chairs. Martha watched him. Then she felt the man's sharp gaze becoming fixed on her. Are you angry? She pinned her flickering eyes on him, returned his look. Defiant: Don't you want your dog to be admired? Why are you bringing him in here? Next time leave him home. She said this under her breath. He stood up and started to move toward her.

Her face darkened, sure that he would confront her, threaten her, insult her. She prepared for battle. She was just in the mood to fight back, not to take anything. He was so limp. He wore powder. She thought: I am certain it is him. If he attacks me, I will strangle him like an animal. I am stronger than he is. He bowed politely.

She was surprised. This she had not expected. She wanted to reply: "I don't dance." Yet she knew that she could not simply pass up the opportunity to make the acquaintance of whoever he may be. She mumbled only: "I don't dance well."

He remarked casually, "We'll see," and picked up her little silk purse that had fallen to the floor.

Martha tried to smile. "You have such a beautiful dog. What is his name?"

"A she-dog. Lebyodka."

"Sounds Polish."

"Russian. It means swan."

"You are Russian?"

"No." He placed his arm around her. "You have a rather deep voice, Madam, don't you?"

Something gave Martha pause. What was this? It sounded like a reproach, but he certainly did not ask her to dance to insult her.

Cymbal and saxophone began to drone, and they danced. The dancer did not speak. And Martha needed the little bit of brain she had left to guess the right dancing steps. It seemed to her that she was doing all right. Near the corner, they got caught up in the crowd and he, probably to disentangle them both by force, embraced the body of the woman more firmly, pressed almost completely against her. Only for a moment, then he let her go again, loosened his grip. A short while later the tumult ebbed. Silently he accompanied her back to her table, bowed, and left. She had not been able to engage him. Martha sat as before.

What did she have now? She had danced at least once, that was all. She had not been able to hold the man, did not attain her next goal. Now she brooded over the reasons like a field commander who had lost his battle. The guests, the neighbors glanced at her scornfully—or was she imagining this? And the light blue girls giggled too—about her? They fooled around, elbowed each other, the brunette pushed the blond off the chair, and then they danced together.

Lebyodka's master was also dancing again. He, the overly slender, weary man, waltzed a coarse woman around the floor. Her naked arms were powerful and bright red. One could easily imagine them pressed against her hips behind a fish trough or a fishing net, if a customer at a weekly market should dare voice a complaint about a purchase. And her crude features were hard and painted over with bright makeup; her lips drooped, puffy and coarse, the color of blood sausage.

"I am not beautiful," Martha told herself. "I am no longer young but compared to this hunk of meat, those clubs ...." Could that woman be his type? He was dragging her around for the second time now. She was not jealous in her heart, for that man repulsed her. Yes, the scum she was searching for, the lecher she tried to track down, had to be repulsive. She had prepared in her mind how she would suppress her disgust, what words she would use to ensnare him. Certainly, she could restrain herself, but he had taken her by surprise so that she had spoken none of these words. It had not been in her plan that he would be so quiet that he would toss her not a sentence, not even a phrase on which she could cast her web. Even what he told her about the dog sounded grudging, curt, and terse.

Was he the one? Was it really he who ... ? In the depth of her being something scampered, crawled, something colorless, feeling its way, blind like a batrachian in a water grotto. She had recently read about those strange animals with their reddish bundles of gills. She was startled out of her thoughts.

The blond girl suddenly stood before her, nonchalantly suppressing a giggle in her bold, fresh face. She curtsied. Martha stared at her. Had she gone out of her mind? She curtsied again, quite cheerfully: "Please—ladies' choice."

Martha remained reserved: "I don't dance with women."

The other one laughed. Under her breath: "I don't either."

What impertinence! She had probably been lumbering like a bear when she was dancing, and now this crazy young thing was making fun of her.

She was annoyed.

"Please, I don't understand. Just leave me alone."

But the creature's hand tapped her on the shoulder, and her lecherous, giggly voice whispered in her ear: "Don't put on such airs. We know what you look like. And I know that Tito, the tall one over there, never dances with women. You are a boy. Well, so am I, in case you haven't noticed yet. I look good, don't I? Do we understand each other now? Why the angry face?"

Martha saw red. She felt blood rise before her eyes. She threw herself somewhere, held on to something, dug her nails into something, an arm, a neck, a cheek. She was on fire and seemed to be growing. She had the strength of giants. Sure the thing fought back, pinched and scratched, but she did not let go. And she felt that she would not let go until somebody tore her hands from their stumps. On the next table a knife gleamed . . . how that riffraff was screaming.

Shouts. Scolding. Bawling and a pair of black sleeves. The brawlers were separated with great effort. Martha's dress was quite ruined, but the fellow was stretched out on the rug in light blue shreds and howling. Somebody said something about . . . making a report . . . calling the police . . . A newcomer, a naive soul. This wasn't done here. One was glad to be left unscathed.

Martha gasped for air. Her whole body was still trembling. At the waiter's demand she nodded and, in mute agitation, she paid her tab and for a broken glass. Then she was shown the door, and she left. Later she was unable to recall how she had gotten her hat and coat.

She stood in the night and breathed deeply, liberated. The air was not cold. The street lights blurred bleakly in the sea of fog. Few people passed. After she had walked a few steps, she came upon a small flight of stairs that led to the entrance of a house. She sat down heavily on the top stone step. A last reserve of strength, which she had taken great pains to sustain, broke inside her, collapsed, and she began to cry.

## Part Two

The pealing of the Sunday bells had long ceased when she awoke. She saw: half past ten and she still did not feel alert and refreshed. Her brain was dull, filled with the tangled rubble of the night before. She yawned, lifted herself up a few times and with a last push, she was out of bed. Barefoot she went to the window and pulled back the drapes. The daylight outside was glaring. The blank hard-blue sky betrayed a dense sun casting its shortened rays mercilessly over the meager, blackish elms, the yellowing, aging crabgrass, and the rotting foliage strewn on the ground. On the windowsill quivered something black and round, like a shred of charred paper. It was a butterfly with folded wings and near death. Martha placed it on her hand and blew at it softly; it moved its delicate feet. She placed it cautiously on the window frame, and it arduously unfolded its wings. A quiet tearful melancholy welled up in its velvet eyes. It trembled lightly. This is the last one, Martha believed; if it dies, it shall die outside, in the free air under the sky and the sun. She pushed it out onto the sill. It fell silent. Then the wings began to move with stronger quivers, and suddenly, still faltering and numb, it slithered away and fluttered, beautiful and sure and vibrant, into the warming light. It would play for a short hour. When night descended, it would be dead. It is good, Martha thought. Why should it die here, piecemeal? It is good.

She felt cold. She closed the window. And just as she was, in her thin nightgown and with tousled hair, she sat down at the table and began to write a brief note to Albert Renkens. Time had passed too quickly the other day; she invited him for the following Sunday afternoon for a more leisurely chat over a cup of coffee.

She held the dress up to the window, against the drizzling gleam.
The only expensive evening dress in her meager trousseau. Burgundy
red silk awash with lace of the same color. She liked it very much,
but had hardly worn it, once to a dance and barely once to the
theatre. Now it was out of fashion. She turned it back and forth,
pondering. With a few quick strokes of the scissors, she severed the
lace trim from the garment—it had been sewn on in a hurry—and
undressed with a few motions. She poured the soft red drizzle over
her naked body. She walked to the mirror. No. Her pale skin gleamed
white through the delicate gaps in the leaf pattern. No. It was not
possible. She looked neither tender, nor attractive, neither voluptuous
nor provocative—not at all gently lewd. More droll. Like the powerful, firm body of an ancient goddess veiled, for reasons of propriety,
in a modish wrap. The thing fell so short on one side that it barely
reached her thighs. Rather than having a clever, seductive effect, it
was simply indecent and crude, very comical. She gave a brief laugh
and tore off the rag. She stood and thought.

She was ready. She knew exactly what she wanted. She did not
delude herself. She did not think of the beginning of a love affair,
of ardent glances and tender words, of the first searching kiss. She
thought in brutal terms: tonight or right now this afternoon he will
be in my bed. He shall cover me, I am hot. I don't love him. But
he shall carry out my will, and I shall have to pay for it. I don't
know any other way. And I have been fasting for a long time and
we shall extract all the lust from us we are capable of.

She breathed deeply. She remembered. She had read about women,
prostitutes, who rest naked on a colorful bed in a southern clime,
on silk cushions to receive even strangers. But for that she would
need a love nest, walls hung with pink damask and adorned with
glittering mirrors, furnished with precious little chairs, silver, fine
crystal . . . What did she have instead? An old wooden washstand
with drawers, flowery bowl and pitcher, a plush green sofa, faded
wallpaper . . . and instead of a chambermaid in a lace bonnet and

apron, she would stand at the entrance herself and get goose pimples. And as she opened, members of the Lange family would come up the stairs or out of the door, and would think she had gone mad and should be sent to Dalldorf. . . .

The joke made her smile briefly. Then sighing, she shrugged her shoulders. She was aware that she was completely devoid of any talent for the art of flirtation, any kind of coquetry or whatever those foreign words were. There are women who are able, even in a nun's habit, to captivate, to suggest the shape of their limbs, of a gift. Not she. She knew only one way to inflame a man: to be as wild and shameless as embers.

No. She could not do it. She bent down, gathered her shirt off the floor, and pulled it over her head. She took out the black, very simple dress with long, narrow sleeves that made her look very slender and tall. The only ornament she wore on her chest was an inherited, old-fashioned piece of jewelry, a flowering golden rose between gilded leaves. She had already spread an embroidered cloth over the little table and had set the table for two with white and golden cups and a beautifully shaped vase of pigeon bluish porcelain. She had dipped four roses in it, three blackish red ones, and one salmon colored. The dusky purple ones were like velvet, the pale one, by contrast, had a redder heart and resembled an alabaster lamp that glowed from the inside. She had bought the flowers a few hours before on the way to the cemetery from a vendor whose pots, bouquets, and wreaths usually found their way to the dead.

She looked around the room. Satisfied: she had done some last-minute straightening up and everything was in its place. Now she carried the cake in from the kitchen, cinnamon cookies, poppy seed slices, domino squares, shortbread, and macaroons. Then she sat and waited.

She waited. She looked at the clock—already a quarter to four, but he was not likely to appear before half past four. She rose to go to the kitchen to sit at the window there but was afraid he might see her from the yard. He should not know that she was on the lookout for him. Every second was too long for her. She had bought a newspaper and had read part of it; she looked at it intently but all events seemed either completely meaningless or hard to comprehend. And she was ruining her eyes. There was a love story:

" . . . Ruth, in light blue silk pajamas was stretched out on a wolf's hide and sobbed. He kneeled beside her.
"Baby," he whispered tenderly, "my doll . . ."

Martha looked in the mirror. Her face was powdered in its natural, ivory tone, but the mouth was painted too bright. It shimmered poison-red and large, a wonderful, mature, cleaving pod. Poison mushroom, she thought, whoever eats of it must die. She wished the younger man no ill, but she felt herself, as she was lurking, like a sorceress, a bandit who lured the wanderer into her cave to plunder and weaken him. For she clung to her plan with that dark determination which we usually apply only to evil deeds.

"'Baby,'" she repeated, "'my doll'—maybe he will call me that sometime." She scornfully puckered her lips.

"I don't have a pair of light blue silk pajamas; it wouldn't be my style."

Deep myrtle green, warm red, those were her colors.

She thought: clothing. She was not one who sought to please the world by decking herself out in pretty attire, not one fond of adornments, and a brain like a box full of ribbons and lace; cheap fashion notions beckoned her in vain, and the seamstress never visited her dreams. Yet she was a woman. She did stop in front of display windows and saw the pleats and took note of the prices, usually without calculating or wishing. Only sometimes did she become suddenly excited about certain pieces of clothing—strange dresses, as in a legend of yore—like the India-yellow silk one or the one of gold and green brocade. She was in the habit of starving such yearnings and many fell from her, limp and gray, after a few days; others persisted. She entered the shop, pointed, asked, left again. Too expensive for me.

She still remembered that as a child she ardently wished for a while, but without ever telling her parents, for a hat like those worn by daughters of the rich. The outside was taffeta or silken, black or dark brown; the inside was usually lined pink, white, or sky blue, and this brown hat was even lined in light green satin. It glittered so nicely; the back of the head was placed into the flat disk and its gleam illuminated the small child's face like a halo. There was a little girl who frequently passed by—her grandfather usually took her for walks on Sundays—carried a scarlet aura above the little ash-blue coat.

There was a sound at the door. Martha got up. The visitor. She had prepared the lamp but had not lit it. Hurriedly, she reached for matches, turned up the wick and placed the jingling milk glass over the long cylinder. Now she opened.

"Oh," he said cheerfully and surprised. "A second oil lamp. There is one burning already downstairs. People really know what to do when the light fails."

Martha smiled. "The light never fails here. It is just that we are still living in the 1880s without gas or electricity."

"That's impossible!"

"It is true."

"Amazing that such conditions should still exist in the western part of the city. You should send this building on loan to a museum. Truly romantic."

She shrugged her shoulders. "Romantic . . . We would have done away with it if the landlord weren't a foreigner and if the tenants could agree on the cost of the installation. Please."

She held the lamp into the room.

"Madam, you know what you look like? Like an exotic priestess in her long, black robe and with a holy lamp."

"In a horribly melodramatic movie, right?"

He laughed.

"I took the liberty . . ." He handed her the tender gift wrapped loosely in silk paper. From a glazed turquoise earthenware bowl rose two slender, noble tulips, their arrogant bronze heads casting orange shadows. Two royal children from a magic kingdom, whose language we no longer know. Martha admired them.

"They are very beautiful. They are much too elegant for my grandmotherly abode."

She poured coffee for him; he fiddled with the creamer.

"The grandmother is very young." He looked around.

"How this little backwardness—I mean your oil lamp—makes everything so nice and cozy here. So warm, so . . . special. Really. Running warm water, electric switches, all that one can have anywhere nowadays. You didn't bake this cake yourself?"

"No, unfortunately not."

"Unfortunately? Nothing against your housekeeping talents, I am not familiar with them, but I wanted to say: That's why it tastes so good."

"You prefer cake from the bakery?"

"Shamefully, yes. There is a childhood prejudice connected with this, I think. That's all. Until I was about fourteen or fifteen I had a terrible sweet tooth—you wouldn't know from looking at me now. At home we seldom had cake; neither our housekeeper nor my father cared much for it. But every twenty-eighth of March we visited Aunt Cecilia with a birthday present. Actually she was not a real aunt, just an aunt of a cousin or the cousin of an aunt. Well, you know, a person one had to respect. Her table was always adorned with a big plate of wonderful things—chocolate pastries, cream puff rolls, or whatever these beauties are called. But she never offered any of them. She would say, 'Try this fresh one first, it is home-made.' The smile that went with it—saccharine. My father and I always had to take it—it was always the same cardboard stuff, inedible. Every March twenty-eighth! I have never seen a guest getting something from the pastry plate. She probably polished it off quietly all by herself when she was alone."

He fell silent, stirred around in his cup, and then exclaimed rather suddenly, as if from deep thought: "But you are not taking any sugar—shouldn't coffee be drunk sweet?"

"Not mine."

He looked directly at her: "You are tough. Or maybe not."

He thought for a while, lowered his head, his hair seemed silvery and soft.

"It is so easy to get fed up. Some women have a . . . certain way with tenderness. Coaxing, playing cute, purring like a little cat, baby language, pouting, and other silly stuff. Such artificial, cheap, perfumed slobbering. Tastes pretty good at first, a bit sticky like baklava; but to have this smearing around every day, especially if one is not the languishing type, then it soon becomes sickening."

He pulled himself together.

"Please you must forgive me. I am spoiling your appetite and mine."

Martha crumbled a macaroon. She had no doubt that he was describing something that happened yesterday or the day before. Again he looked around the room.

"Madame, when your husband was overseas, you did not live here, did you?"

"No, we lived in a new building in Steglitz. I moved here later with my child. My child was," she touched the tulips, "like these flowers."

He leaned forward. Gently: "Madam. It hurts you, I know—you mustn't speak about it."

She flared up. "I must speak about it."

A strangely sharp, almost piercing glance shot from his pale blue eyes. The pupils were very small.

"Madam . . . the other day, you said something strange."

"What?"

"I cannot repeat it."

"That?" she mumbled. "If somebody would help me, would promise to look for the murderer of my Ursa, then I . . ." she hesitated.

"Then . . . ?"

Her hand was still resting on the tablecloth, quiet, but she felt his sliding over hers, felt it as a burning weight she could not fend off. "Then . . . ?" he asked.

A chair was scraping. He whispered near her cheek.

"Then you will reward him, right? What will you give him?"

She breathed inaudibly: "Everything."

She trembled. He threw himself at her. He pulled her up. His lips clung to her mouth, burrowing into it with teeth and tongue as into a red fruit. He removed the gilded rose from her dress and searched for the taut buds of her breasts with hot hands and lips.

She retreated, freed herself. She walked over to the wide brown bed and with a silent grand gesture pulled back the fringed cover.

# . *8* .

She awoke in the night. She had stubbed against something. Something was lying close to her. A strange body. She shot up, sat erect, frightened. Her heart was racing.

Then she smiled: I had forgotten already. I am not alone in my bed anymore, no. Next to her slept a man. She listened, felt his strong breathing. It was pitch-dark. She felt a desire to look at his face by the light of the candle. What did it still know about her? What did she still know about it? But the light would wake him. She felt hot. She shook back her hair, and carefully climbed out of the bedding.

She groped her way. She reached out and felt for the table. She had not even cleared it; the cups jingled softly. There was a tepid, airless stuffiness about the room. She was naked. Barefoot she slid to the window and carefully pulled it open. She drank from the ice and leaned her body forward as in a cooling bath. It felt good. Out of the darkness white flaky crystalline stars drizzled gently and melted on her shoulders and arms. She bent over further. "Ursa," she whispered, "Ursa, do you hear me? Ursa! I am doing it for you . . . for you . . . !"

# Part III

# . *1* .

The few people who disembarked with them dispersed behind the railroad station. Now they wandered past several garden cafés that had fallen into decay. The last one's name was Blitter's Eden. No fence; behind the gray, one-story little house was a fallow lawn with old linden trees. At the other end was a bowling alley. To the right, above the tavern's sign, flapped two little weather-beaten flags, one red-white, the other blue-yellow, hanging sadly withered and faded like leaves on a wintry branch. Brownish red wire mesh fences followed—summer cottages, now orphaned, with mute wooden sheds, empty fruit trees, raspberry bushes, and flowerbeds like cookiesheets strewn with heavy, black moist crumbs. In the corner was the last preserved alder tree trunk. They looked very destitute and hopeless, those abandoned plots of land under a cold sky. A nip was in the air, weary and grayish pale, as if snow were soon to fall—not gentle, soft flakes but hard kernels of hail. The morning had been beautiful. . . . Then came the forest.

It was a mixed forest of grim, furrowed oaks, dusky red, melancholy red pines, elephant-skin beeches. Creeping underbrush. The path was wide but filled with layers of rotting leaves that slithered, screeched, and crackled under their soles. But the grass was green and the green moss was dotted with small specks of snow that seemed to have been dropped with a spoon. Here and there a molehill swelled, foaming brew of dark fragrant earth. Near the path rose a grass bedecked cupola, asleep like the forgotten overgrown grave of a pagan warrior. At times a pit would sink into the ground and form a deep trough of unfrozen brackish water.

The underbrush quivered, crackled. Albert walked over to inspect it.

"It's nothing. Maybe it was a bird. But I have seen deer here on occasion, and wild boars supposedly live farther in the interior. Somebody once told me . . . what are you thinking?"

"Oh, nothing . . ."

"What are you thinking? Come on, tell me." He took her arm.

"I just thought, if you should first have a talk with Bernecke . . ."

He pushed her away, gently. "Oh God, at least out here leave me alone with your inquiries. We are going for a walk, and you . . ."

She replied quietly, "You asked," and fell silent. They wandered side by side without a word and without touching.

The frittering songs of the birds had flown away. Black thrushes stirred from time to time in the rustling of the wilted leaves. A tiny swamp titmouse stood still in the air, hovering near the trunk—such a dainty thing, grayish red with a charcoal cap. Somewhere high up under the crown of the pine tree, a woodpecker hacked away. He could only be heard, not seen. They peered and twisted their heads until they finally found him—a white and black and carmine red bird, a feathered lizard with beak and wings that darted, wagging, around the tree trunk. As they looked for the bird, they began to talk with each other again.

Martha asked, "In America, in the United States, are there the same kinds of birds? Are there woodpeckers?"

"Sure. Just different varieties. But frankly, I don't really know anything about that. I was mostly hanging around in the cities, Boston, then New York and Chicago. One doesn't really think about flowers and birds or about what they may be called. Sure, I saw some flying around from time to time, but I saw them without really understanding—all I had in my skull was stuff like my daily work and having fun. The only bird I really was aware of was some kind of parrot, a strange one from Africa, gray with a red tail. It belonged to a younger woman whom I visited frequently for a while. A Dutch traveling salesman had given it to her. Ugh, disgusting."

She mumbled, "One day you will say 'disgusting' too when you talk about me."

"No."

"Oh, yes."

"No. You know, this Flossie—good God, Flossie!—she was terribly sentimental—sort of phony sentimental. She probably just acted this way because she thought it would knock me over. She always made me sing German songs for her. Germans are so musical; even though I'm not, she listened with delight. I was almost still a kid then and I warbled all kinds of obscenities—she didn't have a clue and that's how I got my jollies. She also wrote me dainty little notes—isn't it sweet? Disgusting."

He hesitated for a moment, then continued, "Once we walked through a park at night and we saw a pair of poor lovers on a bench, quite absorbed in each other. But one didn't have to look if one didn't want to. She looked at them and was indignant about this kind of immoral behavior out in the open. Considering the kinds of things she let me do inside a warm room . . . well, let's forget it."

He pushed a pine cone ahead of him with his iron-tipped cane. "Martha . . ."

She looked at him.

"You—you are really the most shameless woman I know."

She nodded and replied in a hard, clenched voice, "You are right . . . I—"

He smiled. "And at the same time the most decent. There is nothing fake about you, no spring magic . . . blue moonlit nights in the halls of Cupid—you know what I mean, Miriam!"

He often called her that since she had told him that she had been named after her grandmother, whose real name had been Miriam.

"Come." He placed his arm around her shoulder, but dropped it again immediately. Two elderly men appeared, probably on an excursion, under the hunters' hats the camera around the neck. They were absorbed in lively conversation and passed without a sign of noticing them.

A clearing opened before them. A group of small birches stood in the meadow like maidens clad in white, ready to begin their game of round dances in the laughing blueness and sunshine amid the sound of a shepherd's flute and the leaping of lambs. Now they stood frozen, corpse-like, as if under a witch's spell, beneath a pallid, bleak ghostly sky: strange, deaf and spectral souls. In one of the bare treetops were two monstrous crows' nests, stacked on top of each other like black scabs.

Slowly they continued their walk back to the woods. The smaller, crooked black pines brushed against them with their needles, cowering like hunchbacked witches.

Martha said, "I would like to have another tulip."

"A tulip?"

"Yes. Like your two orange and bronze brown ones."

"Mine . . . ?"

"Did you forget . . . ? You gave them to me . . . the first time . . . you came." She looked down. "I just thought some should be blooming in the moss grotto. It is so dusky in there, like a fairy tale, and they would be like lamps."

They found the end of the forest. A boat drifted along, sleepy and listless. At its edge were yellow sheaves, entangled like broad, wrinkled ribbons, and stuck between them was an empty cardboard container. Albert tossed it with his cane and the water splattered and turned murky. Out of the muddy depth welled tangles of plants, tungsten, creeping to the surface, greenish like the tips of fir trees.

There was no overpass. The remains of a torn rope bridge dangled, decrepit and swaying. What could have been worth seeing over there anyway? As far as the eye could see, there were only fields, pallid, treeless and frozen fields.

"This needs a snow cover," declared Albert. "Everything was snowed in . . . then off to a sleigh ride . . . ! "He recalled: "I only visited my Uncle Felix once on his estate when I was a boy—with my father after the New Year for two weeks. Now I believe that even the neighbors were of the party. At any rate, we had about six or seven sleighs. Mine was lined inside with dark blue somewhat threadbare plush. And my two horses wore red and white tassels over the bells. We always drove behind the others to the accompaniment of the pretty sound of the bells, gliding over the soft, cottony ground. Above us stretched a low, heavy gray sky filled with swarms of crows. Before us were fields and more fields, smooth and white and endless like . . . Like what? Like the bedsheet of a giantess. At least this is the way I see it now. Next to me was a little girl, Milda—a real Saxon name—she was holding on tightly to her doll. I don't remember ever arriving anywhere. We must have or I wouldn't be standing here before you now."

Martha stepped close to him.

"Why did you look at me so strangely when you said this?"

"Said what?"

"When you were talking about the bedsheet of the giantess. I am not really gigantic. Just tall. When you picture naked women, do you think of me ... always ... do you?"

He replied quietly, "Martha ... I said it before: you are shameless."

She did not dispute anything. As if by accident, she took his hand and placed it quietly on her clothed lap.

His eyes swam; he whispered, "Who taught you this, not just this, but everything—you must tell me. I have asked you before. Your husband?"

"My blood."

"I don't believe that. You read about it in a book?"

"I don't read such books—they are smut."

"You've had other lovers, have you?"

"No."

"Yet you are not in love with me."

She remained silent.

"But you like sleeping with me?"

"Yes ..."

"You are a whore."

She shook her head without saying a word.

"You are a Jewess."

She had turned away and walked ahead of him with firm strides. He whistled she knew not what—some popular song, probably. They turned their backs on the paltry view and a beech grove received them. Thin, stick-like, splintery trees, sparse and rickety, some grotesquely contorted. The ground was covered with tangled underbrush, hiding places and thieves' nests for stray animals. Humps of shrubbery, with soft, rotting leaves, were pressed into glowing brown balls.

Fallen wood broke underfoot. They tore the ferns as they pressed forward. Within a flat bay was a pond surrounded by wild growth, a thick morass, black like ink. They cautiously descended toward it. Albert tossed a branch into the slimy water to measure its depth.

"No firm ground. Swamp."

# A Jewish Mother from Berlin

Martha was lost in thought.

"You know . . . whatever sinks into this, won't come back . . ."

"No. It would get caught in the bog. Why? Do you want to make me your victim—kill me and bury me in the frog's mire?"

He gave off a brief laugh. She bent down to examine a snail shell. "Not you . . ."

They drifted on, carried on a wave of loose, whitish grass. A malformed tree stump rose like the unseemly, hairy head of a black animal that swelled to the light from the earth's brewing womb. Crackling. Martha stopped.

"Psst. Do you hear something . . . ? There . . . !"

A scampering dwarf mouse sat, gray-brown and delicate on a colorful bed of straw, quietly nibbling on a little sheaf.

"How pretty . . ."

"Do you want it?"

"Leave it . . ." But he was already bending down; the ground was sticky and the layer of leaves was thin; a sudden move with the hand, a second, and he clutched the twitching little creature. It twisted in his naked fingers in its little white vest, endless tail, and squinting eyes, with little teeth that wanted to gnaw, free itself. She felt it.

"Like velvet. It is frightened. Why don't you put it back? There." It hurried away into the bushy growth.

"If I had such little animals for Ursa . . . that . . ."

She fell silent.

Was it only the look that chastised her? This hard, hostile look that lashed out at her from his eyes for a fraction of a second? He rubbed the hand that had caught the little mouse, and said abruptly, in a commanding voice: "Now, we'll turn back. By the way, as you know, tonight we are going to the Fehlandts'."

"You go, if you want. But without me."

"Oh yes, you will. We are living in the world. He has put in a good word for me with the doctor, and has also spoken on my behalf with Leipold. Well, it isn't possible to refuse. His wife especially wants to get to know you."

Martha retorted, "His wife is inviting me? A nice middle-class lady? Maybe she wants to show how open-minded, liberated, and modern she can be?"

"You are wrong. She was his mistress before he married her. An actress."

He added with bitterness, "Do you think I enjoy having beer at Aschinger's with the likes of that professional blackmailer—I am sure he is something of the sort—just on your behalf?"

Martha twitched, pressed her lips together, and said nothing more.

# . 2 .

Dinner was being served at two round, festively decorated tables. Next to her sat Albert Renkens. He had approached her before the meal with a low "If it pleases Madam," and she had smiled. Now she spoke little, staring in front of her with a strange feeling, a little dazed like someone not used to drinking would feel from even a small sip of fire water. She had not been at a social gathering of such a dinner party in years. Her reticence, her aloofness hardly permitted her to make friends.

A few times, when Ursa was still alive, she had visited the Langes' for coffee. But she had always refused whenever Lydia Hoffmann invited her to join her small circle for bread and butter. She remembered, Frau Beucker once took over for an evening. When Martha returned home, she found the child, who was unaccustomed to being alone, still awake in the pillows and crying.

She looked around with heavy, tentative eyes, everything seemed so peculiarly precious and strange—the brown salt breadsticks on the plate, even the rolls, artificially wrapped in a silky, shiny damask cloth, the bundle of violets in a flat crystal vessel set down on a pale yellow lace cover. Asparagus broth was being passed in flawless porcelain cups of exquisite Grecian form. Purple wine swam in a bowl. She did not know which one to drink.

"The red one probably will look better on you," Albert had said. He was satisfied with her. She wore the dress he had given her, softly flowing honey-brown velvet, embroidered with golden flowers. The fact that she said little hardly bothered him. She left him to chat all the more cheerfully with the woman on his left, a very sweet, very young creature with chestnut curls. A slender elf, full of mischievous glitter, who entertained the whole table. She pulled a violet from the goblet and placed it with a delicate hand in Albert Renkens' buttonhole.

He leaned forward, "Young lady, I shall wear it like a medal."

Martha listened quietly. Very slowly she broke off little pieces from her bread and ate them, almost forcing herself to swallow. A few weeks ago, she thought, I became his lover. And now . . . She thought: I am not very clever. He will lose this little flower on the way home. And should it stick, then I will remove it from his suit quietly and burn it in the stove. When he lies with me tonight . . . she smiled, lifted her head a little, her eyes sparkled.

"Madam," said the man to her right. "Madam, we are having a dispute here . . . You are a photographer and must have seen Weege's cinematography exhibit last year . . ."

Martha provided the desired information with listless politeness. Then the maids in white aprons offered turkey meat and red cabbage.

On the other side of the violets was a large decorative piece. A gentleman picked it up and passed it to the other side. A work of art made of milky porcelain: a resting elk with shaggy long hair hanging from his neck, powerful antlers topping the attentive, backward-leaning head, and wide open, quivering nostrils. Albert pushed it over to her—she gently stroked its fur.

The one with the chestnut curls asked: "Is that a reindeer?"

"It's an elk."

"Well . . . Madam, you mustn't get angry with me for saying so, but it is true, you look very much like it."

General giggling. Martha remained silent, inflamed. She belonged to those rare women who are often beautiful, sometimes ugly, but who can never be called pretty. She knew: tonight she was beautiful. This animal was ugly.

Even Albert threw in scornfully: "Young lady, you are as brilliant as you are charming. Look at this." He moved the statue closer.

"But it's true," the young woman defended herself. "I read about it somewhere, there is something fabled about an elk, something eerily dark and wild—something strange—ordinary stags can be seen in Grunewald and not only on Sunday mornings."

She laughed.

"Witty!" lauded a thin, bespectacled gentleman. "Wonderful, Fräulein Lill. Even though this is not quite the way it is, you do know how to find a way out."

Martha felt the jagged horns, she clutched the strong, vaulted, and sensuous mouth with the mighty upper lip. "You are right, Fräulein Lill. I know what you mean."

No one was paying attention anymore. All, including Fräulein Lill, were engaged in a lively discussion whether there still was wildlife in Grunewald or not. And they ate nut ice cream in glass cups with tiny gilded spoons.

Martha tasted a wafer and cinnamon leaf and passed the basket. She thought: the girl is right. This awkward, fire-red, dusky animal, the ungainly, lonely member of a dying species—that is who I am. But the ice cream was delicious. With a golden knife, she too carved a piece from the cylinder of Pückler ice cream.

They had been introduced to each other—Martha, the younger women, the gentlemen, and this pleasant matronly woman. She could not remember their names. During the procession out of the dining room, she had somehow ended up with the group that now sat to the right of the grand piano. The conversation turned to the theatre.

"You have seen *Hudson Lowe,* Madam?"

No. She had hardly read even a scrap of the reviews in the newspaper. But the other ladies knew the play and praised it. Editha zur Nieden as Betsy Balcombe—just delightful. How very young and fresh she was. Only Montholon was a failure. Paul Klisch apparently no longer took acting very seriously, preferred to spend his time on the tennis court . . . God, how can one talk like that? Why should an artist not play tennis? Everybody engages in sports nowadays. Eldersmann is a boxer, for example . . .

Martha nodded. Imperceptibly, she briefly turned her head. Albert stood near the marble sculpture with the host and his friends. Probably talking business. He now had his back turned toward her; he was smoking. He did not seem bored. If we could only go home . . . She saw the tiny brownish mouse he had caught in the woods in the morning, she should have brought it along and set it free among the silvery, ocean-green damask chairs. What a tumult, what sudden screaming in these elegant surroundings. She smiled to herself.

Disruption, moving of chairs, changing of seats, to accommodate new arrivals—Martha used the commotion to steal away from the group. For a few seconds she stopped in front of a picture, the customary corner of Rothenburg, then she slipped, fast as a cat, anxious as a thief, through the wallpapered door that had been left ajar—out of glittering brightness into obscurity.

She found herself alone in a smoking room, small and heavy, dusky from the kilim tapestries and the black wood panels carved in Moorish style. A desk lamp was lit, casting a soft, reddish-yellowish gleam on only the nearest objects. On a narrow shelf that ran along the wall, finishing off the half-high paneling, stood a vase. Extremely pure, gray-blue porcelain of softly blurred colors—a cloud-covered evening sky, a wave, a boat with brown sails. Martha held it with both hands, felt its cool smoothness. She put it against her burning cheeks and for a moment she thought she could feel the icy freshness of the waves, the salty fragrance of the sea. That felt good. . . . Startled she stared at the door: Marie Fehlandt, the hostess. She quickly approached her lonely guest.

"Oh, there you are . . . you runaway! What are you doing in the dark? Is something the matter?"

"Oh, no. I am only admiring this vase."

"Please. Do you like it? My husband brought it only recently from Copenhagen. But why are you hiding?"

Martha wanted to reply.

"Psst! You needn't pretend. I know. I can see you don't fit in with our fun-loving party crowd. I would be satisfied if you enjoyed my dinner."

Martha confirmed, yes. She praised the ice cream, the roast, and, against her will, felt herself captivated by the casual, lively charm of this woman. She had—perhaps impressed by her name—pictured Marie Fehlandt differently: blond, tall, of arrogant demeanor, not at all like this little, wild creature, so petite, with laughing brown eyes and pitch-black, tiny curls.

"Well, why don't you sit down. Though it is impolite of me to leave the other guests to themselves and to my husband—but . . . please do come. I don't bite at all, I am not a dog. I am a cat, says my dear husband, and I only scratch sometimes."

She pulled the woman she had caught unawares down next to her on the sofa.

"First, a cross-examination. You are a photographer by profession. But what else do you do? Do you go horseback riding, do you swim, play golf? No, of course not. Do you like the theatre?"

Martha remarked, "You are an actress. . . ."

"Who, I? Oh, no. Who told you that? I am a dancer—was a dancer. May I introduce myself: Solange Methivet de Vigo."

Martha smiled. "Spanish or French?"

"Both. Also German, as you can hear. Shall I let you in on my origins? They are fantastic enough. My grandfather, on my mother's side, was a Swiss-German who strayed into Spain one day. A Swiss-German, astray in Spain, remember. My grandmother came from Vigo—hence the name. He spoke pitiful Spanish, but he made up for it with excellent German. He taught his daughter German and I learned it from her, my mother. She married a Frenchman, an employee of the Schneider Armaments factory. I was born in Le Creusot—do you have any idea where that is? Pretty far to the east, in Burgundy, Département Saône-et-Loire—if that means anything to you. Pooh, what a sooty town—it crawls up the black hills like a fat caterpillar. There were stairs one had to climb, and right and left the streets run in a semi-circle, built one on top of the other like rows of benches in a circus. We lived in a place off a corridor near the staircase. Downstairs was a big store called "La Cigale et la Fourmi." Bicycles were in one window, sewing machines in the other . . ."

She gave a light laugh. "I'd make a good prosecutor. You were supposed to tell me a little about yourself, and I unpack my entire past instead. Well, let's get serious. You are independent, you have a career. You don't have children . . . ?"

She paused.

Martha did not give herself away. She folded her hands and pressed the palms together; that was all. A flower had bloomed briefly inside of her with a faint fragrance; now it closed up again. Why should she bother revealing anything to this hussy, this dance hall princess, who in a moment's fancy had pushed some kind words on her and would surely forget her within an hour in her flimflam world. My child, Madam, is not for your entertainment. If you are bored, get yourself a few new admirers. Oh, and—"You don't have children . . . ?"

With thin lips: "No."

The other woman seemed taken aback.

"Now I hurt you. Is it so bad? You were married—a widow, right? You could have had children. Children are so lovely. Oh, God if I could have another . . . but you are a cool woman, you don't know anything about this . . . !"

"Oh, I do," Martha said softly.

"No . . ."

"Oh, I do know."

"Oh, what do you know!"

Martha's contrariness provoked her, annoyed her; the little cat claws started to extend themselves, getting ready to scratch. "You . . . you despise me because I am thoughtless. You want to play the genteel, melancholy one, but what goes on inside me, that . . . of that—"

Martha remained calm. "I had a child. It is dead."

Marie Fehlandt fell silent. Finally she said tentatively, "Has it been a long time? How old was the child?"

"Five."

"Oh!" The Frenchwoman contemplated her rings; she wore a heavy, dusky red, glossy tourmaline.

After a short wait she said, "You are lucky."

Martha twitched, looked at her, very amazed but not indignant. Marie Fehlandt sat with a stooped neck, she seemed small and sinking. Then she threw back her charcoal head of hair, a wild flicker appeared in her eyes. She said in a tone that crouched like a beast of prey before the leap: "I am a murderer."

"That's a lie . . ."

"You had your child. I murdered mine before it was born. All my children . . . Yes. I was eighteen then. I was already performing in public as a dancer in Lyons. I had admirers, a friend . . . Eventually I became pregnant. Yes. There was no room in my life for a child. I was referred to one of those witches—you know—who took it from me. It was my first and last one. Now I no longer need to fear a 'mishap,' now I am sterile!"

A short, strange sound detached itself, part scornful laughter, part sobbing. She rose, suddenly composed.

Formally: "I must go back to my guests."

Martha offered her hand. "I shall leave, if I may."

She nodded. "It's all right. I would leave too, if I could. Thank you for coming. Here, use this door, please. I'll see to it that one of the girls unlocks the front door for you."

Martha turned back. "And that's why your name is no longer Solange but Marie?"

"For that reason? . . . No. That was for my husband. He pronounced the name 'so long' and thought it was ugly and stupid. He always teased me about it: Why so long, why not so short? He likes Marie much better."

She added with a smile, "And next time, you will come for tea, cozy, just the two of us."

Martha made an uncertain motion with her head.

"I don't know . . . I have so little time . . ."

## . 3 .

She did not move. The soft coldness spread out like a huge bird, light as a puff of air. She did not cover her bare shoulders and arms, her naked breasts. She rested with a happy smile in the oven-warmth of her spacious, heavy bed with numbed senses which had eagerly embraced what aroused her and had sated her burning desire. She was lying with her hands behind her neck, watching her lover who was doing exercises by the window. He was naked, he was strong and beautiful. He stretched with raised hands. She thought of a picture, a print she had found in a frame shop: a naked youth surrounded by a rocky wasteland, his face turned toward a gleaming bluishness, with huge eagle's wings. She asked him, "Do you want to fly?"

"Where to?"

"Into the sun."

"There is no morning sun here."

"No. Only in the afternoon and evenings . . . fly into my arms."

He ambled over.

"Are you still thirsty? You vampire!"

And yet, in a sudden surge, he threw himself on her and clung to her with a sucking, passionate kiss. Then she let him slide. She had an elongated, reddish mark on her breast.

He closed the window and quickly slipped on a shirt and trousers. He squatted in front of the stove, put wood in, and lit it.

She inquired, "Are you going to talk about it with Apitz, too."

"About what?"

"Of us, of me. When men get together they tell stories about women. I overheard a conversation in the streetcar the other day. 'And where else did you go?' 'To Frau . . . You know.' 'Nice cozy evening?' 'Yes, somewhat strenuous.' 'How is that?' 'Hm.' 'Well, such strong women always demand a lot.' I wouldn't want you to talk like that and yet I know that you do it anyway."

He peeked inside the stove, "I would never admit that it was strenuous."

She laughed softly, "Come!"

"I wouldn't think of it, I have to get going finally. This stuff just won't catch fire today."

She stretched along the edge of the bed, her arm against her cheek.

"I'm sure you won't be back for lunch."

"No. Probably not for afternoon coffee either. I haven't seen Apitz in a good six years. We'll eat somewhere in town and maybe we'll go for a stroll in the afternoon."

"And I'll mark my towels. Not a festive holiday." She sighed.

"You'll have to get used to it. One of these Sundays, I have to take a trip to Tangermünde. Now, let's have breakfast."

He closed the iron flue, lifted himself from the squatting position, and washed the soot off his hands.

Martha got out of bed. She walked around in her Chinese robe, her hair flowed soft and black onto the hyacinth blue silk ... She carried in the dishes. Golden brown crescents beckoned from the basket, hot cocoa steamed in the flowery pot. He filled his cup and ate.

"Another cup?"

"No, thanks."

"Must you leave already? You are so restless today. I wonder if Apitz is in as much of a hurry for this get-together as you are."

"Sure. Six years, that's quite a long time. If you had a close friend from your schooldays, you would feel the same way. You would look forward to seeing her again. Apitz was one of my two most trusted friends."

"And the other was ... ?"

"Ernst Rother."

"Oh yes, you told me already." She thought for a moment. "I am just trying to think if I had a real friend. In the lower grades I had several friends. Later, when we moved away, I was really only friends with Lisbeth Kurnicki. We wrote to each other for several years; then she became engaged and married young, and we just stopped writing. Quietly and painlessly ..."

"Well, Miriam," he reached for his hat, "until tonight." He kissed her briefly on the hand.

## Part Three

When he was gone, she watched him from the kitchen window. Then she slowly got dressed.

She tied on an apron, fed the fire in the stove, and as she did every Sunday, she straightened up the room herself. She had just pulled the chair with the armrest close to the window, and gathered up needle and thimble, embroidering yarn and scissors, and a pile of towels, when the doorbell sounded shrilly. A letter fell into the tin box. The handwriting was completely unknown to her. But her name was on it; she slit open the envelope.

*For Albert Renkens.*

*Dear Albert,*

> *I just telephoned your landlady and since she told me that you were out of town as usual on Sundays, I presume that this letter will reach you. We had planned to meet at four, but I cannot make it before six. Is that all right? If not, call me in the morning at Moabit 4960.*
> *The meeting place remains Cafe Göttl. More in person and*
> *Good-bye,*
>
> *Gerd*

It was from Apitz. She read the words one more time. They seemed inexplicable to her. Cafe Göttl, yes that was correct. But Albert wanted to meet his classmate at eleven o'clock sharp, and Gerd was talking about meeting at four o'clock, after lunch. What was going on? A simple misunderstanding? Betrayal? And Albert had betrayed her after all, had revealed their nights and embraces, had exposed her without consideration to his friend, in letters or on the telephone. How else would this stranger know her address and name? She knitted her brow in vexation.

She placed her elbows on the table, folded her hands behind her neck and stared at the piece of paper as if she absolutely had to discover a hidden meaning in each harmless, commonplace phrase. Even a more jealous or a more alert lover might have believed from experience that some hanky-panky was going on. It was possible that he spoke with his friend for half an hour—one could make it only at four, the other couldn't make it until five, and they really want to see each other, but neither remembered what they had agreed upon. It was not one of Albert's flaws to first say one thing and then another. Apitz might be such a confusing individual, one who jumps back and forth. The thought was alien to Martha. She was used to being as brief as possible on the telephone. The few times she would call her husband or now her business partner, she would say only as much as was necessary. She would never think of engaging with the invisible party in cozy chatter, receiver pressed against the ear. And if Albert said eleven and Gerd Apitz writes about four o'clock, they were no foolish children who gabbed past each other. Here lodged a lie. Like an ugly maggot in a seemingly clear, wholesome piece of fruit, it bored and ate away.

Martha returned to the window and started to embroider the outlined "MW" into the corner of a towel. The stitching and pulling of the thread, the even hand motion calmed her a little. She bent down for a piece of yarn that had fallen and whispered, "It is all right." But then her fingers began to tire and began to dream, and she stopped doing anything.

She had already thought of it—the end. She had delimited in her thoughts, had measured the reprieve with a yardstick. How long would it last? She thought then: not long. Two human beings of the same kind and maturity may join hands, never to part. We cannot do that. He is so much younger than I. And when he came to me, desired me, it was because he had been disgusted by the feline purring of another. My quietness and strong passion will tire him. His next choice will fall on someone still budding, all fresh and gay and lighthearted. Does it hurt me? No. I don't love him. I love his head on my chest, I want his mouth, his loins. He will carry out what I demand, do my bidding, march for my cause, destroy the murderer of my child, and I shall reward him for it. It is a balanced account. . . . She thought: Now the time has come. He did not deceive me. He will meet the friend only in the afternoon, in the morning he meets a girl. Maybe it is the cute Fräulein Lill from the Fehlandts' dinner party. Therefore the great hurry. Now the time has come. I have foreseen everything and have calculated everything. Do I now have to fall from the clouds and be unhappy?

With a determined hand she resumed her needlework. He has not been very useful to me. He has accomplished nothing. At first he had made some efforts, to please me, I recognize that, maybe also because he enjoyed playing detective. But his enthusiasm sagged quickly and I did not press him anymore. He always became a bit impatient when I reminded him. It doesn't matter. He has served me. His service is now over. Whatever has become useless goes out with the garbage. "He can go, for all I care," she said aloud as if to defend the thought to herself. What she didn't know was that she was sighing.

She sighed and looked outside. Flakes were falling, sinking down big and rare and soft like the softest flowers dropping onto a white cover. The naked rods of shrubbery paraded as flower bouquets. Low-growing mahonia bushes with fringed hoods of snow looked like dwarf Christmas firs. And white snakes crawled gently along the barren branches of the trees. On the very top of the tree, against the grayness of the sky, sat a very mighty bird—now it swayed away. A magpie. Down in the street a man was anxiously making his way with his dog. A little old, tremulous man wrapped in a long coat and with a thick scarf tied around his neck. Martha had never seen him before in that park. He paused after every third step under the strain, nodded strangely to himself, scratched the tree trunks with his crutch or poked around in the snow. She thought she heard him coughing. The dog resembled him. A scrawny mutt with a head sunk between its shoulders and a pointed snout, walking weak and stiff-legged alongside its owner. The weak old man and the discolored animal lost themselves in the solitude of the snow-covered garden. Martha followed them with her eyes and a sadness came over her. She wanted to place her tired face into her hands and cry.

Listlessly she looked around the room. The letter was still on the table. She walked over, took it, tore it to shreds, and burned the scraps in the stove. If Albert should ask, she had destroyed only a few useless lines. Maybe he would not even ask.

# A Jewish Mother from Berlin

She prepared her lunch. It wasn't much. Some mixed vegetables, a schnitzel, a small bowl of applesauce. She sat at the kitchen table and pushed the food into her mouth, listlessly, just to still her hunger, without much pleasure of eating. Then she washed the few dishes right away and stashed them in their place.

She stood by the door wondering what she should do. She went to the larger wardrobe and rummaged through it until she discovered it. A flat rectangular, tightly wrapped object. She took it into the room and sat down awkwardly and slightly agitated. Carefully she removed the two layers of tissue paper. . . . She held it and looked at it: Ursa's picture.

It was the first time. Martha had taken the photograph not too long before . . . that time. She had put it away immediately and had never looked at it again. Ursa was so much livelier and more beautiful, warmer and stronger, so much more alive than this thing. Only when she was asleep, lifeless, in the garden of the dead under the yellow rose, had Martha thought of looking for the photograph again. She did not do it. The photograph was good. And she was terrified of it. She was afraid that this smooth print would surreptitiously creep into her memory, cunningly, and drive away the martyred child that was still living inside her, and would intrude in the child's place. She did not trust it. So she left it incarcerated in the dark like some evil fiend. What made her bring it to light now?

It was to help her.

Her child was gone. No, not gone, only less near, only gone farther down below. She still felt it, already somewhat distant, its features less distinct. She had summoned it for guidance: What must I do? But it did not hear her outcry, did not answer her call. So she pleaded with the photograph. She held it like a relic, the picture of a saint who could work miracles—to look at it, touching it was nurture for her soul in need. She hoped and was silent.

The moss-green velvet dress. To adorn her better, the mother had put a delicate necklace with a golden heart on her. Frau Hoffmann made her sit on a stool and gave her a cookie. She studied the scene, cocking her head this way and that. . . .

"No," she said, "it won't work in sitting position, finish eating and come over here."

The child obeyed.

"Which of my things would you like to look at? The fishbowl?"

Yes, the bowl. It was a glass bowl, filled with water, in which fish and a real snake were at home.

"Here—but don't let it drop."

The child took it cautiously with both hands, shaking it lightly. A swarm of brightly colored fish was swimming around in it, and the snake began to slither. The snake had brown spots and the fish gleamed with magnificent scales of blue, silver, and red.

"Now, first look at your mother."

She looked up. The swaying glitter, the colorful pleasure in her toy left a reflection on her face, a quiet, heavenly smile. Martha captured it. The hands were still turning the glass bowl, the little head . . . Oh, God! How lovely she was and how sweet!

No. She sighed. She placed the portrait on the windowsill with a limp, disappointed gesture. It did not come. What she had prayed for so fervently did not come. All this kneeling, submerging in a dead happiness, this holding close, this being in the grip of a burning wave, this becoming swept up in a flood. No, she was not shaken. She did not cry, did not throw herself down groaning and kiss the unfeeling mouth. She . . . she knew not what she felt. She was moved slightly—like a piece of wood drifting on an inland waterway.

She nodded, leaned her forehead against her hands. It was no use trying to force something. Ursa was far away, and the pain was far away, the passionate mourning. She might possibly come back one day when the mother was no longer searching. She looked away. The flakes were swarming closer together. She wrapped herself up more warmly and went out and wandered through the silent streets into the flurry of falling snow, alone.

# . 4 .

"I really don't want to intrude."

"Frau Beucker, you are not intruding. Please come in."

"I am probably disturbing your supper."

"No, I have eaten already." She led the old woman into the room and made her sit on the sofa.

"Yes," she continued apologizing, "I would have called on you some other time, but I thought Frau Wolg is busy in the morning and afternoons she is not home. I have another petition for you to sign."

"Oh, . . . the business with the electric lighting."

"Yes, we finally are to get electricity. It was my son-in-law, you know, who inquired about it and the installer sent a cost estimate. It's coming along. I've almost completed my rounds with the collection list, even the Drachs are willing to pay this time. . . ."

Martha took the sheet of paper and studied it. She went to fetch ink and signed. "Here is my name. But there is no need to run away so soon. You see, I have some darning to do. Why don't you keep me company?"

This was not mere polite talk. She wanted the old lady and her friendly, unexciting chatter that was like a streak of light, her own little lamp with a warm old-fashioned glow, to chase away this weight of gray, ravenous, gloomy insidious thoughts that gathered in the darkness and unsettled her. As a small courtesy she put out a little box of chocolates and kept on stitching while Frau Beucker reported on all sorts of matters of indifferent import, harmless gossip from the building which amused Martha without much engaging her. Oh yes, the Drachs, the "dragons," the drags, they think they finally found a suitable husband for their daughter, though he is supposed to be neither the best-looking nor the youngest, a businessman from Friedrichshagen—a short way from here. . . . Martha pulled her sewing basket closer and asked suddenly: "And how is Elschen, is she better?"

"Elschen? Oh yes, thank God. She went back to school yesterday.

It was just a little cold and fever children get sometimes." And suddenly she fell silent and cast a peculiar, searching look at her interrogator.

This lasted only a moment, but as she was about to resume her chatter, Martha interrupted.

"Is the little one not well? I can see it from the look in your eyes. What is the matter? Why don't you speak up?"

"I . . ." the old woman cleared her throat, and tugged at her white hair in discomfort, her apple cheeks turning redder still. "I just thought . . . Frau Wolg . . ."

"Yes?"

"You mustn't be angry with me for saying so . . ."

"No."

"I just thought . . . Some time ago . . . some time ago, I wouldn't have dared to speak to you about the child."

Martha replied harshly, "Yes, that was some time ago. I know, I was always boasting . . . a bit pompous and became easily excited . . . But now the year of mourning has passed and one can forget the dead. A child . . . what is that to a mother?"

Wanting to calm her, the old woman stroked her arms.

"Oh, now you are offended. I did not mean it that way. I just always had the hope . . . I have often said to my daughter: the poor woman deserves to find peace. Time, it consoles. It doesn't mean that one forgets. Nothing is really lost. Everyone has an angel with God in heaven and one will find him again some day. You must believe it."

Her blue eyes brightened as if she were making a Christmas prophecy.

Martha hesitated a second.

"You speak of a time that consoles. You don't mention the other kind of consolation, but it's on your mind. You know I have a gentleman friend, a lover. Yes, you are aware of that and that's why you're thinking ill of me."

"I don't think ill of you, Frau Wolg," Frau Beucker said softly. "I understand. You are still a young woman, a woman of vitality. . . .

This . . . it probably had to happen. It would be best for you to get married again. Only . . . the gentleman is younger, I presume."

"You have seen him?"

The old woman got flustered. "Yes, briefly . . . I mean my son-in-law saw him the other night."

"Where? Here?"

"Yes."

Martha tried to smile.

"Yes, he is younger than I. You know a husband's faithfulness crumbles so easily, and with an older wife . . ."

The visitor nodded. She made no sound, but her expression betrayed that there was more she wanted to unload, that her desire to babble was fighting an instinct toward reticence. Martha came to her aid: "Frau Beucker, there is more. You still have something you want to say. Please go on."

"But you were already offended once."

"I won't be again. I promise."

The old woman cleared her throat.

"I wouldn't have mentioned it, but since you ask . . . It is . . . it's just . . . my son-in-law saw your gentleman friend near the fence of the Rosskaempfer Inn. He said, a car was parked there . . . a dark gray, very beautiful vehicle . . . no, not quite dark, more silvery . . . and a young lady in a fur coat was walking up and down . . . and . . ."

"And he left with her in the car. That was Thursday night, right?"

"Yes. Oh, then it probably was . . ."

"Guess who? His sister!" She laughed. How unnatural it sounded. But the old woman pretended not to notice.

"Well, then it's all right. Sometimes one worries unnecessarily about the simplest things. And later everything turns out to have an easy explanation. I told my son-in-law right away that one shouldn't think the worst."

Who knows how many people in the building she had already gossiped with about this.

She rose. "Well, now I really must be going. It's already bedtime. They're probably looking for me."

Martha took the lamp from the table and walked her to the door.

"But Frau Wolg, you won't take it the wrong way, will you?"

"Not at all, no."

"Good night, Frau Wolg."

"Good night."

His sister, stepsister. A young girl, a silver blond twenty-year-old. She was a student at the agricultural college near Eutin. A fresh, plain, and simple person, fond of animals and nature, of strong build. Albert had told her a nice little childhood story.

Two little darlings, girlfriends, sat by the brook. Albert, the big brother, happened to be passing: "Well, what are you doing here, you small fry?"

"We are fishing." And they proudly held up a stick with thick twine attached.

"You won't catch anything this way. You need a hook, a really pointed one, and a worm, the fish snaps at it, gets speared, and is stuck."

"Doesn't that hurt the little fish?"

"Well . . . that can't be helped."

"Then we'd rather fish this way."

He had smiled as he remembered.

"The humane way of fishing. I thought they were just dumb little girls; but actually they were right. Most Sunday anglers, who won't trap more than a few tadpoles, should do likewise: just take a rod with a cord and hold it in the water. That was fun enough for them. . . ."

Martha took his hand.

"Ursa would have done the same . . . only she was not allowed near the edge of the water. . . ."

Ursa . . . she thought for a brief moment only, while looking over the mending she had just finished before putting away the sewing utensils. Then again: His sister! Who might this woman be? Maybe Fräulein Lill after all? He had also mentioned a few times a lady friend of his friend Apitz, a beauty, a divorcée. Very rich, very spoiled, but in very fragile health and ailing every few weeks. She might well have a car and a fur coat.

She stared, still brooding, loosened her hair and tossed back the flowing strands. Did she have to assume that it was a familiar face, a definite name—was the enemy not a total stranger? A glittering film star, a charming actress with a well-appointed apartment, precious jewelry, with monkeys and kittens, who travels *à deux* to St. Moritz and the Riviera.

"I am in the mood to travel this summer too," she thought suddenly, "and not just to the Erzgebirge or the island of Rügen."

She had been vacationing with Ursa in Binz the year before last, lounging around lazily in a beach basket, dreaming of greenish glittering waves. Ursa had been playing with other children, collecting shells, building sand castles, digging canals and ponds. Holding her mother's hand, she had jumped fearlessly into the coolness in her lobster-red bathing suit. It must have rained several times, the girl also had an upset stomach once, but Martha had preserved a picture of blue ships, a gleaming sea, beach and sun, a perfectly peaceful contentment.

Oh yes, she thought as she was undressing, Frau Beucker was right. There was a time when thinking about it tore my heart apart. Now I remain calm. . . . I would like to go away somewhere with Albert, a place that is hot and bright, with palm trees, where one can wear parrot-colored silk, blue and green and orange, a place like Andalusia or North Africa or the Canary Islands. How much I would love him there. I love him already anyway. . . . Oh, go away! I don't love him. I would do the same with any other man too—would be just as content. We would go to Spain in autumn. Marie Fehlandt's mother was from Vigo. Wonder where that is?

"Solange Methivet de Vigo," she said softly. A colorful name. Scarlet and gold brocade.

She dawdled as she slipped off her stockings and washed her beautiful strong feet in a blue bowl. The tepid water warmed her gently. It felt good. While she was washing herself with the soapy cloth, she again saw the little Frenchwoman, La Fehlandt, with her devilish sparkling eyes, her curly, pitch-black head of hair. A party cracker, she thought. Maybe *she* was Albert's secret amusement.

She shrugged her shoulders, annoyed, almost furious with herself. "Why should I care about his tarts? Let him play his love games with whomever he wants. . . ." The washcloth dropped with a splash into the wet spray. While she toweled herself off, she repeated, whispering, the same syllables, tasting them like fruit: "Solange Methivet de Vigo." Performed in public in Lyons.

Lyons: What was it to her? A few letters of the alphabet without any magic; the city remained shrouded in fog. But she still saw the dark girl: like a Carmen maybe, a yellow-fringed shawl about her shoulders, a rose between her lips. And how she danced, passionately, wild, ravishing, burning ... And then the embrace, the surrender was only intensified dance, frenzy, ecstasy ... then sudden recognition, fear ... finally, submission, flight into the cave of the seedy old woman ...

Martha did not quite reach the point of imagining all of it. She too had struggled. She had worked to provide bread for Ursa, had known her share of toil and deprivation, illness and sorrow. But no poverty, no suffering. I would have carried it to term. I would have toiled, would have starved my way through. I would have tried to live with it; maybe there is such a thing as mercy. If not ... I would have died with it. I would not have killed it. Never.

She threw her head back and remained erect with a glowering, determined look. The reddish, faded photographs in black frames looked down on her from the wall. A youngish man with a small, sharp, thoughtfully serious face and his little, insignificant wife, a blond Jewish woman. They watched their daughter with a strange look. The father spelled it out, the mother only nodded.

"You are lying. You, too, have murdered your child."

Martha was startled. Never had a voice said this to her before; she heard it for the first time. The paralyzing brew was mixed and administered to her child. Then it fell into a deep sleep. ... Yes ... Did she, the desperate one, do that? Did she have to do it? She pondered. She recalled Frau Ramtow's empty words of comfort: that the doctor and the nurses had no hope from the first day.

And the nurse later pressed her hand: "Frau Wolg, I can only say one thing, it is best this way."

It is best this way. She believed it then. Had she been right, had they all been right: her child truly could not be saved? She seemed so convinced of it, she never had any doubt since then, no pangs of conscience. She had called the miscreant a "murderer" without ever stopping to think!

"Murderer—that is you."

The parents stared down at her. Her lips moved involuntarily as if she wanted to fight back, defend herself; but she remained silent. She pulled herself up in defiance: It is not true. Snap it shut. Yet she held in her hands a leaking vessel; closing and pressing the cover as she might to prevent its contents from spilling, through a crack, a sudden channel, the drops still trickled.

I thought, Ursa would never be able to forget. I thought, Ursa will never be whole again. I thought, the people here know—Ursa will die in agony. I had to watch my child suffer such pain and I had to rock her to sleep. I thought, it was good this way. And now? What if we were all wrong? Doctors and nurses are mortal, shortsighted, powerless, limited. So am I! What if the child had gotten well again? What if we all deceived ourselves? What if Ursa had recovered in spite of the horror, had recovered had it not been for my deed? Or my—crime? "No," she stammered, her fists clenched, "no . . . oh, no!"

Her naked feet slipped off the edge of the bowl, splashing the water and bringing her to her senses. She grabbed the towel and rubbed her feet dry a second time.

"I'll have a piece of chocolate," she said aloud and did it right away as if this ordinary act and these generally understood words would extricate her from the web of her madness. But when she walked to the mirrored cabinet to replace the little box, a strange woman staggered toward her—a sweaty, bloated face with vacant, horrified eyes.

# . *5* .

They walked as in a veil. They walked inside a little transparent skin which enveloped them loosely without being felt, and which only shared its name with the thick, dull, autumn fog. It accompanied them like a wall drawn all around their every step, separating them from the tangible world, and through a delicate web presented them with an unreal, enchanted landscape, gently breathed pastels. The sky gleamed grayish white, and white heavy flakes fell gently on empty avenues, snow-covered gardens with trees and shrubbery like feathery white, ruffled, cowering birds and decaying mansions with scooped gables like the pale headdresses of nuns. Near the torn-up roadway was a pile of cobblestones, more angular and white than lumps of sugar fit for a giant's tin box. Martha and Albert touched each other's hands from time to time. They were the only coarse bodies, the only ordinary living beings in this fairy tale book. The only dark, sober forms. For all around them descended an unnatural, dim brightness without sun, without radiating luminosity: snow.

Albert began again:

"The itinerary goes via Stendal. By the way I am catching the train at Spandau—it works out that way too. You don't know it? There are supposed to be peculiar old edifices."

"In Spandau?"

"No, in Tangermünde. I'm still talking about it."

"Yes." She pressed her lips together.

"You are not very talkative today. Not in a good mood. Do I have to ask you to come with me?"

She only shook her head.

It was stronger than she. Albert had never been much of a talker, and now he lied incessantly about a trip that would never take place, which, if he actually undertook it, would have a purpose totally different from his work.

She could not bear it. If he wanted to leave her, why could he not remain silent? Why not simply say, "I am going on a trip"? She would sooner have bitten her tongue than ask whereto.

She looked to the side. A softness was gliding from the outside staircase onto the lawn, so immaculately pure and chaste. Two goblin-like firs shivered distantly, heavily laden and dipped completely in snow.

"I don't know what's bothering you," he said in a grim tone. Her silence embittered him. "If I have committed some kind of sin, then out with it. Though I am not aware of any fault on my part, one can't put every word on a golden scale."

He waited. He stamped his feet vigorously a few times, kicking lumps of snow off his heels. "A woman pouting without good reason. All right. Here I thought you were different, but—well." With a scornful gesture, he wiped the snow off his shoulders and chest. They continued their walk without a word.

Iron wire-mesh fences, feathery sprinkles adorning them like filigree. A brick building, dusky red-violet between narrow, low-lying windows and a steep, black roof, stood heavy and alone in the snowy space. Martha loved this house in the wintertime. It towered in the far north on the coast of wild swans and the icy-green glass wave that threatened from miles away. The hundred-year-old dark raven, croaking, fluttered off its ridge like a giant into the wasteland.

Albert said, "We are going back now. It's time for me to go. I don't like getting to the station at the last minute. I won't miss much around here. Only this: a woman who keeps on trudging along with me and doesn't open her mouth, just because she is stubborn like a naughty child."

Martha stopped walking. She looked directly at him.

"I don't believe you."

"What don't you believe?"

"Everything."

"The trip . . . ?"

"That too."

He smiled, sure of victory. "Just as I thought. Women are all alike. It is impossible to be away for twelve hours without immediately arousing jealousy. Here read this."

He took his wallet from his coat and pulled out a white piece of paper. "Lauma & Son."

She did not take it. She twisted and turned, repelled and tired. "All right, I expected this."

She walked away, leaving him with his letter by the wayside. He put it away. A darker, ominous redness glowed in his face. From his pale blue eyes, the small pupils darted harsh, hostile flashes.

He quickly marched after her. When he had caught up with her: "Martha."

"Yes."

"I just want to tell you something that is true. I *am going* to Tangermünde. I am going *on business* and *alone.* I am not lying. In this instance, you are wrong. Otherwise . . . you are right."

Martha trembled in her heart. She had known it too well. Now that it had been said, it seemed as if she herself had spoken a word she could not take back. As if she had slammed a door shut behind her forever. As if something had been torn in half, a rope to which she had clung, a curtain before her eyes. She remained in a void, plunging through a space, empty and wide. He did not notice. She should have confronted him at last, should have rebelled against him. His anger was aroused that she apparently still did not deign to do so.

"Of course, you already suspected it, and it does not touch you . . . all the better. I must confess that *my* discovery was more painful. Like a dumb schoolboy I had the illusion that you loved me after all."

"I do love you," she said softly in a strange voice.

"Oh yes? Yes, of course. If you don't, you won't have anybody to run and jump for you like a trained poodle. I've had it. Now you'll put on airs, remind me that you had declared at the beginning of this business deal what you needed me for: to find the murderer of your child and . . . And I searched the streets for you, made contact here, rang a doorbell there, met with every Tom, Dick, and Harry, believing, miserable fool that I was, that you would show me a little more gratitude in return than an occasional night in your bed . . . maybe a little friendliness . . . warmth . . . you obviously have none but the heat generated between the legs . . . ."

Shaking. "Stop it . . . !"

"In a moment. Only one more truth I want you to hear, a very dirty truth: You are a whore. A prostitute, that's all. I run around as your bloodhound, that's how I pay, and for that you sleep with me. Right? Isn't that so? Now we are even. One doesn't fuss much with a whore, no swearing of 'eternal love' no 'union of souls' and so on. One puts the money down, buttons the suit, and is gone. Here is your money."

He threw the base, reviling words at her as if he wanted to smash everything so nothing could be pieced together again.

He turned back one more time.

"Give me the keys."

"The keys . . . ?"

"The keys to the apartment. Hand them over. I am going ahead to pack my things."

His tone was intentionally gruff and commanding. She fumbled in her purse for the key ring and handed it to him. She no longer saw what she was doing. She had the will and determination not to cry, but her eyes were blind. She moved forward, probably took a few steps. He raised his hand in a violent gesture. When Martha recovered her sight, he had drowned in the fog.

Soundlessly the flakes buzzed around her. She walked and walked. Creeping, tired avenues blurred shallow in a hazy sea. Darkness fell on silent islands; the first street lamps opened their yellow, lidless eyes. A large, heavily laden branch hung low over iron lattice bars. Martha brushed lightly against it. It whispered, tossed a few white flowers over her like a gift, like a sisterly caress.

# . 6 .

She rushed. With gliding shoulders, bent over, fists pressed tight against her chin as if to support a drooping head, she paced back and forth in her room like a caged animal. It was a tiger's stride, back and forth between cold walls, slowly extinguishing a soot-black, singeing golden flame. Thus she consumed herself. A chair got in her way; her claws landed on its back as if she wanted to break it. Then she let go of it, continued her wandering. And pondered.

Again and again: Why did I not do this? Why did I not try to say two words to him before he turned away—one forgiving, the other pleading? He met me in front of the Grazietta garden, carrying his suitcase in one hand, my keys in the other. "I am done upstairs," he said curtly, but calmer than before. "I don't think I forgot anything. Wish me a good journey." He tipped his finger to his hat. "So long." And Martha saw him in the street, getting farther and farther away with forceful strides. She stood in silence.

Then finally she was in her dusky room. Alone. He was gone, gone on his journey. But she looked at him with wide open eyes, and spoke slowly: "Go!" He departed, the one who was already gone, and she found peace.

Not for long.

All night she was unable to sleep; senselessly she felt the sheet, she stroked it with mad fingers: suddenly she fell into sobbing.

"Come," she repeated, "come . . . Come!" None came. She let her begging arms drop and said aloud and calmly: "It is over," and she turned on her side.

Thus she struggled for days. Not in the daytime. During the day, her work held her hands and, though less so, also her thoughts. At night she wrestled with the man. She kept tossing him about the way a child tosses a doll, defiantly. "Lie there. I can do without you." She pushed him to the side with a kick. "You wretch. Yes, I did love you and you heaped refuse on me. You smeared me with names, with words that stick to me like mud and excrement. A woman who would bear such filth. . . You can no longer cleanse

147

me. I don't want to forget. Away with you." She gnashed her teeth. Again she constrained him back to her. "Oh you, what does it all matter what you did to me? So what if you hurt me. I love you." She breathed gently. "Call me what you want. Berate me, strike me . . . I am only one thing: I am your whore. See I am lying here, naked and ready . . . Come to me." She shivered. Do you know? The first night . . . when I walked over silently and opened my bed to you, there was your strange look on me, a look that enveloped me, touched me completely, but your mouth said: "You are a woman." As if it wanted to say: "You are a tower, you are a light, a crown." Now I am a whore to you. I hate you. You call me vampire. I want to grip you with my arms, with my bat wings, I want to drink the blood from your veins and lash you away tomorrow like a dog, like a mangy dog . . . You!

Her eyes glowed in the dark. She rested. Her face was hard and sensuous, desirous and self-contained all at once, the face of a sorceress.

And again: His silvery head rested on her breasts, she caressed his hair with her lips. "You beware, I am a Jew. I wish I could do what that Spaniard believed. . . ." The Spaniard came to the studio to have his picture taken. He spoke with Martha, and since he soon found out her racial origins, he demanded to know everything: about sinister secret signs, arts, and rituals of the Jews. Martha knew nothing and denied they existed. He smiled a superior smile. "Nonsense," he said in his foreign accent. "You only not want to tell me . . . The Jews are so . . . refined . . . shrewd. Here will be as in Spain." He shook his head like someone who was not that easily deceived. And at home Martha looked for a book, a thin, worn, little black volume in which she had read as a child the legends of the scholars, teachers, and sages. She had read of Reb Dob Joel Sachs who, so he would reach home before the holiday and not drive his horse into the Sabbath, traversed a river with his wagon faster than on dry land. He was the same one whose raised arm held the wolves at bay that were circling his sleigh. Or Rabbi Akiba Eger who once pondered the meaning of the Kabbalah at midnight. The light had gone out without his becoming aware of it; his cogitating over the sacred pages radiated with a more brilliant beam. She rummaged. But she did not find the little black book. Who knows whether her mother had kept it after her father's death and where it might have ended up. She thought: The Spaniard ... if I could really do that ... Maybe I should draw a letter of the alphabet, try out a certain hand movement, form a word with my lips, then he would wake in the middle of the night, would toss and turn deprived of sleep, would turn on the light, shivering he would go to the desk; then by tomorrow evening his letter would be with me or maybe even he himself. She twitched. Her throat emitted an ugly sound into the stillness of the night. A short derisive laugh.

"I am sick, I am foolish." She squinted and yawned. "I'd better try to get some sleep."

This morning she was so tired out, so weak and miserable, Frau Hoffmann sent her home and recommended bed rest and a hot drink. She had tried to rest on the sofa, but despite her fatigue slept very little—she could not bear it any longer. Now she paced the room, dragging her resolutions, decisions behind her like a loose chain.

Albert Renkens. She built a house for herself, a house of cards, consisting of his worthlessness, his faults, and when it was finished and seemed just right, she toppled it with a single stroke of her hand and resolved to love him. She decided to write to him. This way she could carefully choose her words, weigh them, set down those that seemed suitable and discard those that were inappropriate. In a verbal exchange she might find afterward that she had said the bad things and had forgotten to say the right ones. She saw him ripping the sheet of paper from the envelope, reading it, scornfully shrugging his shoulders with the same grim, merciless contempt he once accorded Miss Flossie. "What do you want with this love drivel? She only wants to do what gives men pleasure and doesn't annoy women." Martha was indignant: No! I won't grovel, I won't kiss the dust from his boots. I am not made for that. She paused. What time was it? Ten minutes before four; he would be home around five o'clock. And as if only instant action could prevent her from aborting the plan she had formed, she tore her best dress from her wardrobe, washed off the traces of tears. She powdered her face in front of the mirror. "I still don't look good," she noted, "sort of famished, haggard. Maybe . . . he will believe my misery and despair . . . will know that I am not lying."

It was a short narrow private street, a dead end, an alley, gray and silent with old, shriveled acacia trees and dusky, once elegant, houses. No greenery, only the second house to the left was set back from a small, fenced-in strip of grass. So that's where he lived; she had never visited him. She stopped for a moment. And when she pushed down the iron door handle and the gate was sliding open and then closing again with a rattle, her heart beat as if anticipating some evil.

The wide steps leading to the house, windowpanes painted with allegorical themes, the carved bench at the landing—all betrayed a more affluent earlier time. Yet the stained walls and the tattered runner on the floor spoke of the present. A porcelain sign: "Von Hettenbrinck" and underneath, a small card attached with a thumbtack. Martha read: "Albert Renkens, Certified Engineer, Kiel, Reventlowallee 9." The place names had been crossed out. She stared at it as at a miracle and did not ring the bell.

Martha rang. A grayish blond woman opened, presumably Frau von Hettenbrinck in person. A painstakingly clean and straight appearance: in her dress with the stiff collar, the old-fashioned brushed up hair above a cool, distant face, she resembled an officer's widow. Her expression spoke of distrust. "Herr Renkens is not at home," she said curtly. Martha hesitated. "He must be returning soon . . . could I wait here a while . . . ?"

Frau von Hettenbrinck showed her into a little room off to the side, which was probably once used to lesser fare, but was now cluttered to bursting with the remnants of a parlor—mirrors, glassware, and damask chairs. A slender blond young man sat in front of a cabinet with musical scores. He shot up as she entered, bowing slightly. Frau von Hettenbrinck offered her a seat. "Please." Then: "Don't let it disturb you, Jobst."

She disappeared. The son hardly paid attention to Martha; after a brief look, he probably found her ugly and old. He sat down at the brown piano and continued his playing.

She leaned back, going over in her mind how she would greet Albert, how she would answer him, how he might respond. The rolling and jingling of the piano playing intruded unpleasantly on her thoughts. Over and over the same boring runs; maybe it was a sonata, an étude, or the like; she knew little about it. What might this fellow be practicing for? Perhaps he was a music student. Or he gave piano lessons, or was an accompanist for dancing lessons to earn his tuition. But this was no dance music. . . .

She could have asked him simply, if she was really that curious. Just then he stopped for a moment, turned on the stool, looked out the window into grayness, at gray walls. One hand still moved over the keys of the piano without sounding them. His name was Jobst von Hettenbrinck. He sat there in another country; she was unable to reach him by calling out to him. He had his back turned toward her and had apparently forgotten the inconsequential, distant woman. He pulled himself together with a jerk and, as if to make up for lost time, he nimbly reached into the keys.

On the table was a thin brochure; furtively she pulled it toward her, surreptitiously, almost like a thief. The cover said: "Hugin— German Defense—Bulletin for Nationalistic Thinking" and between the titles was a raven holding a swastika emblem in its claws. She leafed through it; it contained what she expected.

" . . . Judah has cunningly fashioned the yoke for the Germanic neck." "The true enemy . . . flat-footed, pot-bellied, crook-nosed and swarthy, passes you in the street every day." "The sons and daughters of Israel . . . parasitic plants on the tree trunk of the German nation . . ."

Martha looked up. Her eyes flared the way they did whenever her lover, out of a long-standing aversion and a momentary vexation, derided her people, her origins with fresh disdain. For Albert had grown up among people who threw every malady and weakness of the time at the Jews like stones.

"It is possible that you are right," he said sometimes with some measure of self-recognition, "and I am wrong. But I learned this as a child, now it is so deeply rooted in me that I cannot tear it out."

She lowered her head and continued to read: ". . . and we still do not realize it. Jewish arrogance." She thought: Arrogance? We are not arrogant, unfortunately not. But we might be. Yes, we have a right to it. We survived Rome, have seen Byzantium in ruins; this enemy, too, can kill us only if we undo ourselves. All we need is to muster the strength and courage, sink again, bear again . . . . All we need do is turn inward again, there nobody can pursue us. . . . "Israel is like the dust of the earth, all trample it underfoot, but the dust survives them all."

She nodded and abruptly threw back her head. Her stars gleamed bright into a vast expanse. She replaced the brochure on the table with a rough gesture. Jobst von Hettenbrinck heard a crackling noise and looked around. Martha stood up.

"This is too long for me. I was going to wait for Herr Renkens, but he seems delayed. Will you kindly let me out?"

It was so still—away from the world, from the noise of the teeming city. Martha still walked up and down through reddish-grayish slush, a mix of ash and watery snow on the narrow flagstone path leading from the entrance of the house to the latticed gate. She wanted to wait. And were he not to return until deep in the night, he would find her on the threshold. She felt that she must not leave to try her luck again the next day like a traveling salesman. It was today that she had to seize her fate, subdue and conquer it. Tomorrow she might no longer be in control of it. In the midst of all this an evil thought struck her, not only evil, but also ridiculous. Here she was lying in wait like doom itself, and Albert, wherever he was now, had a premonition and did not dare return home. Meanwhile, an old lady carrying a dachshund came out of the house and tripped past her toward the street. She placed the little dog on the ground with much ado and walked it up and down the street, returning after a short while, not without eyeing the loitering woman with sharp suspicion. The dusky house swallowed her up.

Martha stared after her, brooding. Tired of walking, she followed and planted herself in the niche of the entrance gate. From there she looked out on the miniature garden, but without really seeing it with much more than just her eyeballs. Inside the garden was an empty flower bed, a few low-growing conifers; the rhododendron bush still wore a cap of coarse, gray-brown burlap. Snowdrops bloomed, gentle tufts of milky drops ran along the fresh gleaming leaves. She was aware of it for only a moment, before she could enjoy it, she was already caught again in the web of her thoughts.

She could not bear it for too long. She approached the gate, opened it, and peered down the street. People walked along the intersecting street. A man and a child turned the corner and disappeared inside the nearest house. Cars rolled by, a bicyclist crawled by nimble as a bug. Far away, above the rooftops, she saw the evening colors of the sky standing like a bowl of fruit. The red sun had already fallen down somewhere. But there was still the breeze of a pallid, receding apricot gleam, lilac-pink of delicious plum, grape-dark clouds thickened, a pale banana gold dissolved in the turquoise of the magic fruit. She tasted silently and was refreshed as she turned back toward the earth. But the earth beneath her was buried under stones.

He did not come. The sky sank deeper and turned to dusk, became darker, vaulting higher still. She found no moon. She was cold. Maybe it was not very cold. But her fingers stiffened, her toes were frozen and in pain. In front of the lattice a lantern flickered. Martha circled the sparse light as those women, colorful butterflies, sad moths that flutter under street lamps offer themselves to men for a night. She did not think of it. Two dapperly dressed young men left the last house on the street and brushed by her. One of the men shrugged his shoulders: "Colchicum autumnale." He spoke loud so she would hear it, but she did not quite comprehend its meaning.

A pallid glow betrayed her face. He had apparently seen her from afar before she recognized him. He walked up to meet her. Uncertain: "Martha . . . ?"

"Yes."

He offered his hand. "Good evening. Did you want to see me? Why didn't you wait upstairs?" He tossed off the words in an indifferent, calm manner as if they were good friends. "Come in." They went inside. On the stairs something occurred to him: "I have lost my holder somewhere, my silver cigarette holder—maybe at your place?"

She shook her head slightly. "I didn't find anything." She hardly realized that he didn't ask this because the little tube was important to him but just to make small talk.

He pushed open the door to the rear corridor. "Here, this is where I live." It was a rather nice, spacious room; she paid no attention to it.

"Albert . . ." she began.

"Here, first sit down. And let me talk first. I will be brief, very brief. Well, I am not a boor, I am not a woman—well, you will have noticed that by now—and when I talk nonsense, say stupid things, I don't persist in finding it reasonable afterward. I was very angry the other day, for good reason, and I finally became enraged and slapped you . . . I'd rather not remind either of us of it. You will forgive me, won't you? That is why you came, haven't you?"

"No," she said softly. "I hold no grudge against you. I have nothing to forgive you for, Albert," she said, looking at him as if for the first time. "I love you. Come back."

She reached with her hand across the table. He pulled back. After a pause:

"Martha, I am sorry, but I have to tell you this one more time, I cannot help you. My behavior on Sunday was wrong. As far as the matter itself is concerned, I was right. Something here is dead and I am no magician, I cannot bring it back to life."

She whispered: "Yes, my poor child . . ."

He tapped his fingers on the table.

"I didn't mean your poor child—I meant our . . . our love. It's gone. And what finally had to kill it, was the child's corpse that always lay between us at night."

Her eyes darkened.

"I shall bury it. I promise."

"You cannot promise anything."

"Oh yes, I can."

She showed him a very large envelope with a string tied around it. "Do you know what this is? Ursa's picture. I just don't want to take it out of the envelope—you will spare me this—if you want to, you can . . . later you can examine the cut-up scraps . . . Look here!" She took it as with animal claws and tore it to pieces.

He stared at her. "You . . . and you want to know why I don't love you anymore? By the way . . ." He paused abruptly, fell silent. After a while, very seriously: "You are not a good mother. At first you engaged in an idolatrous cult over your Ursa; now you break the idol in pieces. One is as wrong as the other."

"What do you want me to do?" she pleaded meekly. "Please tell me what you want me to do. So you'll know that I am telling the truth."

He answered with a casual, dismissive gesture. "Only to show me that . . . I am not saying you are lying. But always this excessiveness . . ." He added: "You are very agitated right now. When you calm down, you will see . . ."

"I don't want to see anything. I want to love you, I want to obey you . . . Oh God, you don't understand me!"

He confirmed harshly:

"No, I don't understand you. You run after me. If you had a spark of honor left in you . . ."

"I have none left."

She collapsed. But then she lifted her head abruptly, a spark of fright blinked in her maddened eyes. She pleaded in despair:

"Albert . . . !" And as if he were far away, "Albert, do you hear me? Perhaps you might think this is all just pretense, that I am making such a fuss just to hold you because you are useful for my purpose. . . . You . . . you are wrong. You were talking about a business deal. It is true that's what it was then, a kind of contract. Now . . . I don't want this anymore, this avenging of Ursa. You say I am a bad mother. No. Only today, I remember Ursa with a more tepid feeling and a bit of nostalgia, the way other mothers remember their dead children. At one time, oh God, how I loved my child . . .! More than my life. There was no room for the two of you in me, and you drove her out. That's when she died. A short time ago was her seventh birthday, I carried her to the cemetery and buried her in the earth. Albert. I must tell you something else . . ."

She hesitated. He looked silently at his pencil, drew a few lines on a piece of paper. She wanted to continue, to confess: "I murdered my child, Albert. I confess to you. Now I am in your hands." But she felt the ocean-cold look, an icy drop, run over her head. Clearly: Spare yourself this, Martha. You are not convincing. You may be a good actress, but as a "great criminal" you don't make much of an impression on me. Or even harsher: You're imagining this. You're overwrought. I am no friend of hysterical women.—He lifted his chin, his harsh lips twitched almost provocatively.

"Well?"

She heard herself repeating: "I must tell you something. I want you to know . . . I want to place myself into your hands, then you can send me to jail if I get bothersome. I murdered my child. She was in the hospital, and I saw that she would never be well again, and I administered a potion to her, a sleeping potion. And when it was all over, the nurses said later it was best this way . . . You don't believe me . . ."

He rose. "I believe every word. You are capable of it. Only . . . if something could separate us even more clearly, this is it. You have made me an unwitting accessory to your act. I cannot love a woman about whom I know something like this. I might suspect strychnine in my coffee one day."

She screamed: "Albert!"

"Be quiet. No need to alert the neighbors. And please, go. I don't want to show you the door, but I am afraid of any more of your confessions."

She struggled to her feet, gathered the torn scraps of the dismembered picture, and pushed them into her purse. She spoke in a contained, strangely subdued voice:

"You love another, do you?"

He looked out the window. He thought that she would call out to him once more, bid him farewell. But he heard only her footsteps and the closing of the door. He stood with arms crossed, staring in front of him. Suddenly it occurred to him that he should accompany her, unlock the door to the house. He rushed to the front door. But she was already gone.

# 7 .

She had boarded the streetcar covered with white down as if she wore a dress of feathers. Now as she disembarked, the snow had stopped falling. A gentle, immaculate piece of cloth was spread out over the street; she was the first to tear it, soil it with her shoes. The path was illuminated in a veil of a swan's glow. Snow-dusted branches of the Grazietta garden shimmered, sounded like crystal, as she passed by. But the sky had matured to an enchanting, darkened apple green. The icy moon was diving into the fog.

It was very late. After she had left Albert, she sat in a small, half-hidden café until around midnight only because the ride home loomed before her as a long, arduous journey and she dreaded the lonely, sorrowful abode waiting at its end. She had been reading dated, dusty newspapers by an insufficient light, had hidden from her mind, her heart, behind the humor column and a dumb novel. She had clung to every line, had held on to those lines as if she were walking on a narrow ledge between two abysses and would, if she looked back only once, plunge into the depth of either the one on the right or the one on the left. In the end, she was unable to save herself and she already lay at the bottom of the rocky depth, mute, her limbs shattered. Dead.

What was left to her? Nothing. A few pieces of stiff paper, the torn picture of her child. She had killed Ursa. . . . What else? Nothing. Not even this aching, wretched passion. The love for a man, the desire, her lust was as if touched by the nocturnal cold, frozen, diminished. She stood before the iron gate. She did not push it open. It was as if a creature were waiting upstairs, a miserable, pining creature, she was unable to face in her abject, helpless state, with her empty hands. She despaired.

Opposite the garden area sat a tree stump, enveloped in snow. There she let herself down. She cowered, her arms on her knees, her head between her hands. Her senses dulled, she sat and brooded. What now? What now? I am so tired. I guess I'll soon go upstairs and go to sleep. And tomorrow back to work, the job, the day after tomorrow, and the following day . . . every day. But I take no pleasure in being busy, in earning money. I can do nothing for myself. I always worked only . . . to provide Ursa with milk and bread, even later when she no longer wanted either bread or drink. And then: to wear a pretty dress for the man I loved. Now I don't need it anymore. Now I can grow old; that will go quickly, nothing to hold me back. And God will be merciful and not let me drag myself too long through this life . . . God, yes—

Startled, she sat up. But it was only a clump of snow that had detached itself from the branches, slid off the roof, and crashed with a dull thump to the ground. She stared at the pillars flanking the gate. Each one still carried on its top the emblem of the artistic taste of another era—a mighty stone goblet. A welter of snowflake foam overflowed the rim, then dripped off like slag, a fragrant cream, a sweet dessert. I am hungry. Here I am sitting on this stump by the wayside like a beggar. I have lost everything . . . I am cold.

She raised herself up with a heavy movement. But she did not make her way into the yard of the enchanted maple trees. She shuffled a path through the soft white down to the Spree River valley.

Bright and tiny, the light sprinkles of a distant factory glittered, blinking all night. Not far away were the ugly little lights of the railroad crossing. She looked back. Behind her a snowy slope, a hill suspended in the bluish light of the bleary moon. A flower silence, completely unfolded, so dead, so pure. A shroud. It was woven of silver glass threads, of lilies and the night. This way it gently covered the earth. A shroud. Under its wafting breeze, the frenzy died, the lusting flame was slowly extinguished, fell asleep. Tomorrow it will fade away. The children will trample on it; run over it with their merry sleds. She thought of a winter's evening when she had returned late and Ursa was not at home. She had gone out looking for her. Laughter and screaming came from here, and there was the lobster-red cap with a tassel, the woolen, lobster-red jacket. An older boy was just placing her in front of him on the sled and she raced him to the bottom. Then she climbed back up the hill, little lobster that she was, with some effort but with burning cheeks and beaming dark eyes. "Please, dear mother, please, let me go just one more time."

She leaned forward, held the child in her arms, pressed her against her heart. You. She pushed her fingers under the cap and felt the brown hair. Mine. She was only five years old. And it did not seem at all wondrous or even incredible that she should be embracing her anew. She was simply there. When she saw the strange man fleeing and the door was no longer closed to her, she slipped in with her mother, naturally and without giving it a thought, the way children do things. Now she hung about her neck. "Ursa." She glowed. She smiled. She loved her very much.

A crown of abiding light—which her foolishness had presumed had gone blind, was broken—had soundlessly clarified itself and submitted to her.

She strode through the open rail barrier, crossed the mute tracks, slowly, bent a bit by the breathing bundle she was carrying. She carried it gladly. She was after all no longer a worker, a photographer—no wilting woman or widow, nor any man's lover or a poor woman in despair. She was still the mother with a child whose heart beat against her breast, whose little hands clasped her neck. She was calm. She no longer wanted revenge. She no longer hated. She felt no anger against anybody. She only felt a little anger against herself, but not for long. I killed you once, you joy; God is just: whoever touches you must die.

She stood by the river's edge. The waves slapped in the darkness, breathing lightly. Ursa made herself heavier, nestled fervently against her. She watched her little sun face grow tired and her eyelids close. She leaned forward, slid down. The water rushed. The river closed and continued to run its course.

Newspaper clipping.

*Daily accident report.* On Tuesday afternoon, the driver of a truck lost control of his vehicle at the corner of Brunnenstrasse and Usedomstrasse. The vehicle jumped suddenly from the roadway onto the sidewalk and struck twenty-eight-year-old Heinz Köfer of Charlottenburg. The injured man was immediately taken to the nearest emergency room, but succumbed shortly thereafter to his serious injuries. Both drivers escaped miraculously with light skin abrasions. The hood of the truck had penetrated the entrance of a building and had to be towed away in heavily damaged condition.

# Susanna

## . I .

I am not a poet. No. If I were a poet, I would write a story. I would write a beautiful story, a story with a beginning and an end, a story taken from everything I know. But I cannot do that. I am not an artist. I am only an old governess with graying hair, a furrowed forehead and tear-filled bags under tired eyes. *Her* brow was smooth and gleaming like a sphere of ivory. But I am only thinking of this now because a few days ago a certain woman died: Therese Ruby, née Heppner, at age seventy-one. I read about it in the newspaper on the day before yesterday. A married daughter in Breslau announced her mother's death. *His* name was not mentioned. Only several far-flung cities: Shanghai, Tel Aviv, Parral, San Francisco. Where will *I* be one day? Today, after weeks of waiting, I am still sitting in this rented room of worn, green plush furniture. In the corner, under a locked wooden plank, a large suitcase is waiting, hoping for a second affidavit from Plymouth, Massachusetts.

It has been eleven years now . . . This is likely the last I will have heard of it—this notice in the newspaper. It was also with a notice in the newspaper that it began. An experienced governess was sought, at a good salary, to look after a young girl who was suffering from slight melancholia. I applied. The guardian of the orphan answered and soon several letters were exchanged. For I was living in Mörs at the time and he, a lawyer, did not know anybody in the Rhineland area whom I could have contacted. We came to an agreement anyway, and I packed my belongings and traveled across Germany, from West to East, on a full day's journey.

In the middle of the railroad station, a massive old woman—a peasant woman, in a black jacket, thick skirts and coarse boots, a dark flowery headscarf draping the brown, hard face with Slavic cheekbones—stood motionless. I waited at the ticket counter. An official locked the large two-winged gate behind the passengers; only the smaller door remained open. Unsure of what to do, I walked up to the old woman. "The lady has arrived," she said. "Good." She took the two pieces of my hand luggage and stomped outside.

It was almost nine o'clock. The little town, which extended into raven darkness from the monument square, lit only by a few miserable, shivering lamps, was like many other small towns of its kind. But I don't think I got to see much of it that evening. For I was barely able to hold onto my umbrella in the wind that swept clumped kernels of snowdust, sharp as glass, against me. I observed the back of the pack horse in front of me, trotting along unflinchingly, without turning its head. Even later I never heard her say more than a few sparse words. Her name was Milda Morawe and she came from the Osterland province.

She trudged through a front garden, then up a little staircase, and pushed open the door. While I was still shaking off the white flakes at the threshold, somebody appeared in the hallway to greet me. It was Counselor Fordon. He looked more like an old forester or a soldier in his gray-green short jacket and with his bushy mustache and thick white hair.

I sat on the sofa in the parlor, drank tea from a Bunzlau cup and nibbled gingerbread. He asked questions and nodded.

"With someone ailing . . ." I mentioned by way of conversation.

"She is not ailing."

"I thought . . ."

He interrupted me. "I wrote you about it, but I see that someone who does not know her can hardly imagine this creature. She is like someone always walking into the open under a clear blue sky. The clouds that hang above us are not a burden to her; the walls that stifle and constrain us adults do not exist for her. She is only a child, a cheerful, kindhearted child. Happy as children should always be and often are not. I have seen her cry only once: I had to deny her a new coat, not so much because it was too expensive but because it seemed too flashy to me. She wants beautiful clothes—she loves jewelry—in that regard she is a true woman." He smiled: "But she has no female friends."

"She never had any? Not even earlier?"

"No. Years ago, when on occasion she seemed only strange to

us, she was invited a few times to the house of other young girls, but that did not go well. Her manner was puzzling to the other girls, and she herself was bored by them. She never wished for company; she lives so isolated, and yet does not know what loneliness is."

"And her parents? When did she become an orphan?"

"She lost her mother early. The father only two years ago. Until about six months ago, there was also her nursemaid, Seraphina. I had to send her into retirement. She made well-meaning pandering plans because her darling was already turning twenty, and so she spoke to the child of wedding rings and myrtle wreaths. You must understand, Susanna can never marry!"

I asked why he did not take care of his ward in his own house.

"I am a bachelor, and my housekeeper, if I know her at all, would soon quarrel with her. But mostly, my law practice, the coming and going of clients—that's not for her. To distract her, I gave her the shadow of a dog who never barks, never gets too frisky, and does not gnaw on chairs. Whether it needs to be fed, I don't know. The crust I threw it was scornfully left untouched."

We still discussed this and that point, I forget exactly what— financial matters, no doubt. The cuckoo called out ten times from the clock when I departed.

Back into the darkness. The hot tea still warmed me, but despite the refreshing drink, despite the icy wind and sleet, I sank into a deep sleep as I marched along, and I woke only when I heard Milda Morawe fiddling with the door lock because the key would not turn. Somehow we finally did get into the house and climbed straight to the upper floor where the old woman directed me to my room. The little room with its white tulle curtains, low ceiling, and the few pieces of simple, but good furniture, was homey enough. They predated the style of furniture of the turn of the century with its pompous carved wooden castles, pillars, and sills. The chestnut cabinet was just like one I used to see at my grandfather's house in Filehne when I was a child.

I was ready to turn in. But Milda Morawe returned. She grunted something about Susanna being still awake and wanting to see me. I washed my face a bit, crossed the hallway, and knocked.

# Susanna

I still remember the clear sound of her "Come in!" I pushed down the door handle and remained in the frame without crossing the threshold. This couldn't be. But it was. Something like this existed in books and moving pictures, in advertisements for creams and lotions: a woman like this. The room was dusky. Only one small colorful lamp glowed next to the easy chair. There she sat in a burgundy kimono, her face turned toward me, this wondrous face. A certain kind of beauty attracts only men; but she was beautiful to everybody's eyes. She was beautiful—a perfect, soft skin, the hue of old ivory, a round forehead underneath black hair, a fine straight nose. The eyes radiated dark and laughing; they were of a very deep blue, but that I saw only in the next few days. Her mouth and voice were as charming as her figure; everything about her was grace and sweetness.

She stood before me in her red kimono and asked, using the familiar address: "Why are you so late? I have been waiting for you a long time."

"I couldn't come earlier. I was traveling by train all day."

"Are you very cold? Your hands are cold."

"Your hands are not that warm either, Susanna . . ."

"Oh, mine? I don't have any hands at all. See!"

Her wide sleeves fell back flapping and her hands fluttered like white wings.

"They are wings, they are birds. Seagulls, silver gulls. They have come a long way from the sea. Do you have gray eyes? No, brown. Gray eyes are like the ocean. I saw it once, many years ago. I love being at the sea. It sits inside this shell. I hold it against my ear and hear the rushing. Would you like to hear it?"

"Tomorrow. It is almost eleven. Today we are both too tired."

"Yes, tomorrow. I am going to show you my amber stones, the spherical ones. They are all murky, completely opaque, but the glass-clear one I don't like. When I was still small, I saw some and thought they were caramels and I wanted to eat them. I have more. I'll also show you my fly with the diamond wings and sapphire eyes."

She pointed to the small clover pin on my dress.

"Are these emeralds?"

"Yes, only the one on the bottom is a ruby."

"Oh, I know: ruby." She laughed softly as if I had said something very funny or very silly.

"Ruby.  What a wonderful word: ruby. So . . . dark . . . like embers . . ."

"You can put a teacher to shame, Susanna."

Her eyebrows twitched. Two small folds formed a furrow above the bridge of her nose. She had not understood me.

"I don't think I have ever thought about words the way you do."

"But I don't really think about it—this is just the way it is. Some words one can pick up with the hand. And some one can smell . . . For instance: frying pan. I don't like to say frying pan or the whole room will fill with kitchen odors."

"And what is it that you say then?"

She thought for moment.

"Then I say: rose." And I saw her excitement, saw the breath of her lips bloom, gentle, covered with dew, breathing leaves, with a wonderful fragrance. Rose.

Suddenly a low chair rattled in the corner and a big animal crawled out from under. It stretched as if it was just done sleeping and shook itself a little.

"Don't shake yourself like that!" Susanna called out. "Or Milda will scold you for leaving your hair on the upholstery and the carpet.

> Zoë, Zoë give some shakes
> Throw over me your white flakes!

I made up a beautiful fairy tale for myself—that's where it is from. Come here!"

The animal obeyed. I saw it was slender and tall and wavy and silvery white with a little bit of cream color dotted in places. It came over and touched my hand with its long, cool nose, and looked at me with gleaming, almond-shaped eyes. The old counselor had spoken of the dog as a shadow—that it was. But it was also a dog that was a dream. I caressed it.

"You beautiful boy . . ."

"You must call her beautiful girl," Susanna corrected me. "It is a she-dog and a princess, empress of Byzantium. But she is no longer alive. Her name is Zoë and she lives in a really old century, I don't know which one. And now she is dead. She exists only in the eyes under the fur. But sometimes she gets lost in flight and stays away, then the animal just stands there and does not move and does not respond to being called. I heard a man say once, 'Go already, you big ghost!' The emperor of Byzantium married a lizard, that's where her head comes from. In the old days, humans and animals were allowed to marry, today this is no longer so. Sometimes I think about whom I would have married . . . an osprey perhaps . . . or the sea king. He sits below the waves in a glass house and only rises to the shore at night in the moonlight. On his chest is a wild growth of seaweed like hair, and he has greenish grayish eyes."

"Who told you all this?"

"Uncle Fordon."

"About the sea king?"

"No, about the empress and the lizard."

The guardian had probably explained the name of the dog and joked that this creature with the strange head must have been descended from a lizard and the girl had spun a web of this and that about it.

"Now, we really must say good night, at last—"

"Yes, otherwise we are going to sit around like the men until it is time for *shachris*."

I did not know much about Judaism, my faith, and I took this to be a regional expression; she may not have known its meaning herself either.

"Take Zoë with you. She sleeps in the hall downstairs on a blanket."

She looked at me one more time before I left, friendly and attentive. "You look very different from the way I had thought. I had formed pictures of you in my mind, but now they are all no good and I have to throw them away."

We said good night. I opened the door and the Borzoi immediately ran downstairs.

## . II .

I opened the window. A low, gray dawning sky, no wind. Still slumber and peace.

Below me was a small garden, probably just a cabbage patch: rotting cabbage stalks, dead sunflower stems, a green water pump wrapped in straw, and between shrubs, a refuse pit near the frail, decaying picket fence. Beyond all this, fields, expansive fields, acres whose crusty black soil was breaking through everywhere from under the windswept snow cover. A little, forlorn-looking bridge, an overpass, was recognizable in its midst. Dawn descended in the distance and merged with the dark waves, forest. From a tower, the clock sounded eight times, slowly and seriously and a bit hoarse. I placed my bedding on the open windowsill and went downstairs.

The kitchen was empty and gloomy—the way kitchens are in the gray of dawn: naked tiles, the cold stove, and here also the lattice window, even the neatness of the place added to its sullen look. In a kitchen pots should be boiling, cans steaming, dishes clattering— then everything is cozy and cheerful. I stubbed my foot against Zoë, who was lying on her side; she stretched and raised her head without getting up. I was not important enough for her.

In the living room, Milda Morawe sat next to the coal bucket and stoked around in the stove with an iron hook. My hesitant "Good Morning" was answered with only a grunt. I went upstairs to get my hat and coat, and went out.

The cowering little house was protected on both sides by taller, newer buildings. It seemed like a child standing between two grown-ups. In my mind I saw the simple, old-fashioned furnishings of my room and remembered that Susanna's were no more extravagant. I thought about her father and was surprised that a rich man had been satisfied with such modest accommodations. I did not know then what I learned later: He feared that it would catch the attention of unscrupulous, greedy dowry hunters, who might pursue his daughter were he to flaunt a car and servants and a mansion surrounded by a park. Thus he faked modest means the way others fake wealth.

But it was not possible to hide the money; it shone through the protective cover everywhere.

Meanwhile I steered toward the church, which straddled the roadway. It was probably its peals of the hour I had heard earlier. It was gray, but not venerable, so it seemed to me. I met only few people along the way. A baker's apprentice, who was twirling his empty basket, stared at me. An old woman in a black hood swept the little bit of snow from her doorstep; she was a witch with a broom and met me with the evil eye. The letter carrier, who rummaged through his mail pouch, quickly lifted his head, caught me with a sharp gaze as if I were somehow suspect. I realized that I looked like a vexing intruder in this narrow world, somebody it had to fend off at all cost. Since I did not know where to go for a walk, I soon turned back.

Inside Susanna was already skipping down the stairs, fresh as the morning, cheerful, and cordial. In the parlor the fire was racing in the stove. We had breakfast from grandmotherly dishes with a silver flower pattern.

"Did you sleep well, Susanna?"

"Oh, I? Yes, I slept very well—and you? I had a beautiful dream."

"What was it about?"

"I heard very soft, very distant music. I walked along a road and came to a forest. The trees there were meant to become wood for violins and the violins already sat in the trees, sounding and practicing. There were also crossbills—do you know any?"

"From books, yes."

"Oh, you people always know everything only from books."

"How else should we know about things? We cannot see and hear everything that exists on earth."

"But one can see everything. I see and hear everything. Once I read about the osprey, and at night an osprey flew through the open window and sat on my bedcover close to the footboard, and he looked at me and flapped his wings very slowly. Just opening and closing them again. He was very big and I was afraid of him. He often comes back and flies onto my bed, but I am no longer afraid."

"The osprey is not that big. You are dreaming this," I said, forgetting that I should never contradict her, even in jest, that I could not speak with her as with other human beings.

She immediately wrinkled her brow and twitched her eyebrows, as she did every time her mind was being pushed into a narrow corner, and her eyes flared up like those of a hunted animal.

"No, it is true. When I have a dream, it is completely different."

She unscrewed the lid of the glass jar. "Do you eat honey? I like the kind that is a little bitter, that tastes of wax. Milda gets it from old shoemaker Hentzel. It's made by bees, I was there. I did not dream it. Whenever we took our shoes there, I would go to the beehives near the fence, and there I saw the bees flying around, carrying some yellow stuff. The old shoemaker told us . . . about the queen and the drones . . ."

"You know quite a lot about animals, Susanna."

"But I am an animal."

She said it without smiling. She simply made a statement like someone who will remark when the conversation turns to various types of people, "But I am Polish," or "I am Dutch." Her face closed up, separating itself from me, as it were, and really was no longer a human face. For the first time I felt the slight uneasiness that seizes us in the presence of the mentally disturbed. I tried to gloss over it with a funny remark.

"How about me? Am I an animal too—yes?"

"You? . . . No . . . You must ask Zoë. Maybe she will understand what you are saying to her and she will answer."

Hearing her name, the dog rose and came over, looking at us as if she expected to be questioned.

The sky was gray and like tufts of cotton. The air was still, not cold—soft and foamy and sweet like cream. The flakes fell very quietly, very tenderly, weaving themselves into the pure, infinite covering that spread over the fields. Zoë had blown over the fields, white and whirling, she raced and returned in a trot with hanging tongue and a bad conscience. Susanna scolded her, but under the broad-rimmed, black velvet hat her eyes were smiling.

A vast empty expanse.

A crow came winging along, cawing. A tree stump sat by the

path like an inflated snowgrouse. We came to the dead, frozen river, silver encrusted thorny shrubs on its banks, and we crossed a small wooden bridge.

Susanna ran her hand caressingly over the railing.

"It is always happy when people cross over it. It is all alone here and cold."

Another human passed by, in high boots and padded jacket, his face coarse and red. He stared at Susanna and said hello. She beamed and nodded her head at him.

"Who was that? One of your workmen?"

She shrugged her shoulders and laughed.

"You don't know him? And yet you greeted him as if . . ."

"I always greet all men, and they all greet me."

"They shouldn't do that."

"Why not? All men bow before the king and salute him and it pleases the king when they honor him. So he returns the salute."

"What do you have to do with a king?"

"But I am a king's daughter."

"You?"

"I am a daughter of King David or of King Saul. They lived a long time ago; but we have not forgotten about it. But many other people are not descended from kings. Only I, because I am a Jew."

"So am I."

"You too? Does it make you very happy?"

I hear the words today. No. It did not make me happy. I had forgotten. I was not proud, carried no mark of the royal house; I carried a stain. The stain was quite small and bothered me but little, but I concealed it as much as I could.

"Are you very happy?"

I lowered my head, hastily murmuring something indistinct about the forest. It rolled into the distance, cowering and massive, a dusky menacing, hunchbacked monster.

Susanna saw it that way. "Let's not go there or it will eat us up. We'll go there only when it is no longer under a spell, when it is clear again and filled with trees."

We returned by making a wide turn through the town. There was nothing out of the ordinary. Only a few new tenement blocks among squat, older houses, the new post office, and old St. Mary's church. What was most peculiar was that all the men in town greeted Susanna. Some with admiration, some leering with blinking, brazen eyes, others almost serious and almost with sympathy. The women greeted only rarely and looked at me with curiosity while aiming their thin scorn, their aversion, at Susanna. The mad girl was now getting worse, so that an attendant had been hired as a precaution. That was good and just punishment. For the evil this creature did was to make every woman she met appear washed out and unattractive.

Milda Morawe told me this much later, in a rare talkative moment. Even then I had to put the words together from her coarse, incoherent mumbling.

We were just in time for lunch. Later we sat in Susanna's room and looked at her treasures: seashells, stones, inherited jewelry. I remember a shell that was spotted like a panther, and the one that resembled a harp, Triton's horns, into which the gods of the sea blew; also cowrie shells, coins of the land of the Moors; and the druse of the Cordilleras, a hollow rough-skinned fruit. It glittered and blinked: the meat of the fruit was rock crystal where it was hollowed out and amethyst where it had been broken open. Susanna took out the amber spheres. They were big and a thick, cloudy yellow, probably the last link in a torn chain. She also showed me the fly with its body of milky opal, sapphire eyes, and diamond wings. She also had several pieces from her father: cuff buttons of frozen lava set in silver that had been cut into gems, and his ring of flat, green Brazilian tourmaline. Susanna was able to name them all and knew everything about them; I thought the tourmaline was an emerald. But when I tried to explain to her the roaring inside the shell, she became restless again and crinkled her smooth forehead.

Today I would say that I acted foolishly. But then I was not yet able to suppress my teacher's instinct. I lifted a shell to her ear. We were completely still and she heard absolutely nothing.

She shook her head. "No," she said sadly. "I don't understand it, and it isn't true either. It is the sea and it always roared when I was alone. Now it cannot roar because you are here and you know nothing about it."

She took a matte-gold filigree web out of a little black box, and the spider was a pearl. She pointed upward and I saw on the ceiling in the corner a delicate, gray veiling.

"She is up there. I have often called out to her, but she comes only rarely. She prefers to stay up there in her web. I always think: if only Milda doesn't find her one day and sweep her away. Milda can't stand spiders."

. III .

I had imagined my task to be more difficult. I had expected a moody, easily excitable creature, had thought that I would have to fight rejection and stubbornness. But all I had to do was take care of a grown-up, friendly child. I doubted the acuity of the old guardian's judgment and discounted his opinion that the orphan needed no human friends. He probably denied that she was lonely because the thought would disturb his comfortable bachelor's existence. This was in the very first days—then I came to realize that he had been right and I was wrong. Susanna did not need me. She accepted my presence and fit it into her world since I happened to be there, but she had not longed for me and would hardly have missed me. She would have conversed, as she did with me, with the dog, the shells, the tourmaline, and her osprey. Or for that matter with the spider like Christian II in the tower.

Christian of Denmark and the spider we found in a thick tome Susanna lugged from the cabinet in the parlor to her room upstairs. For in the course of those long evenings, we knitted and embroidered, sewed and darned and alternated reading to each other. Susanna loved books but she had a peculiar way of handling them. To begin at the beginning and end with the end was not for her. She had no appreciation of long stories, developments, complications, and resolutions. First we tried a novel—that was a useless undertaking:

the very element of suspense, of uncertainty, of delaying a decision tired her, the coherence of it all escaped her.

"Why aren't the gypsies there any more? Only Traudel and Hans and the border dispute all the time. That's boring."

So I usually picked only short stories, fairy tales, and legends, sections of travel reports, selections from works of history and the natural sciences, and often also from the Bible.

"Fina said one must read all books starting with the first page except for the Bible. The Bible can be opened anywhere one wants— it is all beginning and end. Because it is God's word."

Fina was the old nursemaid, Seraphina.

We were sitting in my room one evening and Susanna told me one of the fairy tales she had made up. There was an evil stepmother who tormented the poor stepdaughter. But the girl had a white dog whose long, fine hair blew over her completely and she became unrecognizable, covered with fur and an animal herself. And all she had to do was say over and over:

> Zoë, Zoë give some shakes,
> Throw over me your white flakes!

Suddenly Susanna rose, turned off the light and pulled the curtain back from the window.

"Look! How beautiful! We can still take a walk now, can't we? We haven't been outside all day. We'll take Zoë along."

I resisted at first. A nocturnal walk was unusual and the sky spoke of frost. Then we stole away through the garden with secret strides like thieves. For had Milda Morawe seen us from the kitchen door, she would have silently disapproved of our adventure.

The vaulting sky was dark stone, of mercilessly pure harshness. Countless stars were frozen into glittering, splintering ice crystals. The moon blinked silvery and cold. The fresh snow froze and was encrusted with a strong, bluish gleam. The animal turned ashen in the pallid light; it quivered and was transformed into a shadowy being. It disappeared, wandering aimlessly in the darkness of the fields.

Our fur boots sank deep into the snow. Susanna asked: "Do you know what we are stepping on? Do you know what this is?"

"Snow. Fresh snow."

"No. What we are feeling is the sand of the sea. It is glittering white because the moon is shining down on us in the depth. For we are walking on the bottom of the sea."

"But how did we get there?"

"We drowned. We were sailing on a beautiful ship, it was wrecked on a reef and sank. There it rests, they all rest there."

She pointed at the house far behind us, at the town that looked like an eerie ship graveyard, and some of its towers stood out like the chimneys of a steamer, others like mastheads.

"The coolness which is caressing our faces is water. Can you see what is floating around there?"

She pulled on my sleeve as if she were actually excited by something wondrous and rare.

"It has a pointed, elongated fish head and is overgrown with thick, colorless hair that is like whitish seaweed. But it is not seaweed or hair, but whiskers. It is a sea dog."

"I know of seals, but not of sea dogs."

"No. You won't find it in a book, no one has discovered it or written about it yet. For he lives in the depth and is not allowed to come up. When he rises to the surface and is touched by a ray of the sun, he dies immediately and decays and disintegrates and stinks—oh, awful!" She shook herself. "Only the dead can see him. It is a completely pure, soft animal, it is like jellyfish to the touch—"

"Stop it, Susanna! Let's turn back. Soon we will both believe your stories."

"I can't turn back. My ship is a wreck. My clothes are disintegrating and falling off, but I am not naked . . . I am blowing along . . . in a veil of water . . . And the sea king will come and see me and find me beautiful. Do you know what the sea king looks like? His chest has a bushy pelt of algae and his head is as smooth and round as the pebbles on the beach. And he wears a crown of two silvery little fish who bite each other's tails."

"How do you know all this?"

"From God. He can't be heard or seen, but he makes it so that one knows everything. He also created the sea king. Like the humans."

"There is nothing about this in the Bible."

"That doesn't matter. Fina said even if it is not in the Bible, all creation comes from God. For the Evil One cannot create anything, he can only destroy. So any creature that exists comes from God."

"Does the sea king exist?"

"You are dumb."

I laughed. "And you are not very polite."

"Let's go home. I want to go to bed and wait for the sea king. He only comes at night."

"Fairy-tale woman . . . !"

"It's not a fairy tale," she said seriously.

We went home.

While I struggled with replacing the lock on the door with the knocker, Zoë went to the refuse pit and sniffed around. Milda Morawe stood in the dark with a garbage pail like a reproach turned into a picture of stone.

A chair had fallen over. Or maybe it was something wooden that had hit the wooden planks of the floor. I sat up in bed and listened. All was quiet. Maybe I had been mistaken. Perhaps it was a clump of snow sliding off the top of the roof. I listened. Everything remained quiet. I threw myself back, stretching comfortably, desirous of going right back to sleep. A rapping sound . . . What was it? It wasn't Milda Morawe. She would have stumbled down to the kitchen from her little attic room with heavier steps. This was very soft, sneaking . . . prowlers? I was startled. The dog did not bark. But then she never barked. I rose in the dark, groped for my housecoat, and stepped into the hallway.

There I saw—Susanna's door was flung wide open. Susanna was downstairs. What was she doing? She was walking in her sleep through the rooms . . . She awoke, was confused and was looking for her sea king, her phantom . . . A sense of horror of the deranged woman fluttered after me in the night, a scornful fear. I wanted to turn back, rush back into my room, and turn the key twice. I should have switched on the light. But I was as mesmerized ... After a few moments I regained my composure, pulled myself together and softly descended the stairs.

I heard voices coming from downstairs. Susanna's voice, muted, and then the whispering of a man. I felt my heart beating. I got to the kitchen, the door was ajar, and I stared ...

A cold breeze blew at me. The window was wide open. On the windowsill stood Susanna, her hands gripping the lattice, her body pressed against the rods, pushing outward. Her black hair breathed like an animal. She stood there in a long silk nightshirt that gleamed pearl white in the icy silvery moonlight. She stood there barefoot and quivering, laughing softly and beguiling.

The man stood somewhat lower, in the garden. Her body concealed him from my view. Only when she leaned to the side was I able to see a corner of his hat. He spoke in muted tones, but the stillness of the night carried every word to me.

It was a dark kind of pleading:

"Susanna!"

"What is it now?"

"I beg you ... I beg of you, go!"

She laughed. "But I don't want to."

"You are freezing and you will catch cold."

"I am not freezing at all. But you are trembling in the frost and want to go home."

"Susanna ... you know ... Why do you mock me?"

"Because you are bad and are sending me away. And I have come to give you pleasure."

"Give me pleasure ... go get a coat ... please ... in this thin shirt ..."

"Don't you like seeing me like this?"

"You torment me."

"I don't want you to torture yourself. I am going in a moment to put on a coat."

"You are really not cold?"

"No."

"Then ... stay ... stay another moment ... please ..."

A brief laugh. "You don't know what you want."

"Oh, I know . . . I know what I want . . . Susanna!"

The name was like the smile of someone suffocating.

"Yes?"

"Lean down . . . I have to whisper it in your ear what I want . . ."

She leaned slightly forward.

"I . . . oh, I am melting away . . . I am burning . . . my clothes are on fire . . . I want to tear everything off in front of you . . . in the winter's night, you . . . oh, you . . ."

She extended her arms through the iron bars. "Come."

I was frightened. I felt sweat breaking from my pores. And I stood there and stared . . .

"My precious stone . . . yes, that's what you are, my deep red . . . ruby."

"I am all blood and desire . . . Susanna."

She bent down, knelt, and did something, but I was unable to see what it was.

"That heavy scarf must go and the collar . . . wait . . . the button . . . there . . ."

Quiet.

"Do you like doing this, Susanna? Do you like stroking the fuzzy hair on my chest?"

"It isn't hair. These are algae—black-green algae. You are a sea creature. But nobody knows it, because you wear human clothes over it. Nobody knows, only I."

"Only you."

"What are you doing?"

"Your hand . . . it is like a little, warm animal on my chest . . . I must kiss it. . ."

"Yes, my hand is warm, only my feet are getting cold."

"Did you come barefooted?"

"No. My slippers are somewhere in the kitchen. I can't kneel anymore. Close the collar . . . neatly . . . nobody is allowed to see who you are, nobody . . ."

She raised herself up.

"Give me your foot . . . Let me warm it . . . cover it with my hands and with my lips . . . what delightful feet you have, Susanna . . . so white . . ."

"Don't all women have such white feet?"

"Not all . . . oh, you . . . I would like to take you completely . . . not just your feet . . . cover you completely . . . oh, go!"

"Yes, I am cold."

"You are cold? Go, my darling . . . go . . ."

She squatted down, she seemed to crawl into herself and her face searched something along the window lattice. And for a moment I saw his head next to hers, and they were one.

"Farewell. You will write to me?"

"Yes, my darling, I will write . . ."

I was unaware of his leaving. I did not hear him go. But Susanna turned and glided down from the windowsill. I stepped from the threshold sideways to the wall. I forgot about the chair that usually stood in the corner and I stubbed my foot against it.

"Psst." Susanna called out with muted voice. "Zoë stay down."

She closed the window and scurried past me. When she came to the dog's bed, the animal stirred and rattled its chain. Her nightgown shimmered spectral, pallid. She seemed to be bending down. Maybe she was putting her hands around the dog's head and caressing it.

"My darling," she whispered. "My white, white, beautiful beast, my friend . . . you . . . I am happy!" There was such deep, secret jubilation in her whispering that I was able to see the glow of her face even in the dark. Then she stole upstairs.

And I still clung to the chair by the wall, shivering and unable to rise and go to my room. A welter of thoughts spun through my brain. Everything was tangled without form or sequence. I was too tired. . . . The love of those two was obviously not what people call pure love, what, at that time, even I would have called pure love. (May God forgive me . . . ) A love that kisses only with the soul and shies away from the body, one's own as well as that of the other. That man trembled with burning desire and Susanna longed to hurl herself into it. Why did he not devour her? It would have been easy for him to lure her into the garden, into the snow. She would have liked to let him in and rest in his arms. Why did nothing happen? Why did they place the lattice between them?

Amidst all this, the thought flashed through my mind that Susanna had planned our walk to erase her friend's tracks in the snow ahead of time with our stomping around. Be that as it may, it was hardly necessary. Milda Morawe carried the trash can to the ditch every night, and her feet were not small. The thread snapped suddenly and another ran crosswise: I had heard Susanna's footsteps, had gotten up, and followed her; I saw everything, but did not prevent anything. Now it was over. What was over? Nothing surely. But Susanna might come down with pneumonia by tomorrow. It would have been my duty to get her away from the open window; to chase away this man. I could have done it without a loud word or a raised hand, by calmly crossing the threshold. Or was I mistaken? The man was a stranger to me and I did not know whether his flaming scourge might whip him into a fury and into resistance. Maybe I secretly feared him and hesitated out of fear. . . . Perhaps. But what I saw seemed so unreal, the white girl, the window lattice, the moon, and the lover in the garden, all as if taken from the pages of a story book. Maybe it was the quality of unreality that held me back. Perhaps. I still ask myself today why I hesitated and as then I have no answer. A poet must always try to illuminate the cause of human action; life saves itself the effort and leaves all motivation in the dark. What I am writing here is what was experienced. But the old counselor would demand an explanation; he would cross-examine me sharply, would scold me. I would have to lie . . . What if I didn't tell him anything, if I remained silent and waited? That would be best . . . yes . . . I was already nodding off. I pulled myself up and dragged myself to bed.

. IV .

Susanna was sick. The doctor called the illness "grippe." I was glad he did not have a worse name for it. My secret burden was lightened a little because Susanna would be unable to escape from me right away, into the garden, into the snow-covered fields, or to the lattice window. She suffered gently, in an amiable frame of mind. She sneezed and coughed, perspired and shivered. Her cheeks, red and feverish, her nose, sore and swollen, she lay there bearing it all for the sake of a lover with the tired, relieved smile of a happy young mother. On the second day, she took a little key from her night table and asked me to check the mailbox. When I returned empty-handed, she was quietly disappointed. But on the morning of the third day, I presented her with a strong, bluish gray linen envelope that carried neither stamp nor address. Her eyes gleamed quietly as she took it and placed it on her quilt. A little later it had disappeared. I did not see her reading it. From then on I found several letters in the box and delivered them all loyally without any questions.

No, I did not ask. I only said, letter in hand: "Today you are contented again, right?" She nodded. I hoped that one day she would take me into her confidence and would spontaneously open her heart to me.

I did not mind that it did not happen right away. For whatever she might have told me, I would have been obligated to report to her guardian, who, well-meaning as he was, would then have wiped the dew off the wings of the colorful, quivering butterfly. This I didn't want. He came to visit several times and brought the patient Yaffa oranges and little packages of candied fruit. She was always a good, lovable, harmless child.

I spent most of my time in the sickroom, doing a lot of mending and darning. Susanna asked me to read to her, but I never did for very long, because listening was strenuous for her. Once I read to her the story of Solomon's judgment from the Bible.

"It was then that two women came before the king."

She interrupted me, amazed: "Does it say women? It used to say whores."

"It still does." I wriggled out of the noose. "I just thought you wouldn't know that expression and said 'women' because it is a more commonly used word."

"And I thought it had disappeared." She pondered for a while. "Tell me . . . is it possible? Is it possible for words to disappear from a book? The print fades gradually until it is very faint and finally a word is no longer there. And in the empty space a new word slowly begins to form: at first the letters are unclear and gray and then they become more and more distinct and black ... And this way completely new stories are created inside books, but perhaps also sentences nobody understands. Is that possible?"

I shook my head.

"No? That's a pity. It would be a nice surprise, every time one opened a book. But you can say 'whores.' I know whores are women who love." She lifted her eyebrow lightly and looked at me. "Is that something bad?"

"Yes," I explained. "It is bad. Because one can only love one man, right? But they love many. They don't really love anybody properly, but only pretend to. They always want to get gifts like jewelry and clothes and money from the many gentleman friends they have."

Her voice became frightened and meek: "Isn't one allowed to get any gifts at all when one is in love? Not even chocolate?"

"Of course, when one is in love one can accept everything. But one should not pretend to be in love in order to get things. And that's what these women do. They want only rich men, then they plunder them. If a man is poor, they pay no attention to him and they look for another. That's bad."

"Yes, that is bad," Susanna confirmed gravely, adding: "Fina said that whores and prostitutes are the same thing."

She fell silent and I was about to continue with the reading when she asked: "But if they are not really in love, then they are not happy."

"No, they are not happy."

I read a few sentences and then I stopped. Susanna was reclining quietly and I saw that she was thinking about something; I saw the small, vertical furrows of her brow. She thought for a long time. Then she said fervently, with conviction, as if she were making a timid confession before God, not before a human being: "No, I am not a whore."

I wanted to take her into my arms and press her against my heart, the way one holds a child.

"There are toads as brown as the earth," Susanna informed me. "And some are grayish green with dark spots and small red dots. Why aren't you sewing anymore?"

I had discovered among her things a piece of green and gold brocade which I was making into an evening purse for her. She liked it although she did not attend social gatherings. All that was left to do was to baste in the lining, and I had started with that already.

"The yellow spool is empty," I replied. "And I don't see another matching thread in my case. Some other time."

"No," Susanna pleaded. "Today. It is still early. Why don't you go to Abramowicz? Abramowicz's in 'Frog Town'—they are sure to have yarn and wool and sewing thread."

"Where?"

"Frog Town—I used to go there with Fina because her sister lived there, only a few houses away. I can describe the way for you."

She described the way and I went. Thirstily, I breathed in the fresh air after days of being locked up indoors. Snow was falling. Big flakes fell, very gently and intermittently, settling patiently under shoes and muffling the harshness of the step. They lovingly enveloped the hopelessly plain façades of the houses, swathing them gradually in white hoods. People gliding past each other became incorporeal as shadows, separated from each other by vast spaces. Yet there was no fog, only a very quiet, feminine, melancholy grayness; invisibly the sun was dying. I was in a mood to wander for hours in the gray light, in the muted softness. It carried me forward as on the back of a mighty, gentle creature. All that edgy brooding and worrying seemed blown away, buried—only a faint remembrance. A dream ... But I did not walk for hours after all. I soon arrived in Frog Town. A rivulet wound its way through crooked streets with uneven pavement and old dilapidated houses and one feared that the iron railing along the banks of the little stream might smother it to death. This railing was surely newer than the three decrepit little wooden bridges that crossed it in short intervals. In between, children were sledding and ice-skating. An older boy shouted orders and with his broom he swept away the powdery layer of scraped-up ice that constantly gathered again.

The store of Aaron Abramowicz contained more than it promised. From the outside it made a miserable, sickly impression. Inside it was narrow but deep, and its green drawers, adorned with brass handles, seemed well stocked. But to select a roll of thread, since it was too dark inside, I had to go to the door. I barely was able to make out the features of the dark, wizened little gypsy mother who waited on me. I bought a few other things. She talked about the weather, about winter, and the coming of spring.

"But you won't be staying very long now that the young lady has gone away."

"The young lady has not gone away, she is ill," I explained curtly.

She made a strange little sound, almost as if she was suppressing a chuckle.

"Never mind . . . never mind, what gossip . . . it's quite all right. You have to say that . . . why should you tell people the truth . . . they know it already anyway. Ridiculous."

She apparently had gotten something into her head and I did not try to straighten her out. I just felt the colorful wool strands with my hands without responding. Her black, piercing eyes bored into me. Then she remarked: "Yes, what should one believe . . . others may be more *meshugge* than she is . . . but with her they make such a fuss."

I nodded and she began to dish out all that the tongues and ears of this small town relished as the absolute truth. The beautiful girl was nowhere to be seen, and so she was being kept locked up. The guardian had secretly placed her in a locked institution where she would have to remain from now on.

"And in two weeks, she will have recovered and will go out for walks again."

"From your lips to God's ear," the woman said doubtfully. Suddenly she yelled out, scolding: "Albert, go already . . . what are you hanging around here for?"

I turned around. He had emerged from the rooms in the rear of the store and I had hardly noticed him. I looked at him startled. The dark, Eastern head of a boy with beautiful sad eyes was pushed down deep into the shoulders of a malformed, emaciated body above a hunched back. He carried a string bag in his hand.

"Don't forget the apples."

"No."

He made an awkward sign of greeting and left.

"You see," she said, the voice less sharp, her eyes less penetrating. "He is such a smart boy, such a *gebensht,* blessed boy . . . How he studies! What a misfortune! You have the same with your girl, only the other way around . . . the back is straight and the *sechel,* the mind is crooked . . ." She sighed. "*Shem b'ruch hu* [God, blessed be he] will know why he made it this way . . ."

I paid. Outside Albert was still lingering near the railing and watched the frolicking on the ice below. He had been waiting for me. When the door of the shop fell shut, he turned around, startled, and then walked over quickly to meet me.

"Tell me," he asked in a pleading, shy tone. "Is the young lady very ill?"

"A bad cold, but she is already better."

"Oh, . . . I am glad . . ." He smiled and his sad eyes gleamed.

"Shall I give her your regards?" It was hard to guess his age. I did not know whether to address him in the familiar or the formal way.

"No, oh no . . . not that . . ." He blushed as if I had proposed something that was inappropriate. "And . . . I thank you." He quickly stumbled away.

I wandered along the bank of the little stream, and was getting covered with snow. The flakes whirled and scattered. From the other side of the stream a man crossed the second bridge. Then he stopped and as I was about to pass, he lifted his hat.

"Good evening . . . allow me, please. My name is Ruby. I am a friend of Miss Susanna. I saw you from afar and would like to ask how she is doing."

"She is still feverish."

"I am sorry about that. Please give her my regards and I wish her a quick recovery. I already told you my name: Ruby . . . Good evening."

There I stood, as he walked away, beside myself and confused.

I was overwhelmed. I had often imagined how I would sneak up to the enemy, how I would confront him, seize him, how I would interrogate the man, pressure him, rattle at his conscience as at a gate, and now nothing had happened. . . . Nothing had happened. We had only exchanged the usual meaningless words. And I had prepared myself . . . armed myself for this meeting . . . so many times . . .

I have never been loved. Susanna's friend, of whom I had barely caught a glimpse, but whom I had pictured since that night, was the beautiful youth from a book. He was a tall Greek youth, slender and curly-haired, whose voice flared fire as he pronounced the beloved name. I knew nothing, but the most beautiful girl could belong only to a beautiful youth. But this most beautiful girl loved this not very tall, stocky man of at least thirty, loved the straight, thinning hair on a round skull and unmitigated, sharply Semitic features. He uttered the enchanted name and his voice did not quaver; his quiet politeness was an insurmountable, impenetrable wall. I knew nothing. I had never been in love.

Susanna greeted me with a smile and asked: "Do the shops still have rose-beetle shoes?"

"I don't know. I did not pay any attention to Prilotz's window today."

"I would like to have some rose-beetle shoes again. I had a pair once when I was a child. You do play the piano, don't you?"

"Yes."

"Then you must play and I want to dance. Then I will jump out of the rose-beetle shoes and they will dance all by themselves! How good it smells."

"What?"

"What is wafting from your clothes—the freshness, the outdoor coldness. Do you know what I would like to do? I would like to walk in the woods . . . my fur boots would like to stomp around in the woods, in the thick snow like little black bears. For they *are* bears: sometimes I hear them growling when I am about to lock them away. Tell me, are the men all sad because I don't come out?"

"They did not *all* tell me."

"But some?"

"Two."

"Who?"

"One was Albert Abramowicz."

"Oh, he is still a boy. But I like him very much even though he is ugly—as if only his head were human and the rest were not . . . he is very obliging. When I come to the store, he always wants to wait on me and then he does everything wrong. Once he also climbed a ladder, which he is not supposed to do, and he dropped a whole box of ribbons. You should have heard his mother scold him! And who was the other?"

"Which other?"

"The one who is also sorry that he cannot see me anymore."

"A Mr. Ruby."

"A Mr. Ruby . . ." She clapped her hands together like an exuberant child. "A Mr. Ruby! A Mr. Emerald! A Mr. Turquoise! A Mr. Diamond! All gentlemen gems. Good morning, Mr. Amethyst, how is Mrs. Tourmaline?" She laughed. "Amethyst is small and weakly and blond with pale blue eyes, and Tourmaline is dark and tall."

"But it is a person's name!"

"No, not a person's name. It is a gem, my gem, my blood-red gem . . ."

"Why yours?"

"Because I love him and he loves me."

I stood there, stood and looked at her. This is the way it was. I had been searching for a key, had fumbled with the lock, had tapped at the walls: and here the little box had opened by itself without my doing anything. I looked inside and did not know what to say at first.

"Susanna, you mustn't . . . you mustn't joke about things like this."

"But I am not joking . . . I am not in the mood for jokes . . . I am not at all happy."

"Weathervane! You were just laughing and now you say—what is the matter? Susanna! Child!"

She burst into tears.

"No, oh no . . . I . . . oh, I am so alone."

She broke into heartrending sobs. I bent over her, frightened, and stroked her temples, her hair.

"Be calm . . . be calm . . . stop." This was no jest, she was in love. She wept. "Oh, I can't . . . I can't. I am lying here, sick, and he does not come! I want him to come. Just once. Oh, I love him so."

I sat close to the bed and took her hot hands in mine.

"Susanna . . . my dear heart . . . you must be good now. Don't excite yourself, so you will get well soon. So you will be able to get up. Then we will write to him and ask him to come to the other side of the street, then you will go to the window and you will see him and nod at him."

"Oh, yes . . ." Her mouth was already smiling. She wiped her eyes and whispered, "You are good." And she threw her arms passionately around my neck and pulled me close to herself and twitched and burned and embraced her lover.


. V .


I reflected. No, I could not do that. I could not lecture Susanna, reprimand her, warn her. I would sooner have been able to reprimand the poplar that gives itself to the wind and disseminates its catkins, or the female blackbird, or warn Zoë, the dog, to beware of her many suitors. Her all too many suitors. Whenever I opened the backdoor I was greeted by the expectant eyes of a strange dog—a bristly terrier, or a German shepherd, or even a griffon and a mutt whose breed could not be disentangled. They jumped through the gaps in the fence and Zoë was not allowed to wander around the garden as she used to do. Several times a day I walked her on a leash, and even then I had to fend off the persistent beleaguerers.

About this time, I tried to befriend this animal, to get closer to her, to talk with her the way Susanna did. It didn't work. I was not Susanna. When I called two or three times, the dog rose hesitantly, almost unwillingly, from her resting place, walked over and stood before me looking bored. Whenever I wanted to stroke her, she ducked and turned her head from under my hand, as if she could barely tolerate my touching her. When I would bring her a snack, she did not fall on it, but consumed it with care and without haste, thanking me only with a weak wag of her tail. At other times she simply stood there motionless, staring dully at the ground. When I spoke and scolded to wake her, her indistinct, sadly gleaming almond eyes looked at me in a strange and distant way.

"See how happy she is! She is laughing!" Susanna said one evening.

But she never laughed for me. "You don't love her enough," Susanna remarked. "That's why she is sad. Whatever is not loved enough is sad." And she told me the story: "One day came a hurdy-gurdy man, a Croat, with a huge long-tailed monkey. The man was sad and the monkey too was very sad. It was very cold that day and the monkey shivered. The man played his hurdy-gurdy and we gave him money. But the following year he came alone; the monkey had died. 'I guess I shall die soon too,' he said to Fina. And he never came back."

I was watching Zoë, who had trotted over when we called her. She stood there, her back hunched, her head lowered, staring in front of her as if she was following a bug, a spider, or a tiny crawling creature on the floor, ready to snap it. But there was nothing except the Turkish pattern of the rug. She stood there . . .

"Why are you staring like this?" Susanna asked.

"I am staring because Zoë is staring. I want to find out what she is thinking. Probably nothing."

"Oh, but she does think. She is thinking something, and I know what it is."

"What is it?"

"She thinks: murdered . . . murdered . . . murdered . . . I murdered my husband, the emperor of Byzantium . . . her nose . . . she is sensing something. . .there is some fine, colorless powder spilled on the rug, a tiny bit only. We don't notice it, but she can smell it. And she stares at it: poison . . . poison."

"Susanna, stop it!" I almost shrieked.

She looked at me with big eyes. She had said these terrible things in a soft, urgent tone, but without intending to make anybody's flesh creep, without intending to frighten or torment, without knowing their horrifying nature. She had not made up anything in her fantasy; she had invented nothing. She just knew what Zoë had done and what she thought now. She revealed it to me because I had asked and was surprised when I interrupted her. She remained a stranger to me. She lived inside an enchanted, impenetrable circle. At times she came out to meet me, but I was never admitted inside.

"Child, drink your milk at last; it's already getting cold. It will be all cold soon if you keep stirring it."

Susanna was permitted to leave her bed. Soon she walked around the room in a brown velvet housecoat or a burgundy kimono, still a bit unsteady on her legs, but cheerfully calm and at ease. One thing worried me, and also disappointed me a little: despite that short, violent outburst, she did not call again for her lover. Occasionally I would still find a stiff gray-blue linen envelope in the morning: she would take it, thank me with a smile, and read it when she was alone. She never spoke about it. The letters disappeared somewhere and I did not look for them. But then one day, when I came in I found her beaming and holding an opened letter in her hand. She asked me in a sweet tone to go to the garden gate that evening after dark.

"What do you want me to do there?"

"Don't you know?"

Of course I knew. And the meeting was not completely unwelcome. This time he would not catch me off guard and he would not get away from me so easily.

The evening came. I was almost as excited, as filled with anticipation, as Susanna. She sent me out much too early. But when I waded through the slippery slush for the second time, I spied a shadowy figure behind the lattice gate.

"Good evening."

"Mr. Ruby?"

"Yes, it's me. Thank you for coming."

"Don't thank me. I came only because Susanna asked me. I have been looking a long time for an opportunity to talk with you about what you are doing. For what you are doing is not right."

"I don't understand you."

"You don't want to understand me."

"If I did understand you, I would ask you not to interfere in my affairs."

"I am interfering in your affairs because they are also my affairs. For I have been appointed to guard and protect the child."

"She is no longer a child."

"Thanks to you perhaps. No, I don't mean to insult you. I don't want to argue and I don't want to beat around the bush. Susanna is extraordinarily lovely and beautiful and I can understand that ... Only what do you want with her? If you were an unscrupulous seducer then I would know, but I don't take you for that. Susanna can never marry, and I presume you have not really been thinking about marriage. So where should all this lead?"

He nodded. "I have often asked that myself," he said slowly, his voice expressionless. "But now the answer has been found."

He fell silent. Since I did not say anything, he began again after a while: "This is farewell. I am taking the early morning train to Berlin. And I shall not come back here."

He waited, but I said nothing. I had nothing to reply.

"Well ... I ... I am fleeing, yes. But I was not playing with the girl. I want to talk about it, because now it is all over. You see, we have been in this town less than nine months, my mother and I. I came from a big city. During one of my first nights here, I walked across the fields, and in front of an open gate to a garden a girl was romping with her white dog. I beckoned the dog to come and caressed him. The girl was charming, she allowed me to chat with her and smiled; she addressed me in the familiar form and she lived alone in the little house. I asked to meet with her one night. We stood in the moonlight in front of the fence, but there was something so peculiar about her, she made such a strange impression that I did not follow her inside. The next day I heard who she was and learned her particular story.

"Well, I knew it then. But the spark remained in my blood and continued to smolder. Once I met her accidentally, with her Fina, at the bakery. Of course, I greeted her and spoke with her. I met her two or three more times in rapid succession. I believe now that the old woman arranged it that way. Shortly thereafter she was dismissed, but her work had been done. Now you may judge. I don't think that I deserve a jail sentence."

"No," I mumbled.

He took a few steps. "My mother will soon move to Breslau to live with my sister, so I won't be coming back to this town. But Susanna must think that the separation is only temporary. She would not understand . . . If she knew she would come to me today . . . tonight . . . she is a marvel. Tell me, is she still confined to her bed?"

"No, she does get up."

"Then . . . will you allow me to come inside to tell her good-bye, a good-bye of weeks for her—forever for me."

"No. I am sorry, but I am not allowed to do that."

"I thought so. Maybe it is better this way, I am not very strong . . . But you will give her this letter?"

I took it together with something in a soft wrapping, probably flowers.

"Once again: I thank you. And . . . Susanna is so obliging, so defenseless, please protect her from a man who might have less of a conscience than I have."

"Have a good journey." I extended my hand through the fence, he pressed it, turned, and disappeared into the darkness.

I entered Susanna's room.

"What is this?"

She reached for the rustling tissue paper and exposed four soft, orange-yellow, half-closed roses. She lifted them to her face, and touched the petals while deeply inhaling their strong aroma. "How beautiful . . . I would like to wear one of these in my hair when he comes . . . in my black hair . . . that will give him pleasure . . . please get a glass . . . the best . . ."

I went downstairs and found a blue crystal vase.

When I came back, Susanna held out the letter to me with a fearful, blazing glance. "No . . . do you know . . . ?"

"I know. He is going to Berlin for a while. A short stay."

"I don't want him to go."

"He probably must go. He has to work, earn money."

"He can do that here too. I want him to stay here with me, always, forever and ever."

"Be reasonable, Susanna. I am sure it won't be all that long . . ."

"That makes no difference. I don't want him to go just the same. Where is my writing folder? I shall write him that I don't want him to go. I don't want him to go. I don't want it . . . I love him."

"But," I lied to prepare her, "the mail will not be forwarded tonight and he is leaving early in the morning."

"He won't go. I am writing to him . . . he is good."

The corners of her mouth twitched. I knew I had better not stoke her agitation by contradicting her. I went to my room and left her to herself with her letter. It would not find a messenger, and I informed Milda.

We were sitting in the living room downstairs around the supper table when I was startled by something that crackled and splattered against the windowpanes.

"A pile of snow from the roof. It is melting." But Susanna tore open the window before I was able to hold her back.

"Albert? Are you back?"

"Yes."

"Did you deliver the letter?"

"No. I rang the bell four times, but nobody opened. They probably weren't home. So I put it in the mailbox. Is that all right?"

"Sure. Thank you, it's all right."

"Don't mention it."

"Good night."

She closed the window and sat down again with her egg cup. She beamed. "You know. I wrote him everything and then I thought who could deliver the letter for me? And I thought, let me look out the open window, maybe someone who knows me will pass by and will do it. But I was unable to distinguish the people because it was too dark. Only Albert Abramowicz, he is so bunched up, him I recognized right away. Besides, he had been lingering in front of the house for quite a while. I called him and asked if he would do it. I wanted to give him a bar of chocolate, but he said he would do it just the same. He said I shouldn't toss the letter down or it would get wet and he wouldn't find—so I went downstairs and handed the letter to him. He was supposed to bring me an immediate reply; but he didn't want to ring our doorbell. He was too shy in front of you and Milda . . ."

"This was very careless of you. I hope you didn't catch cold again. Is his name on the letter?"

"Yes. He will read it and he will stay with me and everything will be all right."

Was everything all right? Consoled, Susanna went to bed. But my head was full of unpleasant, gray thoughts. In my dream poor Albert was standing by the light of the street lantern, his hopeless eyes raised to Susanna's window.

## . VI .

A knock at the door jolted me from my slumber. "Come in!" What was the matter . . . I stared at the door in horror. But Milda moved ponderously like the rook on a chessboard. The black rook. If the rook had been able to speak, it would have uttered the words in the same heavy, laborious, and clumsy manner.

She said that the little granddaughter of Frau Kors had just stopped by. Her grandmother had twisted her foot on the slippery ice in the early morning darkness and was unable to come today. Yes.

She fell silent. I did not grasp immediately why she disturbed my sleep with this news.

Meanwhile, she continued: Well, yes, but after all the laundry had already been sprinkled and arrangements been made for use of the steam press, and it wasn't all that far to go, but she couldn't carry the basket all by herself. Usually Frau Kors helped her, lent a helping hand, but now . . . She paused again and looked at me expectantly.

Well, if that was all. Let her wonder about the alacrity with which I offered my services. I flung back the covers, washed and dressed quickly. At the kitchen table, I poured down a cup of burning hot coffee.

We marched off, each holding a handle of the laundry basket.

The sky was pallid with frost. A biting east wind pinched the ears, my fingers stiffened from holding the braided wicker handle. We walked along carefully watching our step, frequently groping, through the empty morning streets. The snow that had melted the day before in the drizzly weather was now like glass under our soles, few entrance ways had been spread with sand or ashes. Only here and there was a grumpy, sleepy house, yawning and stretching, from which a man emerged with a bucket and shovel and began to spread sand. The man greeted Milda Morawe and gave me a questioning, disapproving look. What did I have to do with the basket of laundry? That was Frau Kors' job. I was the intruder, the stranger, and was only allowed to go for walks with Susanna after ten o'clock.

The mouth and eyes of the woman in the little variety shop opened wide when we entered. Maybe it was her stupefaction over my unexpected appearance that prevented her from finding the key to the pressing room right away. We must have worked at the steam press for about half an hour when we turned back with the pile of folded laundry through a now much livelier town over an already less dangerous pavement.

I acted like the variety shop woman; my mouth and ears opened wide as we entered the vestibule of the house. A strident female voice came from the parlor. But first I had to help Milda Morawe take the basket upstairs. Then I took off my coat and went downstairs. I knocked only lightly and entered.

"Ah, Miss! Good that you are here. Very good that you're back. I am sure you will support my efforts . . . that you will agree with me. You do not know what I mean? I am glad, I am really glad about that, because it shows that you are not in cahoots with this young person here, your charge."

"Madam, I don't know you and I don't know . . ." I began stupefied.

"No, no. You don't know and, as I said, I am glad about it. But you should know. You don't know me? Perhaps you have seen me

or heard my name . . . I am Frau Ruby. The mother of a son whom
this young lady has drawn into a relationship. For I am inclined to
believe that it was she, not he, who instigated this. He is hardly as
madly in love with her as she would wish; she would like him to
neglect his duty, waste his time around here instead of going to
Berlin. And what does she do to keep him here, to tie him closer to
herself? What does the innocent creature do? She makes him a
written offer, yes, an explicit offer . . . I, an old woman, would turn
red if I told you more about it. Well, what do you say, Miss?"

I said nothing. I remained silent. I remained silent and did not
express my displeasure more clearly. For her words did not ooze
with anger or indignation, rather they dripped cold, compressed,
corroding hatred and scorn, and she played the role of mother. Part
of this role was the lorgnette that dangled golden from a gilded
chain over her gray taffeta blouse. She lifted it slowly as she spoke
and eyed Susanna with it: she looked at the strange, lower creature
from a fitting distance as if it were an animal or a plant. The
poor girl sat there stupefied, with a pale, fearful face, devoid of
understanding . . .

"Susanna, go upstairs now. You are not even properly dressed.
Madam, I would like to have a private talk with you."

"That would suit you just right!—No, my child, you won't get
away from me like this. You are dressed enough, even if your attire,
this red silk, was probably meant for eyes other than those of an
old woman. And what you want to tell me privately, Miss, I can
well imagine. You will present a miserable, unhappy waif who is
not responsible for her actions and who, in the end, may be more
in need of being comforted than of being scolded. That may be so.
It may well be that there weren't brains enough for learning arithmetic
in school. But this letter, which my son did not find, this letter is
worth a plus point. She has had good teachers and has been a good
pupil, this beauty!" She reached into her bag. "Here. Would you
like to read this?"

"No, thank you, Madam. Susanna probably wrote from the sim-
plicity of her heart a very foolish and incredible letter. But you say

yourself that your son did not read it and he has already left for Berlin or will do so soon."

"He left on the early train. Fortunately, he did not check the mailbox before leaving."

"And if Susanna does not know his address, then the bond should be dissolved. You could have destroyed the letter instead of coming here . . ."

"Yes, instead I came here . . . instead I came here . . . Would you like to know why I came?" She raised herself up, belligerently; harshness gleamed in her eyes.

"My son could recently have married a nice, fine, intelligent girl; he gave her the cold shoulder and now I know why. But I won't stand idly by and see him squander his happiness, I won't stand idly by as he throws his life away, I won't stand idly by as he attaches himself to a man-crazy, dim-witted whore. I don't know what has been going on behind my back up to now, but what might happen in the future I shall seek to prevent with any means I have, even if you do not support me, any means! Of that I can assure you! And that's why I came here."

I was about to reply. Suddenly Susanna said, slowly and almost in a daze: "No, I am not a whore . . ."

"And what are you then, my child? Whether a woman offers her charms to a man under a street lantern or commends them to him in a letter makes no difference. I can't call you anything else."

"Madam, you are covering yourself with guilt . . . my God!"

Susanna had become enraged. A quick move—her hand clawed the collar, the woman's thin neck. The other woman tried to fend her off, gasped. I threw myself between them, I screamed and forced her hands to release their grip. Susanna persisted. I hurt her and she fell against the edge of the table. Her eyes were totally black with fury. She looked like an animal that had been deprived of its prey.

I yelled at the woman: "Get out of here! Get out of here immediately!"

She retreated, still hissing and spreading her poison: ". . . the authorities will hear . . . a raving maniac who should be locked up." I followed and locked the door to the house behind her.

When I came back, Susanna stood in the middle of the room, languid, drained, breathing through her open mouth, and a face that was frightened of herself.

"Susanna . . ." I touched her gently.

"Why . . . why is she so evil?"

"She is not that evil. She is his mother, Frau Ruby, and she thinks that the two of you did something bad, her son and you."

"But we didn't do anything bad . . . oh, she is evil, very evil."

"Susanna, she does not know you, she does not know . . ."

"She does not know me, but she says, 'You are a whore.' But that's not what I am. I don't want money or clothes or jewelry. I just want to love him. Why can't I do that?"

I knew no answer yet.

"Oh," she lamented. "Now he is gone and did not even read my letter. I don't want to stay here either. I want to go away too and be with him. I don't want anything, no presents. I don't want him to believe what she says . . . I just want to see him again. I shall go and look for him . . ."

"You cannot look for him, you won't be able to find him, the city is too big. We have to wait for him to write to you and when we find out where he lives—"

"I can't wait! Oh, why are people not good? They always scold and quarrel and don't want people to love each other."

Tears . . . I held her and stroked her neck.

"Come now, be good and wash your eyes and put on a dress and a warm cardigan and then the two of us will have breakfast. I am really hungry, aren't you?"

She obeyed. But all morning she sat at the window in her room, looking out, brooding. She hardly spoke with me.

How strange it is! So much of what is most important is forgotten and trivial things, ridiculously worthless things are well remembered. To this day I know that we had noodle broth and liver with mashed potatoes and applesauce. After lunch, Susanna announced that she was tired and wanted to rest. I prepared a bed for her on the small sofa and went to my room. It had been an ugly, stormy morning, a bit of sleep would do us both good. I lay down right away. I had planned to rest for only twenty minutes, for I wanted to write to my family before afternoon coffee. But my good intentions did not help much and I woke after an hour. I tidied up and went to see Susanna: her room was empty. She was probably in the parlor or in Milda's kitchen. I was about to go downstairs when a thought came over me, a premonition—

I tore open her wardrobe.

And I saw: neither her green velvet dress nor her fur-trimmed green wool coat was there, her hat was not on the shelf. I felt the floor of the wardrobe; between the shoe boxes should be a red cowhide suitcase, but it was not there anymore. I flew down the stairs, tore open the doors, roused Milda Morawe. She helped me into my jacket without a word, and I stormed outside.

To the railroad station. The ruddy young man at the ticket counter did not know Susanna, but he knew immediately of whom I spoke. Yes, the young lady had been here, maybe three quarters of an hour ago. She had emptied her purse and had asked for a ticket to Berlin. "But this is not enough." She did not understand him at first, then she begged him urgently, almost crying. "But I must go to Berlin. How shall I get there?" "Why don't you follow the tracks, you will get there eventually, even if it isn't today." He laughed at his joke. I was seized with fright. I thanked him for the information and left. I ran.

To Counselor Fordon. The gray housekeeper growled at first. He was having office hours and two clients were already inside. But I insisted, ordered her. Against her will, she waddled inside. Counselor Fordon came out right away and showed me into the dining room. Without a word, he listened to what I had to say. I confessed almost everything. Almost everything . . . I couldn't tell him about what I had seen on that certain night . . .

He did not reprimand me. He put the blame on Seraphina, the nosy one, the pandering witch whom he detested. He asked his clients to return some other time. We went to the police. Then he sent me back home. In the parlor, the table was set for coffee and cake. I was unable to eat or drink anything. I sat in the dusk without light. Everything darkened around me and inside of me. From time to time I rose in the midst of brooding and walked restlessly back and forth.

Before darkness fell, two policemen called at the house and took Zoë with them. After half an hour they brought the dog back as useless. She lay down on her blanket without a care. Soft, like a doe, she lay there, but when I leaned over, she lifted her head and in her elongated female eyes glittered a hardly discernible, playful fine scorn ... knowing ... At that moment, I hated her and could have kicked her with my foot. I stayed in the kitchen all night, without speaking. We were surrounded by darkness. The old woman sat disgruntled by the hearth, feeding the embers from time to time. Their red glow illuminated the immutable stone face of a black goddess of fate. Very late, the counselor stopped by. The railroad tracks and all roads nearby had been searched, but in vain.

Near dawn, I finally fell asleep for a while on the hard kitchen chair. The rattling of the oven door woke me. I tumbled into my room and threw myself fully dressed on the bed. I slept, plagued by nightmares, restless and numb, but not for long. I went downstairs tothe parlor and knew not what to do. I took out a dust cloth and began to polish the furniture. Milda Morawe, who usually did the cleaning, would not have tolerated such an intrusion into her jurisdiction on any other day. The fact that she let me do as I pleased was the only sign of how deeply affected and agitated she was.

Only once, while cleaning the oven, did she say quite directly: "I wanted to bake her a gooseberry pie. She liked it so much. We still have some canned berries left."

I shook my dust rag out of the window again. And I saw: on the other side of the street, two men walked along, one with an official's cap, carrying a ladder horizontally and on the ladder something dark was stretched out, almost like a sack. And the poor misshapen boy trotted alongside. They turned and crossed the roadway. When they were close to our house, Albert Abramowicz spotted me and with a twitching motion, he lifted up a blackish, red leather suitcase. He wept ...

The newspapers, the people in town spoke about suicide due to mental derangement, but I knew it was otherwise. Had she recognized that she had been abandoned, she may not have wanted to live anymore, but she was so unsuspecting, and had only one thought: I am being harried, spied upon as long as it is daylight. Now she had crawled out of her hiding place and wandered at night along the tracks, as the railroad official had recommended, on her way to her lover . . . I don't know whether he soon heard about it and whether he returned once more; for a few days after the funeral, I left for a stay with my family. Then I had a position in Drossen and another in Stettin. And the memory of all this came back to me now because this woman had died: Therese Ruby, née Heppner, at age seventy-one.